the woods at barlow bend

A STORY OF
LOVE, LOSS, AND RESILIENCE

JODIE CAIN SMITH

The Woods at Barlow Bend

1st edition published 2014
Republished 2nd edition 2021

ISBN: 978-1-955119-12-2 (Paperback)
ISBN: 978-1-955119-11-5 (ebook)

Cover Design by Michelle Fairbanks
Interior Design by FormattedBooks.com

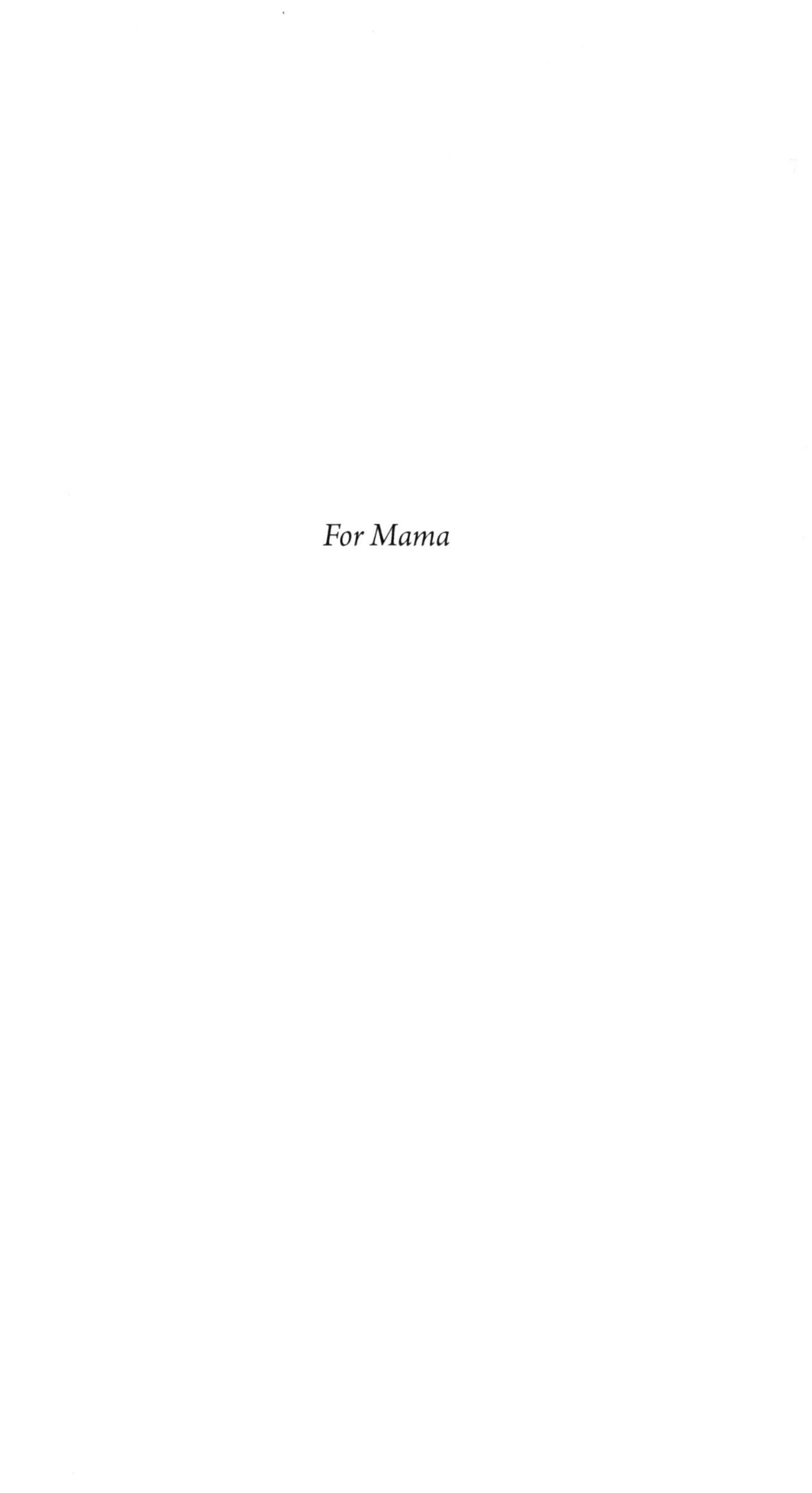

For Mama

introduction

I believe ghosts walk among us. Lives unfinished, they guide us toward what they did not complete. My Catholic upbringing called this Purgatory, a period of repentance—God's gift of a second take. Walking through the pine trees and kudzu of the thick Alabama woods, I feel the presence of my ghosts. I hear their whispered taunts and encouragements urging me to live a life fulfilled, find the right path, make up for their shortcomings, step carefully at times and wildly at others, or maybe, ask forgiveness for their sins.

In 1993, during my junior year at McGill-Toolen Catholic High School, I was given a simple assignment for my AP History class: Discover what life was like during the Great Depression. I decided to interview my grandmother as part of my research. I needed an A, and thought a personal reflection of the time might be effective.

I expected to record the typical story: A young girl struggling alongside her family to put food on the table and clothes on everyone's backs. What I got that day from Granny, sitting at her dining room table—me with my list of sterile questions and tape recorder, her with her Carlton 120's and simple housedress—was shocking.

Before that afternoon, I knew little of Granny's past. Her parents and husband were dead. She had a sister and two brothers I rarely saw and could barely pick out of a crowd. She seemed content to live by herself in her three-bedroom home, but also appeared to long for a companionship she could no longer have. She always seemed slightly homesick and a little heartbroken, surrounded by artifacts from her past: Old record albums stacked neatly next to an ancient record player; furniture covered in scratchy, plaid upholstery; figurines that small fingers mustn't touch; oil paintings created by a young version of my mother. Granny's house was neither completely lit nor completely dark. The sunlight danced around the rooms, creating shadows that were cold and comforting at the same time.

Granny looked to have stepped out of the pages of an old nursery rhyme with her housedress, socks with sandals, and soft, white curls. But she had mystical powers, too. She made okra grow from the dark, Alabama dirt, and transformed those ugly, fuzzy shoots into the most delicious fried wonders ever eaten. She turned the process of snapping green beans into a delightful, hazy afternoon spent on her back steps; her affection for me present in every crisp snip. Her generosity knew no boundaries. She spoiled me with trips to McDonald's for French fries and Gayfer's for new outfits. Summer day trips to the beach were frequent and always included an ice chest full of fried chicken, pineapple sandwiches, and cold Cokes. Her hope for my life was in every conversation we had. I felt her urging me to a life full of adventure before she ever said the words aloud.

Granny was also full of mystery. Children in my family learned that questions were to be asked quietly and rarely, and answers were to be given hurriedly so the adults would not get caught talking about past tragedies or scandals. None of my aunts or uncles ever talked about Granny's past. Granny never mentioned her childhood or parents. As far as I knew, Granny came into the world wearing a housedress, socks with sandals, and soft, white curls. I never heard mention of Granny as a young girl from Frisco City, Alabama. Before that afternoon, I never thought to ask about her past.

On that February afternoon, part of me felt like I was intruding on Granny's privacy, but I knew Granny would give me what I needed to protect my fragile GPA, and I only needed a few slices of everyday life during the Great Depression. Granny gave me much more than that. Much to my surprise, she brought me into her private world, one that I had no idea existed. She told me the story of an idyllic childhood in rural Alabama, one virtually untouched by the typical hardships of the Great Depression. The story was perfect for my project. But then, she continued to talk. What Granny told next, over several cups of coffee and half a pack of her Carlton 120's, was the story of the incident early in her adolescence that permanently altered her world, the tragedy that ended her childhood.

I don't know why Granny chose to tell me her story or let me into her private world. Maybe, she told me because she knew I loved a good ghost story. She knew I loved her old, jazz records and her accompanying tales of the glamorous, exciting singers featured on the covers. Maybe Granny wanted me to know the exciting woman she knew when she was a young girl, the woman who left her far too soon. Maybe she was still trying to figure out exactly what happened in the woods of Barlow Bend in Clarke County Alabama back in 1934. Maybe she told me because I was the only person who dared to ask. Maybe she had been waiting sixty years to finally tell the story. For whatever reason, Granny chose to share her ghosts with me that afternoon.

For six decades, she carried the assumptions, rumors, and heartache alone. For sixty years, she had walked with her ghosts, taunted by questions that could not be fully answered, taunted by an unfinished life. That afternoon, Granny saw her chance to give her ghosts away, to rid herself of the story that had haunted her for so long. In her dimly-lit dining room, with plumes of cigarette smoke swirling between the shadows and sunlight, she introduced me to Hubbard and Addie, mother and father to Hattie, my Granny.

The Woods at Barlow Bend was inspired by the story Granny told me that afternoon. Many names were changed, and conversations were invented. Through months of research, as I unearthed secrets buried long ago, I pieced together Granny's adolescence and the events that molded her life story. Discovering Granny as a teenage girl helped me better understand the woman I dearly miss. I hope that her story will motivate others to respond to the taunts of their own ghosts, but what if some secrets should never be revealed? That is the question I may never be able to answer. All I do know is, as I typed each word, I felt Granny's arms around me again.

prologue

January 31, 1934
Barlow Bend, Clarke County, Alabama

The water was like glass. The winter chill had finally settled into lower Alabama, and the sun hadn't burned off the frost yet. It was too early for that. Dawn had broken over the horizon, providing just enough light to see the opposite bank.

Hubbard glanced at the bottom of the boat as he rowed across the river. He was surprised by the amount of blood that began to fill the seams between the planks despite his hope that the wool blanket would soak up most of it or at least keep it contained. Instead, the thick, dark liquid mixed with the dirt and debris on the bottom of the boat, forming a gruesome paste. He tried to focus on his rowing, to keep the tiny vessel as still and steady as possible. Finally, he reached the opposite shore and pulled the bow up on the beach.

Hubbard lifted the soaked bundle out of the boat, careful not to expose any of Addie's 100 lb. frame, especially not her face. He didn't want to see her face again, not like that. Even in the shadows, he saw the light leave her eyes instantly. She was looking right at him when the gun fired. One single shot was all it took. She was gone before her body hit the ground. He closed his eyes for a moment to let the feeling of it pass.

Hubbard laid Addie on the riverbank. He had to rinse out the boat. The small skiff was used by anyone needing to cross the river at Barlow Bend, so he couldn't leave it in its present condition. The next hunter, or whoever might come along, would wonder what on Earth had left so much blood. Luckily for Hubbard, the next traveler would probably think that someone had scored a large buck or a prize turkey, but was too lazy to clean up after himself. A few buckets of water washed out most of the blood, leaving the boat in an acceptable condition. He couldn't linger on the riverbank any longer. He had to get moving.

Hubbard put on his pack which contained the sparse supplies his wife, Addie, had packed for the morning, and the two guns they brought safely tied to either side of the canvas. With Addie's body still wrapped inside the blanket, he gently lifted her again into his arms and set out for the two-mile hike to the car. Addie always insisted upon hiking deep into the woods on their hunting excursions. She felt it was more of a sport that way: go deep into the prey's territory undetected so that the prize was even more deserved. He regretted letting in to her as he realized the considerable distance ahead of him. Two miles through the thick pine and underbrush while carrying such a load would take considerable time, but he quickly realized that time didn't matter to his Addie anymore.

As Hubbard walked, he was struck by the stillness surrounding him. The only sounds he heard were the crunching of pine needles beneath his boots and his own breath. His load was getting heavier with each step, and his arms were beginning to burn. He wondered for a second about how many other hunters had taken the same path, and if he might run into any of them. It was the last day of rifle season, so he feared the woods would be teeming with hunters hopeful for one last, great morning in the woods. He hoped he could avoid them. Hubbard didn't need the distraction of having to tell the story of what happened or the waste of time to ask for help. Addie was beyond help.

"Stop it," he said aloud, and pressed forward.

Hubbard mapped out a plan in his head. He would hike to the car and drive the approximate 30 miles from Barlow Bend to Jackson, where he hoped his cousin, Stephen, would be on duty at the Jackson police station. The upstanding Andrews name was synonymous with law enforcement in Clarke and Monroe counties, at least until Hubbard came along. Hubbard would tell Stephen the story, and hopefully, he wouldn't have to use too many details.

Stephen would know what to do with Addie's body. Once that was taken care of, Hubbard would then drive the sixty miles back to Frisco City and try to wash up before the children saw him. They didn't need to see him like this, frozen from the chill in the air, sweating at the same time, and covered in their mother's blood. He would tell Hattie first, she was the oldest. Then, the two of them together would tell Meg, Billy and Albert. For a moment, Hubbard's thoughts went to the children. Where would life take them with no mother as guide? Hattie would help the younger ones cope, Hubbard reassured himself. He knew Hattie and Meg were old enough to remember, but maybe the boys were young enough to forget.

Hubbard finally reached the car, Addie's ragtop 1930 Model T Ford, and laid her carefully on the back seat. The blanket had shifted during the hike so a glimpse of her hair fell into view. Hubbard touched it, sticky and cold, the deep, coffee-colored brunette now streaked and matted with her blood. Suddenly, he was struck by the thought that he would never stroke her hair again, never hold her face in his hands, never hear her infectious laugh, never feel her heat. He became numb.

PART 1

rumors & wildflowers

chapter one

August 8, 1933
Frisco City, Alabama

"I poured it out in the yard. If you want the whiskey so bad, go out back and lap it up like a dog." Momma stared right into John's eyes as she said this. Momma wasn't a teetotaler by any means, but she didn't like how drunk Uncle John got during these family get-togethers, so she took matters into her own hands. Rather, she took Uncle John's whiskey into her own hands, and watered the azaleas.

It was the night of my thirteenth birthday. The house was full with friends and family, ready for music and dancing. Meg, my younger sister, played the piano while Momma, Daddy, and the others danced in the living room, but Uncle John became handsy when drunk. Daddy got irritated when Uncle John got handsy.

"Nothin's gonna ruin your party, Hattie." Momma, as usual, fixed the situation to her liking.

Momma stared at Uncle John's heavy eyelids and scruffy complexion for a moment, probably wondering for the millionth time why her older sister, Audrey, married such a worthless man. Not even really a man, but a pitiful being ready to beg for scraps.

Momma knew how proud Uncle John was of his whiskey. "A family secret passed down from my papa," Uncle John would proudly announce, as if we all hadn't heard that statement over a hundred times.

Pouring out the whiskey was a little mean, but I think Momma enjoyed angering Uncle John, and I loved her fearlessness.

"Audrey was pretty before John. She could have done much better for herself," Momma told me earlier that day when we were making the cake for my party. I loved being in the kitchen with Momma. Even if it was to help make my own birthday cake, an afternoon alone with Momma was a gift. Each story she told was like a secret shared just between us. And Momma had plenty of stories about Uncle John, his whiskey, and the way he treated Aunt Audrey. Momma also thought that a real man would at least attempt to argue with her when insulted or tricked. When John's only argument manifested as incoherent and pathetic huffing and puffing, she couldn't help but laugh.

Uncle John stormed out the back door of the kitchen with Aunt Audrey chasing behind him.

"Jesus, Addie, why do have to be so hateful?" Audrey squeaked at Momma as the screen door slapped the frame. "John, Honey, come back to the party!"

I wondered for a second how these two completely different women could be sisters. Aunt Audrey's face was weathered and splotchy, probably from long hours spent in the fields trying to salvage the meager profit Uncle John had promised during the spring planting. Momma, on the other hand, had a perfect porcelain complexion that would glow a beautiful bronze in the summer, but always returned to a smooth, soft cream by mid-fall. I had also never seen my mother chase after Daddy when he stormed out of a room.

"Hattie, Honey," Momma said as she turned toward me, "Promise me you'll never waste your time on a man like that."

"I promise, Momma," I said.

"That's my girl." Momma kissed my forehead, shook her shiny, wavy hair, trimmed smartly just above her shoulders, and turned to walk down the hallway into the living room with a pitcher of sweet tea and glasses balanced on her favorite serving tray. Daddy stopped her in the doorway and shook his head. He didn't care for John Howard too much either, but he did like the man's liquor. It was the smoothest in the county. Momma knew Daddy would be disappointed, but she also knew how to be forgiven—tilted chin, coy laugh, piercing blue eyes staring straight into his.

Addie and Hubbard Andrews were each better looking than the other. Who could say whose blue eyes were more powerful: Daddy's clear, ice blue, or Momma's nearly cobalt, like beach glass washed on the shore, smooth and shiny? I was witness to Momma's subtle, yet mesmerizing ways of winning on several occasions. She knew exactly how to be forgiven for every impulsive action.

"Sorry, Hub, but John's barely tolerable sober, much less lit up like the Fourth of July."

Then, Momma made the move that made Daddy forget the whiskey. Momma gently, but intentionally brushed her body against his as she passed him through the kitchen door. Her hair brushed his chin and she dragged her fingertips along his waist. Daddy stared at her, fixated by her every move as she exited the kitchen and disappeared into the parlor without spilling a drop of tea. The room always seemed a little darker after she left.

chapter two

October 1933
Frisco City, Alabama

I heard them as they stepped on the front porch. The front door swung open so hard that it hit the wall and bounced back. Momma and Daddy had gone to an adult social at the Methodist Church that night and were home earlier than I thought they would be. I had just crawled into my bed when I heard Momma's voice on the porch. They were fighting again. Meg, of course, was already fast asleep and engaged in her heavy, rhythmic breathing.

"It's bad enough that I have to hear the hens whisper about you, but to watch you! And right next to me! You'd think you would've finally learned a little self-control after what you did, but no!" The hurt caused by whatever Daddy had done echoed in every word Momma spoke.

"Addie, Honey, I…" Daddy tried to explain that he was just being friendly, but Momma kept at him.

"They're never going to stop!" Momma was in the mood for a good fight and determined to have one. "Do you know what they say about you? About me?"

"And there it is!" Daddy raised his voice loud enough to silence Momma. "You're not worried about what I'm off doin' or not doin'. You're not worried about what I did. You're only worried about precious Addie Izora Andrews and how you look to all of them! Well, to hell with them and with you!"

The door slammed again, and then silence. I knew Daddy had left. Momma would stand her ground and stake her claim on a room, a piece of land, or an argument until it was reduced to ashes, but Daddy would retreat. He couldn't stand being next to Momma when she was in one of her moods. The flashes of heat coming off her could suck the oxygen right out of a room and force Daddy to search for fresh air so he could breathe, or at least seek cover until she grew bored with arguing, which was usually the only reason one of their arguments came to an end. That summer and fall, the arguments came more frequently than in years past.

According to Momma, I came from very strong-minded and strong-willed stock. Momma claimed that as soon as she and Daddy first laid eyes on each other, the battle for control began. I think that was probably what attracted the two to each other to begin with—the need to rule their own small piece of the world. Neither of them wanted to rule over someone weak. The weak offered no challenge, and, therefore, no reward. Momma and Daddy met at the First Methodist Church in Luverne, Alabama, 90 miles east of our home in Frisco City. Both claimed to have picked each other and that once his or her mind was made up, the other had no choice but to go along with the match. Of course, I always privately believed Momma's version of the story more than Daddy's.

Momma claimed that for weeks every Sunday morning, she stood in the choir box and looked out onto the humble congregation, heads bowed in prayer. Every head bowed except one. Throughout the service, Daddy would stare at her with his delicious blue eyes, then linger by the door afterward. Enjoying the game of chicken far too much to end it so soon, Momma would walk coolly past him and down the street with her sisters in tow, not even giving Daddy quick glance.

Momma's four sisters; the Lowman Girls as they were known across the county, would beg her to speak to the dashing Andrews boy; youngest of the eight children born to General Jackson Andrews. General—no military affiliation, just a name—Andrews owned a large plantation on the north side of Luverne and seemed to have his hands in all county business: from farming, to politics, to which moonshiners were allowed to prosper in Crenshaw County. The Lowman Girls considered an Andrews boy a great catch.

Momma would smile and tell her sisters, "Maybe next week," knowing that Daddy would be back in the middle pew the next week, and their game would continue until she was sure he was completely hooked. After a few weeks of the game, Momma finally paused on the steps and spoke to Daddy. She accepted an invitation to accompany him to a dance the following weekend. Two short months after their first conversation on the front steps of the modest wooden chapel, the two stood there together again as husband and wife.

By that evening in October of 1933, Momma and Daddy had played their game of chicken, trying to find out who was in control of whom, for fourteen years. Lying still in my bed, I held my breath so I could hear Momma. Whenever they fought,

I waited to hear if she would cry afterward. If she did cry, I never heard her. What I did hear, was Momma's pacing, fast and hard on the wooden floor, and then a kitchen cupboard creak, a glass on the counter, the thud of a thick, glass bottle. I knew Momma was still fuming because all of her movements sounded more deliberate and animated than usual. I decided to stay in my bed. Momma was a force when angry, and I didn't want to get caught in her path or end up a casualty in tonight's match. Sleep would give way to a calmer morning for both of them.

As I lay in bed, my heart pounding too hard to fall asleep, I fantasized about my future life. I hoped to marry a simple man, a local shopkeeper or a man who worked for the town, not one who traveled all over selling his wares and who owned a hotel in the next county that required him to be away for several nights at a time.

"I go there to check on the hotel, Addie. That's all!" Daddy's constant explanation rang in my ears.

In the stillness, I heard Marion Harris singing *I'm Just Wild About Harry*. The tune bounced from the radio set in Mrs. Williams's front parlor across the street, and through my open window, "He's sweet just like chocolate candy and just like honey from a bee. Oh, I'm just wild about Harry and he's just wild about me."

I swore right then that I would marry someone like Harry from that song, someone that's sweet like chocolate and wild about only me. And I would be wild about him. We'll live quietly without worrying about who's winning or losing the game of chicken that I will refuse to play.

The next morning, I woke to the smell of coffee and my mother's lilting, sparkling laughter. She was teasing Daddy about sleeping in the barn like a dog, too scared of his "tiny, little ol' wife" to come back inside. Luckily for Daddy, October was still a warm month in Alabama. Not all the nights he spent in the barn were too comfortable. At least, when I heard the front door slam night after night, I always assumed he went to the barn.

But on that morning, I had no idea what was ahead of me. On that morning, I was just a teenager who wanted her parents to stop fighting. I softly padded down the hallway and to the kitchen as Momma and Daddy continued to flirt and tease each other.

"Wicked woman, I should have drowned you last summer when I had the chance," I heard Daddy say as Momma howled with laughter, and I paused in the hallway.

Daddy had taught all us kids to swim over the years, but Momma was content to float on her empty Karo Syrup cans, one neatly tucked under each arm.

"If the Good Lord intended me to swim like a fish, he'd have given me gills!" she would playfully snap at Daddy as she gracefully floated on her cans. Daddy would beg her to at least try to swim, tickling her until she threw her arms around him for support when her cans floated away. When Momma and Daddy were good, they were fantastic.

"Hubbard, you worship every hair on my pretty little head." Momma playfully lunged at Daddy who was leaning against the kitchen sink.

Maybe to prove how much stronger he was than her, Daddy picked Momma up and spun her around as if he was holding a small child. He kissed her neck, and she laughed even louder. He held her there for a moment longer. Her feet dangled nearly a foot off the floor, and her blue eyes danced with his.

As I watched my parents from the doorway of the tiny kitchen, the song from the night before came back to me but the lyric changed. *Addie's just wild about Hubbard, and he's just wild about her.*

chapter three

January 31, 1934
Frisco City, Alabama

I rose early that morning. I always woke up early on the weekends. I didn't understand sleeping late when there was so much to do. The possibilities were endless on the weekends, especially with Momma. All week long at school, I daydreamed about how to spend my two glorious days. With Addie Andrews at the helm, I never knew where I might end up.

Often, Momma would sweep me, the oldest, and Meg, second in line, off on a day trip. She never planned where we would end up; she would just rush us to the car and off we would go, Meg in the backseat, and me, next to Momma up front.

In her charge for the winding country roads, Momma often forgot to pack us a lunch. We would be 30 miles away from home, in the middle of nowhere, and suddenly, Momma would remember that she didn't bring food. Luckily, in Alabama, blackberries and honeysuckles were delightful summer treats. Pecans littered the ground in the fall and scuppernong grapes, although they were a bit sour and made my jaw all tingly, would do in a pinch.

I had made the sweetest batch of blackberry jelly from picking blackberries in one of the forests we explored that last summer with Momma. That morning, I grabbed one of the two jars left from the batch out of the pantry, along with flour, sugar, salt, and buttermilk from the icebox. Momma and Daddy left way before dawn to hopefully nab one more wild turkey and, God forbid, some nasty little squirrels before season's end, and wouldn't be back until lunch. Therefore, breakfast duties were left to me. I didn't mind. I relished the few moments of peace and quiet in our little kitchen. I just hoped that Albert, the baby of the family, and Billy, number three, didn't end up with the sticky mess all over themselves, the table, and the floor. Albert, especially, had a way of wearing rather than eating the food set in front of him when he was away from Momma's watchful gaze.

Of course, my hopes for a peaceful, civilized breakfast were dashed soon after the boys came to the table. Meg tried her best to keep Albert focused on actually eating breakfast, but he preferred to mush my beautiful biscuits and jelly between his fingers until he formed a grayish purple paste. Billy ate most of his biscuit, but a considerable amount of crumbs littered the floor around him and blackberry jelly was smeared on his chair, his pajamas, and in his hair, causing it to matte on the side. He would never have acted that way if Momma were at the table.

"Enough." I efficiently and effectively declared breakfast over and bath time to begin. Meg, thankfully, took Billy and Albert to the bathroom where she stripped them down, put both of them in the shower at the same time, and turned the water on their heads. Judging from Billy's and Albert's loud yelping, the water must have been ice-cold. I couldn't help but laugh as I pictured Meg trying to wrestle the jelly and crumbs out of the two boys' hair. She probably ended up splashing more water on herself than the boys.

"Meg, they don't have to look perfect, just rinse 'em off!" I yelled toward the bathroom.

Momma and Daddy had left instructions for the four of us to head down Bowden Street to Aunt Matt's once we were up, fed, and dressed. I loved spending time with Aunt Matt, a kind, colored woman with a big, soft body and thick, strong arms that used to spin me around when I was little. She was so strong that she could make you feel like you were flying through the air, but completely safe in her mighty grip. Of course, by 1934, I was too old for all that.

Over the weeks leading up to that January, Aunt Matt had been teaching me how to make all my favorites: fried chicken and okra; pot roast with thick, dark brown gravy; and fried catfish caught by her equally jovial husband, Henry. Henry had promised to take the boys fishing that day after he finished the morning shift at the railroad station, so they would be out of my hair and out of my way. I figured Henry would love the leftover biscuits, and hopefully, Aunt Matt would be pleased with how far her pupil had progressed with biscuits. What had started out as hard, flat little bricks and were now flaky and tender. I wrapped the leftovers in a clean kitchen towel to take with us down to their house.

I glanced at the kitchen clock and was stunned at how fast the morning had passed.

"Meg, hurry up with the boys! We need to get over to Aunt Matt's!"

I wanted Aunt Matt to help me prepare a hearty lunch for Momma and Daddy to enjoy and now, I only had a couple of hours to complete the task. I quickly wiped down the table and Albert and Billy's chairs, swept up the crumbs, and was on my hands and knees with a soapy rag trying to get the blackberry jelly off the floor, when I heard a car door shut and footsteps on the porch.

"Meg, I think Momma and Daddy are home!" I yelled, not sure why they were home so early.

I had just thrown the wet rag in the sink when Daddy and Aunt Matt walked into the kitchen. Usually, he came barreling into a room, announcing his presence, as if his heavy footsteps weren't warning enough. Today, however, he barely made a sound.

"Daddy, y'all are back early," I said, rushing to return the broom and dustpan to the pantry. "Aunt Matt, you didn't have to walk all the way down here. I was gonna walk the kids over myself."

Aunt Matt usually greeted me with a big hug and an almost lyrical, "How ya doin', pretty girl?" but she was silent and had tears in her eyes.

"Where's Momma?" I asked.

Daddy sat at the kitchen table, a large, sturdy piece made of solid pine that he had built himself.

From the doorway of the pantry, I saw Daddy's face, tired and pink from the cold. His tanned, youthful complexion had turned dull and grey; making his prominent cheekbones cut harsh angles under his eyes. I noticed stains all over his shirt, pants, and hands.

"So, did you get a big one? Is Momma out admiring her prize?" I walked to the sink and peered out the window just above it to catch a glimpse of Momma with her latest kill, but only saw the black car.

I hoped that they would come home with a turkey rather than squirrels, which, in my opinion, were tough and gamey no matter what you did with them. No amount of Momma's artistry or Aunt Matt's expertise in the kitchen could improve the little creatures. For a moment, Daddy and Aunt Matt both stared at me soundlessly.

The look in Daddy's eyes scared me. I had never heard him so quiet or seen him look so distant. I took a seat and looked at Aunt Matt who was seated in my usual place, and reaching for my hand. Squeezed in hers, my hand looked so small and pale wrapped up in hers—big, and dark, like soft, wrinkled leather. I wanted to say something to break the tension, but instinct made me freeze. The look on Daddy's face was too intense. Aunt Matt was breathing harder than usual and she kept looking from me to the table.

Daddy spoke softly, "Sweetie, your momma had an accident." I stared at the dark stains all over Daddy's clothes.

I had always considered myself to be quite capable in a crisis, so I immediately sprang to action. "Let me tell Meg. She can stay here with Albert and Billy, and we'll go to the doctor's. Momma must be hungry, so I'll bring her the biscuits I made earlier. Aunt Matt, you'll be so proud. They're fluffy and tender, just like you taught me. I was going to give them to Henry, but he'll understand, won't he?"

I waited for Aunt Matt to return my smile, but she reached for my hand again and muttered a "Dear Jesus," toward the ceiling. Why was she crying? That wasn't like her.

"Hattie, Sweetie, sit down," Daddy said, more to the table than to me, "Your momma and I went over to Clarke County near Walker Springs. We crossed the river at Barlow Bend, and were walking into the woods. She heard some squirrels in the vines of a big tree and was tryin' to scare them around for me to shoot. She was creeping around that tree when… Sweetie, her gun went off. She didn't suffer. It was real quick." To this day, I don't know why he didn't look me in the eye.

As I sat on the hard seat, stunned and not quite comprehending what I just heard, Aunt Matt tried to comfort me, "Now, Baby."

Why did she call me "baby"? She hadn't called me that in years. What happened to 'pretty girl?'

Aunt Matt started again, "Now, Baby, your daddy's gonna need your help with Meg and them boys. Me and Henry gonna do everything we can. Oh, Baby, I am just so sorry, just so sorry."

Aunt Matt calling me baby made me angry. I was no longer a baby. I wasn't even a child. My childhood ended as soon as that shot was fired, and I knew it. The thought of Momma being gone rushed over me. Every inch of my body began to cramp, and my chest got so tight, I struggled to breathe. I rushed out the back door to the car, and stared at the brown stains on the floorboards.

"Where is she?" I yelled as I looked in the car. There was a small pack with two guns, but Momma wasn't there. Tears burned my eyes, and the cold air stung my lungs.

Aunt Matt grabbed my hand and pulled me toward the house, "Come on, Baby, come back inside. You gonna catch your death out here."

That's when the frost began to sting the bottoms of my feet and I started to shake.

chapter four

February 1, 1934
Frisco City, Alabama

The next day, I held on tight to Albert's hand as we walked down the aisle of the First Methodist Church of Frisco City. The church was full with nearly everyone from town. Daddy and Reverend Howlington walked in front of me with Meg and Billy behind us.

As we passed each row, the people seated on the ends looked at me with such sad eyes. One woman, as I passed her, held a handkerchief to her lips. I remember thinking, *Is she sad that Momma died, especially in such a horrible way, or did she feel sorry for Addie's four motherless children?* I couldn't tell.

When we reached the first pew, Daddy stood at the end as we filed in and took our seats. Reverend Howlington walked to the pulpit. When I sat, I noticed the choir at the altar. I didn't recognize the song they sang that day, but I think Momma would have liked it.

Before that day, we never sat in the front row. Momma usually chose a pew toward the center, proclaiming that the center rows were "Close enough for God to see you, far enough back so He won't see me pop your behind if you act up." She would look at us very sternly as she said this, then smile and wink at me.

But, there we sat, in the front row with Papa and Grandma Andrews. Grandpa Lowman and Aunt Audrey sat on the pew directly behind us. Cousin Stephen and more family were on the third row. Aunt Audrey hadn't stopped crying since she'd arrived at the house earlier that morning. I looked around for Uncle John, but didn't see him. I assume he stayed outside. Aunt Mittie, Momma's twin sister, and Uncle Melvin, Mittie's husband, weren't there. I would learn later why they didn't come to Momma's funeral, but at the time, I couldn't understand why Mittie didn't show up. Maybe saying goodbye to a sister was too hard for her, but she should've been there. Momma would have been there for her if Mittie was lying in that coffin. When I turned to see who else was in the church, Aunt Audrey looked at me with such sadness that I quickly turned back around. Sitting in the front row, on display to the entire town of Frisco City, I smoothed the dark fabric of my dress, crossed my ankles as Momma always told me, and folded my hands neatly in my lap.

I held Meg's hand in mine and tried to focus on anything but Momma. I gazed at the sunlight streaking the altar. I examined the robes worn by the choir–the pleating and piping surrounding the collars. I even listened intently to Aunt Audrey's sniffling, but all I could feel was the absence of my mother.

Reverend Howlington spoke for a really long time about Momma, but I couldn't concentrate on what he said. I heard syllables and some full words, "beauty," "spirited," "charming," "devout," but all I thought of was Momma's face. I wanted to see her light up with pride when I told her how I got Billy and Albert neatly dressed in their suits and kept them out of the backyard so they wouldn't mess up their church clothes. I wanted to see her smile when she saw how pretty Meg looked in her navy dress, white stockings, and French braid.

I wanted to hear her say, "Chin up, Sweetie, what's all those tears for?"

I wanted her.

After the church service, we rode over to Union Cemetery on the outskirts of Frisco City, about half a mile from our house. Momma's place was near a magnolia tree. Momma loved magnolias. A few feet from Momma's site was a tiny, unmarked grave, barely two feet long. To the right, were the headstones of a couple I never knew: Frank something or other and Fannie, beloved wife of Frank. I wondered what Momma's headstone would say.

Once again, we were seated in the front. Albert and Billy had been quiet all day: Divine intervention I guessed. Everyone else gathered behind us. I decided then and there that I don't like front rows. If I looked forward, all I could see was a coffin, a coffin that had Momma in it. If I looked to the sides, I saw Daddy's face, older than the day before, and Meg, all red and splotchy rather than her usual creamy alabaster. Albert looked so angry and hurt, like he'd been robbed of his favorite toy, only much worse, and Billy hadn't lifted his gaze from the ground once since we left the house that morning. I think pieces of all of us were buried with Momma that day.

Behind me, I heard whispering: Soft, feminine voices talking about how Daddy carried Momma over two miles through the woods, and then drove to Jackson with her body in the back seat. Male voices whispered questions about why Daddy left her body with Cousin Stephen at the police station in Jackson.

There was talk of gunshots, women who hunt, and the gruesome aftermath of a rifle misfire. I heard trite sentiments like, "Those poor babies," and "She was just lovely, so charming." Liars! With every word, I felt my anger toward them growing.

I wanted to turn around and scream at each one of them, "Stop it! You didn't love her! She didn't love you!"

I knew what the truth was. I knew that everyone in Frisco City loved to gossip about Momma. I knew they thought she was insane to go off on unchartered road trips alone with Meg and me. They thought she laughed too loud and that we spent too much time in a colored woman's kitchen. They thought Daddy was a womanizer and that Momma flaunted her beauty, but I also knew that when Momma and Daddy were on a dance floor, not a man or woman in the room could keep their eyes off them.

I didn't scream at them, but Momma would have been proud of the searing glare I gave them. She would have been proud that when I glared at them, no tears rolled down my cheeks. I kept my head up and held their glance for a moment, willing them to shut their stupid mouths without ever saying a word.

As I looked across the field, I saw Cousin Stephen near the back of the crowd. Uncle John spoke frantically in Stephen's ear. Stephen looked annoyed by Uncle John, but every time he tried to move away, John would grab my cousin's arm and force Stephen to stay with him. Momma always said Uncle John was rude. Well, "uncouth" and "worthless drunk" was her actual description of him. Even at her own funeral, Momma was right. What could be so important that he felt the need to ramble on at a time like this? I couldn't believe how angry Uncle John looked, but couldn't make out what he was saying. In his wrinkled suit and loosened tie, he probably reeked of whiskey, even on a Sunday.

Unfortunately, Uncle John was too far back to meet my stare.

chapter five

April 16, 1934
Frisco City, Alabama

Aunt Matt stayed with us since Momma died. I kept telling her that I could take care of everyone and that she could go home, but she insisted on being there.

"Pretty girl, your Momma would want me here."

Secretly, I loved having Aunt Matt with us, and Henry, too.

Henry would come by every evening for dinner. He would tell us wild stories of his work with the railroad. Henry worked at the station loading and unloading the boxcars as the L&N came to the Frisco City station. He helped the passengers with their luggage and unloaded the shipments of fabric and other sundries shipped to our little town. He would tell funny stories of stow-away critters and sad stories of dirty, exhausted men looking for work. Most of these desperate travelers kept moving past Frisco City, unless, of course, the cotton or peanuts were ready for harvest. Sometimes, he would find a stowaway sleeping in an empty car. Henry would leave them be, though.

"They ain't doin' no harm. Just lookin' to get by," Henry would say.

Somehow, having the seats at the table filled by Aunt Matt and Henry made losing Momma a little easier. I didn't want Momma's chair to be empty, but I couldn't bear to sit in it myself.

* * * * *

Aunt Matt and I were sitting on the porch that afternoon in April. We were shucking some butter beans for dinner from our small garden out back. Momma, Meg, and I planted the butter beans along with green beans, cucumbers, lettuce, turnips, and okra the prior fall. The butter beans were the first to come in, so Aunt Matt and I picked some and planned to add them to a pot of ham hocks. The beans and hot-from-the-oven corn bread would make a nice supper. I was already looking forward to corn bread crumbled in milk for an evening snack when two police cars pulled in front of the house. Cousin Stephen, accompanied by a serious-looking man in a dark jacket and scuffed boots, got out of one car, and Marshal Brooks of Frisco City, got out of the other.

"Hattie, where's your daddy?" Stephen asked. Daddy must have heard the cars pull up, because he walked out of the house as Stephen, Marshal Brooks, and the strange man stepped up on the porch.

"Stephen, what are ya doing over in these parts?" Daddy asked as he looked from man to man and stopped at the strange man in the dark jacket, "Billy, what are you doing in Frisco today? Ya sure Clarke County is safe with two of their finest over here?"

Frisco City was located in Monroe County, one county over from Stephen's jurisdiction. Daddy seemed to know the strange man, but I'd never laid eyes on him. He was a big wall of a man with thick, dark hair. I wondered for a second how many yards of fabric Momma would have had to use to make a jacket that big. I wondered if Momma had ever met this man and what she would think of his unruly head of hair.

The presence of two police cars on our typically quiet street created a spectacle. Several of our neighbors gathered on their porches and strained to hear what the men were discussing. At least they were honest about their eavesdropping.

"Mister Andrews," the strange man said with a deep, steady voice, "we need you to come with us."

"Hubbard, we've got some questions about Addie," Stephen told Daddy, and then quietly, "Hub, John Howard has been running his mouth. I'm sure we can clear all this up at the station."

Daddy stiffened at the mention of Momma. He hadn't talked about what happened since that Saturday in January. To be completely honest, he hadn't really talked much at all. Aunt Matt kept saying that he would "brighten back up once his heart don't hurt", but over two months passed without much from him other than short orders to Aunt Matt and a "be back later" to us as he was already through the front door. Other than sitting in the parlor listening to the radio most evenings, going to bed earlier than he ever did before, and leaving most mornings before the rest of us awoke, I didn't know how he spent his time. I assumed he went to work and solitary walks after dinner, but he never said, and I never asked.

Without a word to Stephen, Marshal Brooks, or the strange man, Daddy squeezed my shoulder and turned to Aunt Matt. "I won't be long," he said.

With that, Marshal Brooks escorted him to the back seat of one of the cars. Stephen and the strange man got in front. Marshal Brooks went to the other car, and then both cars pulled away.

I looked across the street to see the neighbors staring back at me. Several of the women held their hands over their mouths and whispered to one another. The men shook their heads in disbelief before going back to the business of the day. I pressed my fingers hard into the sides of the bowl of shucked peas until my fingertips turned white and felt my anger, just as strongly as the day of Momma's funeral, turn my cheeks red. I turned sharply to Aunt Matt, searching for an explanation. What did Cousin Stephen mean by *questions about Addie,* and what did the strange man in the dark jacket need with Daddy? Why did the neighbors think it was any of their damn business? Aunt Matt didn't answer. She just gathered up our bowls.

"Go on, get in the house." Aunt Matt rushed me in without looking at the neighbors still gawking from their porches.

Later that evening, I lay in my bed, pretended to sleep, and tried to make sense of the day. Earlier, Aunt Matt and I finished fixing supper. She hurried us through dinner, then put the little ones to bed. Aunt Matt, Meg, and I listened to the radio for a while before she ordered us to bed as well.

I kept asking her when Daddy was going to be home, but she just said, "Baby, don't you worry about that. Your Daddy will be fine." Daddy had to be fine. Of course, he would be fine.

As I lay there in my small bed with Meg sound asleep next to me, I heard Henry and Aunt Matt talking on the porch. I don't think they knew my window was open or that I was still awake and could hear their conversation, even if I did have to strain a little. Mrs. Williams, the old widow across the street, had left her radio on as usual. I swear, as soon as Old Man Williams kicked the bucket a couple of years before, Mrs. Williams ran down to Hendrix General Store and bought the fanciest, most expensive radio Mr. Hendrix had for sale. Rumor has it that Mrs. Williams spent every dime Mr. Williams had saved on that radio. So, every night since, Mrs. Williams fell asleep in the rocker in her front parlor with the window open and the radio blaring. On this particular night, Viviane Seal's piercing soprano was being broadcast from Mrs. Williams's window for all of Frisco City to hear. However, if I held my breath and kept perfectly still so I wouldn't rustle my bedcovers, I could just make out what Henry and Matt were saying on the porch.

Apparently, Henry had gone into town to find out what happened with Daddy. Henry said that all people could talk about was the police showing up at our house.

"They're saying it wadn't no accident. They say he shot her out there in them woods and then made the whole story up," Henry told Aunt Matt.

According to Henry, Daddy was being questioned about Momma's death, and the Clarke County solicitor was determined to get an indictment from the Grand Jury, stating that Momma's death was no accident and that Daddy was responsible. My head started to spin. I squeezed my eyes shut and tried to tune their voices out. I tried to concentrate on Vivian Seal and whatever song she was singing, but all I could hear were the words Henry said. Daddy wouldn't do something like that. He couldn't. Momma's death was an accident, a terrible, awful accident. Daddy was a good man!

I lay awake for most of the night, waiting for Daddy to come home, but I must have drifted off sometime near dawn. When I woke up, I rushed into the kitchen to see if he was there, but only Aunt Matt was sitting at the table.

"He's come and gone already, Sweetie. Now, you go on and get ready for church."

* * * * *

John Howard has been running his mouth. Cousin Stephen's words haunted me for days. I finally found out from the twin teenage boys next door, what Uncle John had been busy with since Momma died. According to what the twins heard, Uncle John had been talking to anyone who would listen, including Aunt Audrey, Aunt Mittie and Uncle Melvin, Grandpa Lowman, and every man within ear's reach of the barstools of whatever honkytonk Uncle John found himself in for the evening. He was suspicious of Daddy's story and was all too eager to distract others from his own shortcomings with a tall tale about a crime supposedly committed by Hubbard Andrews. The way I saw it, this was Uncle John's chance to finally do something right in the eyes of the Lowmans, to finally be something other than the family disappointment, to finally have something bad to hang over Daddy's head. Uncle John wasn't going to miss this chance.

According to Momma, Uncle John showed promise in his youth, but WWI changed him. After the war, he came back to Crenshaw County, Alabama, with a temper and taste for whiskey. He made his living as a small-time farmer, and was content with rotating a couple of fields every few years between meager cotton and peanut crops. A garden and a couple of dairy cows kept his family of four fed and, until Momma's death, kept Aunt Audrey occupied and off his back. According to Momma, Aunt Audrey did most of the work around their little farm, and Uncle John did most of the "big talking". It was only in the last couple of months that Audrey started to tell John how disappointed she was in him.

In Uncle John's opinion, Aunt Audrey changed when her sister died. She was consumed with grief, and obsessed with how little her baby sister approved of her choice in husbands. Momma was quite vocal of her dislike of John when she was alive. After Momma died, her disapproval seemed even louder. John began to hear Addie's contempt for him in his own wife's voice. He sought solace from the constant judgments in the dark shadows of the local honky-tonks throughout Clarke, Monroe, and Crenshaw counties.

Uncle John was even more fed up with the Lowmans' concern for Daddy. Before Uncle John started to voice his suspicions, the entire Lowman clan seemed eager to console Daddy while he wept for Momma. They wanted to help him with his business ventures in Frisco City and Grove Hill while he grieved.

"The Good Lord would want us to help Hubbard in his time of need," the God-fearing Lowmans would all agree as they gathered around the table for Sunday supper in Searight, Alabama, just south of Luverne in Crenshaw County.

Malachi Lowman, or Papa Lowman as we called him, was even trying to save enough money to purchase a headstone for Momma. After John learned this one Sunday afternoon, I heard him mutter that the Andrews clan didn't needed financial help, and that if Hubbard Andrews wanted a fancy headstone for Momma, then "Hubbard should pay for the damn thing himself!"

Uncle John couldn't afford to hire the help needed for his fields or fix the dilapidated farm equipment that littered the small patch of land behind his home. Papa Lowman had never offered to help John Howard, not even when John went to him with his hat in his hand. Uncle John couldn't stand the idea of spending good money to memorialize a woman who seemed to enjoy torturing him while she was alive and continued to torture him after her death.

I guess Uncle John couldn't help but run Daddy's story of Momma's death through his mind. Suspicion of whether or not Daddy was telling the truth apparently started to grow in his mind during Momma's burial in Frisco City. Daddy's cousin, Stephen, had shared the tragic story of the accidental shooting and of Hubbard's hike through the woods with Momma's body. John thought the story lacked plausibility and suspected that the investigation into Addie's death was insufficient, if there was an investigation at all during the twenty-four hours between the gunshot and the burial. Uncle John was certain that no Andrews in the great state of Alabama, especially Hubbard's trusted cousin, Stephen, would look for the skeletons in any other Andrews's closet. John was sure there were plenty of skeletons to be found.

Uncle John shared his concerns with Papa Lowman. Why were Hubbard and Addie alone in the woods with no porter to tend to the boat? How would Addie know there were squirrels hiding in the vines if it was still dark out? How was Hubbard able to carry Addie, two rifles, and their pack for two miles through the heavily wooded area? How did Hubbard go unnoticed through the woods on the last day of the hunting season? Why did he choose to seek the assistance of his cousin in Jackson, thirty miles away, rather than the authorities in Barlow Bend or Willow Springs? Both towns were much closer. For that matter, why did he choose to drive thirty miles west to Jackson rather than thirty miles east to Frisco City after Addie was shot? Uncle John was also all too familiar with the choice gossip running rampant since Momma's death. The rumors told of sordid affairs between Daddy and several women in Clarke County near the hotel Daddy owned; Hubbard's *real business* in Grove

Hill according to Uncle John. All of these questions and rumors in Uncle John's mind added up to only one scenario: Momma's death was no accident, and Hubbard Andrews should pay for his obvious crime.

I overheard Uncle John and Papa Lowman arguing after supper one Sunday in March of 1934. Papa Lowman told Uncle John to clean up his act and stop drinking so much. He told John that he expected a lot more out of a son-in-law. Uncle John admitted he had faults, but insisted he was at least better than my daddy was to Momma.

"I didn't shoot my own wife, did I?" Uncle John yelled at Papa Lowman. "I'm not runnin' around on Audrey am I?"

John kept at Papa Lowman, insisting that Papa should listen to his suspicions about that day in January and Daddy's actions. He insisted that Papa Lowman at least consider that Daddy may have shot Momma in cold blood.

Uncle John may have failed many times in his life, but he succeeded in planting suspicion. I didn't know it then, but a seed of suspicion began to grow in Papa Lowman's ear that evening, then Aunt Audrey's mind, and finally, the Clarke County Sheriff's Office. On the night of Daddy's questioning by the Clarke County Sheriff Department, two and a half months after my mother's death, John Howard raised a toast of his best home brew to his own personal form of justice. *Everything evens out in the wash,* he probably thought to himself, unaware of how the cards would play out in the end for him, for Daddy, or for me.

chapter six

April 2, 1934

Daddy was so quiet in the weeks after Momma died, and didn't tell us anything other than "Your momma had an accident."

Even though I wanted to, I hadn't asked Daddy about that morning in the woods. I didn't want to make him angry or more heartbroken than he already appeared to be, but the appearance of Cousin Stephen and the strange man in the dark jacket proved that I couldn't ignore my curiosity any more. I decided that, as soon as I could get a moment alone with him, I'd ask Daddy what happened out in the woods. In my opinion, at the age of thirteen, I was old enough to know exactly what happened to Momma. I was no longer some little child who needed shelter from terrible things. For God's sake, the most terrible thing I could ever imagine had already happened. What else could I possibly need shelter from? Let Meg, Billy, and Albert be hidden from the truth. I needed to know.

I had also, in my opinion, earned the right to answers. I helped Aunt Matt each morning with breakfast, and got Billy, Albert, Meg, and myself ready and off to school. I was still at the top of my class despite coming home directly after school each afternoon to help Aunt Matt with dinner and daily chores. On the weekends, I made sure that all of us, especially Daddy, had fresh clothes for work and school the next week. I tended to Billy and Albert during church on Sundays, and had perfected Momma's *sit still or you won't be able to sit at all* look that she used to give all of us in the middle of Reverend Howlington's long-winded sermons. I cleaned scraped knees, soothed upset stomachs, and drove away the boogeyman from under beds in the middle of the night. My shoulders were perpetually waterlogged from the tears of my siblings. Daddy worked, took long walks, went to Grove Hill to check on the hotel, or did whatever he did that made him disappear at odd times of the day and night. I kept this family afloat.

I also heard the whispers of Frisco City. From the co-op to the schoolyard, I heard the whispers. Momma was always a popular topic of conversation in our little town, but since her death, she was all people could talk about. At first, the good people of Frisco City appeared concerned for Momma and for us kids, as if they shared some deep, binding friendship with her. Once Daddy left in the police car, the outpouring of sympathy and pity turned to curiosity, suspicion, and downright nasty gossip.

According to the running mouths on every front porch and dusty street corner, Daddy visited with several disreputable women all over Monroe and Clarke counties, especially over in Grove Hill. They said the visits started long before Momma died. In church one Sunday, two old biddies sitting right behind me had the audacity to suggest that Daddy was carrying on with a woman right there in Frisco City! They hid their shame behind their fans when I turned to glare at them. One unbelievable yet popular story was that Daddy knew the woods near Barlow Bend so well because he had a girlfriend out that way. I couldn't walk into Hendrix's General Store without the place going silent. I constantly seemed to interrupt the debate of whether or not the dashing Hubbard Andrews shot the lovely, yet unconventional Addie Andrews in the woods at Barlow Bend.

Many believed Daddy regularly went by the alias Hubert Anders when circumstance required a surname other than Andrews. This, I found most curious. At the time, Andrews was a highly-respected and revered name in Alabama, especially Clarke, Monroe, and Crenshaw counties where every third house seemed to have some relation to the Andrews name. According to Daddy, our people, the Andrews, went all the way back to the Revolutionary War. He said that our people proudly fought the British tyrants from our plantations in the Carolinas before heading south to Alabama. Why would Daddy ever use a name other than Andrews when our name should make any man proud?

Many of the men who spat tobacco juice like grasshoppers while loitering in front of the shops in downtown Frisco City appeared to relish the theories of Daddy's guilt. They speculated on every detail of Momma's death from the type of gun that was used, to the thick brush in Barlow Bend to the best squirrel hot spots and hunting techniques. They argued that Addie Andrews was too skilled to make such a fatal mistake. Several months before all of this mess, these same men would have gathered around Daddy as if he was the hunting messiah sent from God above to teach all of them how to hit the tiny head of a varmint from seventy-five yards out. Since Momma died and the police came to our house, these same ignorant men became self-proclaimed experts, overflowing with squirrel hunting wisdom.

Some of the inhabitants of our little town defended Daddy, saying that even the best hunters have accidents, and that Momma, however skilled she may have been, made one careless mistake. They also adamantly argued that Daddy wouldn't have carried Momma through the woods for two miles if he had killed her. They said a guilty man wouldn't have put himself through such a chore, that only a strong, enduring love would motivate a man to such a heroic act. Well, at least, Mr. and Mrs. Hendrix, proprietors of Hendrix's General Store, offered me their support when I stood at the counter waiting to pay for the flour, sugar, and lard needed for one Saturday supper.

Tilting her face to the side, Mrs. Hendrix professed, "Your daddy carried your poor momma through those woods to bring her to rest, bless his heart." She always placed a hand on her heart when she said this, a convincing, even if unnecessary, touch added to her frequent sentiment.

The worst part of the local chatter is what they said about Momma, "Crazy Addie was always so careless", and "how could any man deal with her as long as Hubbard did?"

I heard them talk about her being mad, that our adventures throughout Alabama were strange, inappropriate, and unacceptable. They said that Meg and I were better off without her, and maybe the Lowman sisters would show us the proper way for a mother, and subsequently, young ladies, to behave. Some even said that momma had it coming; that they always knew her "wildin' ways would lead to a tragic endin.'"

Mrs. Williams shared the most hurtful rumors to a small gathering on her front porch one Saturday morning. Unfortunately, Mrs. Williams was hard of hearing, as one would guess from the bellowing of her radio every night, and didn't realize just how loudly she spoke. I heard every word crystal clear from my seat on our front porch.

"You know, I heard Addie Andrews did plenty of carrying on herself! I guess she didn't want ol' Hubbard to have all the fun." Mrs. Williams waited a few beats for the laughter of the small crowd to die down, and then, "Well, why else would she go gallivanting around the way she did? And with those sweet girls in tow? I only pray that our Lord and Savior will forgive her sinful ways and welcome her into His fold."

I wanted to yell to Mrs. Williams that Momma didn't need the prayers of a sad, lonely, old woman, and that no matter how much preaching she did from her front porch, her flock would always be just a bunch of pathetic gossips. I wanted to, but I didn't.

I knew they were wrong about her. They were jealous because Momma always seemed bigger, better than Frisco City. She was too special for the confines of this tiny little town tucked away behind the thick pines and gray moss of Monroe County. She was unconventional and adventurous, but loving and everything a mother should be at the same time. If the sun was up, Momma was moving. We always had clothes that fit right; pretty dresses for every occasion, carefully stitched by her delicate fingers. She taught Meg and me how to bake cookies and tend the garden. Our table overflowed every day with scrumptious meals, prepared by her loving hands. The house was immaculately kept, with clean linens and fresh flowers in every room. We never missed Reverend Howlington's sermons on Sunday mornings, and were reminded of his lessons every time we slipped up.

Sometimes though, I think Momma got bored of her daily chores. I think the walls of our little house started to suffocate her on occasion. Sometimes, she needed to remind herself that adventures could be found right around any corner.

"You just have to make the turn," she would say to me as we rode with the ragtop down, feeling free as the wind whipped through our hair. Momma's smile was never bigger than it was from behind the wheel, flying down an open road. In my mind, the world belonged to Momma. Momma shined in the center of our lives like the sun, and the rest of us were warm in her light.

I had to know how and why that light was taken from me, so one afternoon in April, as my siblings and I trudged home down Bowden Street after school, I decided to ask Daddy how Momma died. Ignoring the rumors around town had become too difficult, and I felt that Daddy owed me an explanation. I needed to hear exactly what happened from his lips. When our little house came into view, Billy and Albert took off running toward the back yard. Being forced to sit still all day on the hard benches of our schoolhouse was pure torture for the two of them. Meg had plans to meet up with a couple of girls her age that lived two blocks over, so she handed me her lunch pail and borrowed books, and headed down Oak Street. Off she went, leaving me to walk the last block home by myself.

While I was consumed by confusion in the months following Momma's death, Meg seemed to bloom, despite the grief that enveloped our home. At nearly twelve years old, Meg's childish appearance of chubby cheeks and stocky gait had given way to the beginnings of a lovely young lady with porcelain skin, soft, honey curls, delicate features, and Momma's blue eyes. Meg's heart was crushed when Momma died, but if she was plagued by the same curiosity that kept me awake at night, she never let it show. She floated through life as if protected against the true reality of our situation. I must admit that I was a little envious of the peace she had found.

With the boys out back playing, and Meg down Oak Street out of earshot, that afternoon would be my only chance to ask Daddy about Momma's death. When I saw him sitting on the front porch cleaning his pipe, I mustered up every bit of courage that Momma instilled in me. As I climbed the three steps up to our porch, I heard Momma's voice in my head, "Speak your mind, Child. Whatever has put that look on your face is just itchin' to get out."

I sat down next to Daddy, took a deep breath, and spoke the words quickly so I wouldn't chicken out mid-question, "Daddy, what really happened to Momma in the woods?"

Daddy turned and looked at me sharply, grasping his pipe tightly in one hand. "Hattie, I told you what happened."

"You told me Momma had an accident, but you didn't tell me how." At this, Daddy got up from his chair and leaned against one of the front columns. His back was turned toward me, but I pressed on, "Daddy, people are saying you did it."

I held my breath, waiting for a switch to come at my legs or for Daddy to order me to fetch his belt for saying such a terrible thing to my father. Momma always encouraged us to speak our minds, but Daddy reminded us to use respectful tones and engage only in approved topics of conversation. Sometimes, his reminders were harsh. Asking my father if he killed my mother was certainly not acceptable in the house I grew up in.

Daddy's response surprised me. He didn't chastise me for asking such a question or for listening to the town gossip. He didn't banish me away from him or even ignore my question. Instead, he turned and looked straight into my eyes. He was crestfallen and weary, all of a sudden appearing exhausted.

"Hattie, Sweetie, I would never hurt your mother. She meant the world to me." With that, he turned and went into the house.

I would never hurt your mother. That short sentence didn't contain the details I craved, but it told me what I needed to know. Daddy didn't do what the pathetic gossips of Frisco City couldn't stop yammering about. He didn't hurt Momma. He never would. His love for her and me was right there standing on our porch. At the time, I decided that was all I needed to know.

Daddy remained silent through dinner and left soon after on one of his walks. Aunt Matt and I cleaned the kitchen and got the boys to bed. Meg drifted off around nine. I lay awake until I heard Daddy come up the porch stairs just before midnight. He must have tripped on the last step, because I heard him curse the planks after he stumbled. I considered getting up so I could make sure he was all right, but decided to let him be.

chapter seven

September 1934

The Monday after the policemen questioned Daddy, he had gone back to work as he did nearly every day since Momma died. Along with owning a small hotel and café in Grove Hill, Daddy worked as the Raleigh Man for Monroe County. The usual stock of ointments, salves, and kitchen sundries seemed to move in and out of our house as they normally did in February and March, but in April of that year, sales slowed down to a standstill. Boxes bearing the trusted Raleigh name started accumulating first in the pantry, then the parlor, and finally, stacked to the ceiling near the back door. All through April and most of May, Daddy went door-to-door without much luck. Most of the good people of Frisco City tried to conjure up decent excuses for not buying Daddy's stock, blaming their lack of money or bad timing.

"Oh, bless your heart, I'm plum full up from my last order," Mrs. Williams told him one morning as I was leaving for school. Unfortunately for Daddy's pride, that bellowing voice could be heard two counties over. She might as well have yelled, "Lock your doors! The boogeyman is comin'!" Three months earlier, Daddy couldn't keep the products in stock. Now, most of his former customers wouldn't even answer his knock at their doors.

For weeks on end, Daddy left the house at first light and was gone until late evening as he peddled his wares to nearly every small town in Monroe County. Finally, after several weeks of trying with very few sales to show for his efforts, he decided to get out of the Raleigh Products business.

Daddy blamed the low sales on the economy, saying, "Nobody has money to spend on this stuff right now," but I knew the truth: No one wanted to give his or her hard-earned money to a man who may or may not be a murderer.

The rumors and speculation spread like wildfire through the county. Most chose to avoid Daddy altogether to appear that they weren't taking either side. His reputation in Monroe County was damaged beyond repair. Not even the upstanding Andrews name could bump sales.

By June, the overt chatter had evolved to hushed tones. The sympathetic sighs and tilted heads had turned into suspicious and curious stares. Daddy stopped attending church on Sunday mornings with us, claiming that he had too much work to do. I knew that was a lie. Daddy just couldn't take the stares anymore. I, on the other hand, must have had more of Momma's spitfire running through my veins than I first thought. I gladly met the challenge of walking into the Frisco City First Methodist Church every Sunday morning with my eyes fixed on the pulpit in front of me. I may not have had Momma's pretty singing voice, but I sang every bit as loudly as she would, louder still if the choir was singing one of her favorite hymns.

At the end of June, Daddy threw in the towel.

"Dinner will be ready just as soon as the grits are done, Daddy," I told him over my shoulder as I stirred a few potential lumps out of the grits.

Henry and the boys had caught a bunch of catfish, and after the fish were cleaned, fileted and deboned, I fried the nuggets to a golden brown. Paired with grits, fried catfish was one of Daddy's favorites.

"Sweetie, I sold the house," Daddy said as he sat down at the kitchen table. He speared a big piece of fried catfish with his fork.

"You what?" I wasn't sure what he meant.

"Frisco City just ain't workin' anymore," he said through a mouthful of fish and breading. "I think we need a fresh start."

"Okay?" I said and then, "um, where are we gonna live?"

"I was thinking we go on to Grove Hill. To the hotel."

"But this is Momma's home." I couldn't bear the thought of leaving her, leaving the house that seemed to keep her. "I don't want to go, Daddy. Please."

The walls of the little kitchen began to close in on me. The hot June air, combined with the heat from the stove was too much. I turned from the grits to open the back door, hoping for a breeze to slow the spinning in my head.

"Sweetie, it's done and it's the best thing for us," Daddy said.

"Maybe you could buy it back," I begged. Why would Daddy sell our house without asking me if I wanted to leave?

"No. We're going." Daddy dismissed my pleas without hesitation.

I stood in the doorway stunned for a few minutes, and then turned back to the grits. Unfortunately, the lumps had formed despite my early attempts at stirring, and I could feel the bottom of the pot sticking. I turned the flame off, but the damage was done.

"Well, these are ruined!" I snapped and tossed the pot into the sink.

Daddy retrieved the pot, gave them a quick stir, and said. "The grits are fine. Now, go on and get your brothers and sister and let's eat."

I did what Daddy told me to do. As always, Billy and Albert were far too slow coming to the table, but eventually, we gathered around the table for cold, fried catfish and lumpy, slightly burnt grits. After washing the dishes, I spent the rest of that evening wiping tears and consoling broken hearts. Frisco City was our home, and none of us were ready to leave.

Soon after Daddy sold our little house on Bowden Street, we prepared to move to his hotel in Grove Hill, Alabama. Daddy tried to make living on the top floor of a hotel and running a small café on the first floor sound exciting, but my mind painted a more realistic picture. I knew as soon as he told me that he sold the house, my life was about to change again, and probably in ways I would not like. Aunt Matt wouldn't be in Grove Hill to help me with Albert and Billy, the laundry, or cleaning our new home. The rearing of my two young brothers was now entirely up to me. I feared that my days would be filled with washing linens, dusting windowsills and baseboards, mopping floors, and cleaning up after customers in the café. And we would be miles and miles away from Momma. Without even starting my new life and tedious daily chores, I yearned for one of Momma's road trips.

I worried about Aunt Matt and Henry. Wouldn't they be lonely back in their little two-room shack without the four of us around? I couldn't stand the thought of spending Saturday mornings without Aunt Matt humming in our kitchen as she fixed biscuits and gravy for us.

On my final day as her student, I tried to focus on her lesson. "Should I add more lard or is the sausage grease enough?" "How much flour?" "How brown should the roux be?" I hoped that if I asked enough questions, we would stay in that kitchen forever, Aunt Matt and me.

"Baby," Aunt Matt said, "them hungry men at that hotel is gonna pay a pretty penny for this gravy. You just teach that cook Aunt Matt's secrets." She chuckled with delight as she tasted my first successful batch before we left our home and the kitchen that I loved.

On our last morning in Frisco City, Meg and I brought fresh flowers to Momma's grave. We had gone into the woods behind our house, just the two of us, and picked a big bouquet of wildflowers. Momma always told me that wildflowers were the best flowers because no one could tell them where to grow or how to bloom. The wildflowers followed their own plan. We placed the big bouquet on the ground next to the small marker with only an etching of her name. My heart sank knowing that we were leaving Frisco City, leaving her there without a proper stone on her grave that declared how special she was and how desperately we loved her. Aunt Matt promised me that she would tend Momma's grave and make sure that she placed fresh wildflowers near the marker as long as they bloomed.

As we pulled away from our white house with three bedrooms, a big parlor, an indoor bathroom, and the little kitchen that I loved, I tried to memorize every detail, from the big oak tree in front, to the painted cedar trunks that Daddy had used as columns on the front porch. Daddy had leaned against those columns when he told me he didn't hurt Momma. Those columns meant that he loved everyone inside the house.

Those columns also showed our corner of the world how unique my mother was. Momma said that when Daddy built this house, she made him leave the knots on the trunks rather than smoothing out the odd shapes and bumps so that the whole town would know that inside the house were very special, unique people, free from the boring expectations and limitations of our town.

I stared at our home until we turned left turn off Bowden Street, onto County Road 38, and our little house disappeared. I turned back around in my seat, closed my eyes, and sucked down the cry that was welling up in my throat.

Somewhere along County Road 38, between Frisco City and Grove Hill, Daddy laid out my new life. He quickly confirmed my fears. He needed and required my full attention in the café, which meant going to school was a thing of my past. I had dreamt of going to teacher's college, but that dream was replaced with an apron and kitchen utensils. He wanted Meg and the boys to finish grammar school, but I was in the ninth grade. I had all the education Daddy required. Paying customers ranked over a high school diploma.

"Hattie, I don't need you in school. I need you at the res'trint," Daddy told me in a tone that left no room for compromise or argument. "Now, you'll help me out in the café, and next year, when Meg's done with eighth grade, she'll start work, too, and then the boys when they're done. That's just how it's gonna be." Meg and my brothers slept right through Daddy's plan for the family.

By September of that year, we were all settled into our new routines and new home in Grove Hill. I celebrated my fourteenth birthday in the hotel cafe with a cake that I made from strawberries bought at the corner market on Main Street in Grove Hill. Before that cake, I don't know if I'd ever had store bought strawberries. The hotel was right on Main Street, in the heart of Grove Hill, and seemed to be constantly surrounded by the typical, exciting hustle and bustle of a county seat, but we had no place for a garden. The week of my birthday, Daddy gave me a few extra pennies for strawberries for my cake. He also gave me a new dress made of blue cotton gabardine with tiny pink and yellow flowers on it, from the dress shop two blocks over. It was my first store bought dress.

Meg, Billy, and Albert left for school every morning at eight o'clock. The school was only a few blocks away from the hotel, but Meg complained daily about getting the boys to school as if she had to wrangle cattle on a drive through the open plains of Texas.

Meg met her new responsibilities with a frequently expressed sense of martyrdom, "Hattie, you will never understand how challenging the boys can be! Running ahead or lingering behind. By the time I sit down, my nerves are so frazzled; I can hardly concentrate on what teacher has to say. At least Miss Springer understands the extraordinary challenges of my life!" Meg had perfected a flair for the dramatic.

I didn't share my intense jealousy of my sister getting to go to school. I was fairly certain that Meg would revel in the idea that she had something I wanted, and there was no way I would give her that satisfaction. I loved going to school back in Frisco City. I found nearly every subject fascinating, except arithmetic. Reciting multiplication tables and practicing long division didn't appeal to me or challenge me in any way. I raced through our arithmetic lessons, checking my work once before turning in my paper long before my classmates. Those of us who quickly finished those monotonous lessons were given the privilege of selecting a book from Miss Hendrix's personal collection. She had fairy tales and adventure stories, science fiction and mysteries. She would even let me borrow books to take home. Miss Hendrix trusted that I would return the books in pristine condition and quickly, and I kept her trust by doing just that. Momma called me a "voracious reader", and I liked the idea that I was voracious at something.

I missed Miss Hendrix terribly. She was a lovely, petite woman in her early twenties. Every day, she would pin her blonde hair back just above her ears. Her cotton dresses were always immaculately presented, as if freshly pressed each morning, and she would greet each of us at the door, with her gleaming white teeth and soft, pink cheeks. Once, I asked Miss Hendrix why she had not married. She grew up in Frisco City, the daughter of the general store owners. She returned to Frisco City and her parents' home on Oak Street right after attending teacher's college in Birmingham. I couldn't understand why a woman as delightful as Miss Hendrix was unmarried.

"We all must choose our own paths, Hattie," was her simple yet cryptic reply. Before Miss Hendrix, I had never heard of a woman choosing not to marry.

My current path at the hotel and café in Grove Hill was certainly not of my choosing. School had been replaced by seemingly endless days of mindless tasks. I woke well before dawn, dressed in the dark so I wouldn't disturb Meg, and headed down to the café on the street level of our hotel. I started the coffee first. When the hotel was full, we went through several pots each morning, so I had to make sure we had several in reserve when the guests arrived for breakfast and quickly drank their first, second, and sometimes third cups. Next, I helped Henrietta with the biscuits, making them exactly according to Aunt Matt's recipe. Miss Henrietta had no problem using Aunt Matt's recipe, especially because it was the same as hers. Country ham was heated on the stovetop in a large cast iron skillet that was so heavy I had to use both hands to lift it. Luckily, Miss Henrietta, a colored woman who only needed one hand to lift the cast iron skillet, was a very good cook and a tireless employee. No matter how early I headed down to the kitchen, Miss Henrietta was already fast at work.

Daddy and the children would come down the stairs around seven. I served the kids breakfast at a little table tucked in a corner of the kitchen, and then turned my attention to the customers in the dining room. Daddy, Meg, and I served the guests as they arrived downstairs from their rented rooms or stopped in for a bite on their way to work.

Most of our hotel guests were migrant workers in search of a new start at a mill or factory, but only earned enough money for a couple of nights before moving on to the next stop on the L&N rail. Many of our café customers, however, were long-time residents of Grove Hill. The Clarke County Courthouse was three blocks down Main Street from our café, so several of the attorneys, bailiffs, sheriff deputies, and clerks stopped in for breakfast or lunch. Sometimes, I would linger as I cleared away dishes and wiped down tables just to hear the men debate their latest cases over bowls of stew, sausage gravy, or fried pork chops.

The café was small, but lovely. Each table was pre-set every night with coffee cups, silverware, napkins, a small vase with a fresh flower, and a small jar of jelly, usually blackberry or strawberry. Often, guests would comment on how good the homemade jelly was, sweet and bursting with fruit. I found it hard not to swell with pride when I heard their compliments or saw how quickly our hungry companions devoured breakfast. I liked talking with the guests and listening to their stories, especially the odd court cases and stories from the railroad, but I wondered if that was all my life was going to be: serving breakfast, lunch, and dinner to guests crowded around twelve café tables, and listening to the stories of strangers rather than having my own to tell. As each guest finished, Daddy worked the register, making sure that every penny was accounted for, and I returned to the kitchen to help Miss Henrietta wash, dry, and put away stacks of dirty dishes.

After Meg and the boys left for school and the guests were off to work, Daddy and I would sit down to breakfast. Every morning, without fail, Daddy laid out the day's chores for me. A woman named Ruthie came by every other day to change the linens on the twelve guest beds in the little hotel, but most of the other tasks were my responsibility. Daddy dictated the lunch and supper menu as I made a list of any items needed from the corner market. He also reminded me of the rotating cleaning schedule, which I knew by heart: Tuesdays and Saturdays, we mopped the floors; Wednesdays, we dusted all surfaces; and Thursdays, we wiped all windows and sills. The floors were swept and the indoor bathrooms, one on each floor, were cleaned daily. Meg, Billy, and Albert would all pitch in with the list after school because most of my day would be spent in the café, prepping lunch and dinner, washing dishes, waiting on customers, and wiping down tables after each service.

My reprieve came on Fridays when the Tuscaloosa Bookmobile came to town. The bookmobile was a large, older model black wagon. Behind the cab, the rear sides folded down to reveal hundreds of books. The first time I saw the bookmobile's sides fold down, I couldn't believe how many books were waiting on the shelves for me. A bookmobile didn't stop in Frisco City, so I had never seen one before. Miss Hendrix's collection paled in comparison to the treasures before me. Each week, I returned my picks from the week before and checked out at least three new novels, mainly romances and mysteries.

Both librarians knew me by name and marveled at how quickly I tore through the pages.

At night, after I put Billy and Albert to bed, made sure the dining room downstairs was set for breakfast service, and the kitchen was spotless, I liked to lie in my little bed and read. I was always tired to the bone, but my mind raced with my new responsibilities as café waitress, hotel maid, and mother to two young boys and a girl who believed wholeheartedly that she was all grown up at twelve years old.

I craved the distraction I found between the musty pages of my books. Each contained the possibilities of new friends and formidable enemies, desperate circumstances and paradise settings, all in sharp contrast to my humble and mundane existence in the hotel. The fourth and top floor of the small hotel I called home was a far cry from the luxurious suites I read about in my novels.

I liked to lie in bed and read, but Meg demanded, night after night, that I turn off the little lamp that barely lit our room.

"Hattie, turn off that dreadful light right now! I am plum exhausted and can't sleep with it shining in my eyes!"

Meg's whining made finishing a novel in the comfort of my bed impossible. In order to keep the peace, I turned off my lamp and tried to force myself asleep. Some nights, I was successful, reciting prayers from our church in Frisco City in my head until I drifted off, but other nights, most nights, no amount of tricks would work. As soon as I closed my eyes, Momma's face would appear. Her blue eyes and bright smile sparkled in my mind. I could hear her laughter, full and contagious. Some nights, I could almost feel her lying next to me, the warmth of her body pressed against my side as we squeezed together in my tiny bed.

On the nights when I missed her too much to lie there in silence; when I felt the pain of her absence welling up in my throat; when the loneliness that her death created seemed to take my breath away; I snuck downstairs. Quietly in the dark, I would go to the kitchen first. My favorite late-night snack was corn bread crumbled in a glass of milk, but crackers in milk would also do if the corn bread had all been eaten. I would take my glass and book and sit at the far corner table in the dining room. By candlelight, I read.

After a couple of hours alone with my book, my candle would have nearly burnt away and my mind would finally, albeit momentarily, be quiet. I made sure to leave the table as I found it, removing any evidence of my midnight retreat. I would sneak back upstairs—my feet snugly encased in socks—and creep inside our bedroom making sure not to disturb Meg. Then, finally, I closed my eyes, and slept. I didn't choose to leave school to work in a hotel with my father, Miss Henrietta, and Ruthie; to raise three children at the age of fourteen; or to lose Momma; but each week, I would eagerly go on countless written adventures with my newfound heroes and heroines, pirates and detectives, damsels in distress, and quick-witted villains. In those pages, I found a new education and a lifetime escape route.

chapter eight

September 1934
Grove Hill, Alabama

My Saturdays were so much different than they used to be in Frisco City. Before the last time Momma went hunting with Daddy at Barlow Bend, I waited all week for Saturday, eager to find out what she had in store for us. Would we spend the morning in the garden and the afternoon listening to her stories on the front porch? Would we spend the day in the kitchen with Aunt Matt canning vegetables and making jellies? Would we be hurried to Momma's car and carried off to theater houses or dance halls, open pastures or moss-covered woods?

In Grove Hill, Saturdays were utterly predictable. My day was spent in the café. The businessmen of the workweek, with the exception of a few from the courthouse held over for long trials, would transform into family men. Our little café became crowded with mothers in fine crepe and silk dresses; seated between fathers in polished welts; and children in their best cotton frocks. The fascinating conversations centered on crime details and trial strategies were replaced with shopping lists and pleasantries about the weather. If Saturdays in the café weren't so busy with every family from the surrounding countryside coming to town for the day, I would have been bored to tears.

* * * * *

On September 15, 1934, I went about my regular duties as café hostess and waitress. The breakfast service was typically slow for a Saturday morning, but the lunch service was one of our busiest yet. Miss Henrietta fried every piece of chicken we had, and nearly all of the catfish and pork chops as well. Daddy seemed extremely pleased with the booming sales, and after the last table from lunch paid their bill, he carried the drawer to the back room to count the register with a big smile on his face.

Just as I was wiping down the last table and about to set the tables for the dinner service, the strange man from that day way back in April in Frisco City walked into the café. I recognized him immediately. He wore a white buttoned-down shirt, black vest, and navy pants, and was just as big as he seemed before. He was sweating from the warm temperature even without the large, dark jacket he wore in April. Who could blame him in this heat and with his thick hair? His thick, unruly mane must feel like a wool hat pulled tight down to his ears and collar.

"Good afternoon, Sir. Sit wherever you like," I smiled at him as I motioned to the empty dining room, "We are out of chicken, but still have a few pork chops and catfish. Can I get you an iced tea?"

"No, Miss. I'm looking for Hubbard Andrews. Is he here?" He stood directly in front of the door and scanned the café with his dark eyes.

I told the man to wait there and went to the back to get Daddy. When we returned to the dining room, Daddy first and me directly behind him, two deputies wearing Clarke County badges had joined the strange man. Daddy stopped suddenly when he saw the three men standing between him and the door.

"Hubbard Andrews," the strange man said and revealed the handcuffs he was holding in his giant hand, "You are hereby under arrest for the murder of Missus Addie Andrews."

PART 2

motive & opportunity

chapter nine

September 1934
Grove Hill, Alabama

"Stop it!" I leapt toward the strange man and struck his chest with both of my hands bound tightly into fists. All of the anger I felt toward the gossips of Frisco City came out of me in sharp blows. One after the other, I struck the man with every bit of strength I had. "Leave us alone! Leave us alone!" I cried as I continued to strike him.

That was what my heart wanted to do, but, instead, I froze. My lips allowed no sound. My feet were still, as if bolted to the floor, and my limp arms dangled at my sides. Daddy was arrested right in front of me. Daddy was handcuffed and treated like a criminal, a murderer. Daddy murdered Momma? The sheriff thought Daddy looked into Momma's beautiful eyes and pulled the trigger of his rifle. These men thought Daddy took her away from me.

Before I really knew what was happening, the strange man, who I would later learn to be Detective William Murray of the Clarke County Sheriff's Office, handcuffed Daddy and told him that he could keep silent if he wanted and that he would be given an attorney.

Daddy glanced at me and said, "I won't be long. Don't worry." Then, the three men took him away.

The front door slamming felt like a slap in the face. Daddy was supposed to fix the hinges on the door that afternoon so it wouldn't slam shut every time a customer walked through the door. I guessed the door would continue to slam until Daddy came home. I just didn't know when that would be. As the sting faded, I realized that I was holding my breath.

"Were handcuffs really necessary?" I asked to the empty room.

For a moment, I looked around, wondering what I was supposed to do. *Do I tell Meg, Billy, and Albert that Daddy was handcuffed and taken to jail? Do I finish getting the dining room ready for dinner service? Do I tell Henrietta that Daddy was just arrested so I have no clue what we're supposed to do with the hotel guests or dinner service? Do I run four blocks over to the jail and beg the men inside to let Daddy go?*

"Henrietta, I'm going out for a bit," I yelled toward the kitchen.

I propped the *Sorry, We're Closed* sign in the window, and rushed through the café door. I ran down Main Street and then turned right onto Jackson Road, dashing passed the few pedestrians sauntering down the sidewalk. In four short blocks and what felt like mere seconds, I was standing, out of breath, in front of the Clarke County jail. My heart raced and beads of sweat streamed down my back under my cotton frock and apron.

I must have appeared insane sprinting down Jackson Road, with my apron on and clutching my pen and tablet, one in each hand. The old biddies back in Frisco City would have loved each delightfully embarrassing morsel of the scene I surely made. I quickly took off my apron, wiped my face with the hem, then rolled it into a ball around my pen and tablet. I smoothed my hair and tried not to look as crazed as I felt. As I walked into the foyer, I tried to remember all of the legal terms used in the murder mysteries I loved to read, but, much to my disappointment, I just felt incredibly aware of standing alone in a jail looking for my father.

"May I help yew, Miss?" asked the officer seated behind a desk toward the back of the room. The way he squished and dragged out the 'yewww', made the hair on my arms stand up, and reminded me of the voices of the men outside Hendrix General Store in Frisco City.

I approached him and said, "I am looking for my father, Hubbard Andrews. I think he was brought here just now."

"Speak up now," he said, "I can barely hear ya, girl."

So much for discretion, I thought. I repeated myself loud enough for everyone in the entryway to hear.

"Uh, huh," the officer muttered, "And why do you think that?"

"Because they just arrested him in our God-forsaken dining room!" My voice cracked as tears filled my eyes. I swallowed hard and forced myself not to cry. I looked the officer directly in the eyes—after all, what did I have to be ashamed of—and asked, "Will you please see if he was brought here? Mister Hubbard Andrews?"

"Wait here, Miss. I'll go check."

I sat down on the hard, wooden bench and waited for what seemed like an eternity until the officer finally came back.

"Miss Andrews, your daddy was brought here," the officer said, then gave me the all too familiar head tilt of sympathy, "Seems the charge is murder. Your momma?"

"Are you asking me if he did it?"

"Oh, no, Miss. Just...well, he was brought here. They're processing him now. He'll have to stay here a while."

"When can he come home?"

"Well, it bein' Saturday and all...Judge Bedsole won't be back till Monday. So, the judge will decide Monday."

"Decide what?"

"Oh, ya know, bail, trial dates, all that," said the officer as if Daddy was arrested for murder every day of the week; as if Daddy being arrested was common or mundane. I wanted to smack him hard, right across the face, but thought better of it.

"So, he can't come home yet?"

I felt like I was six years old again lost at the State Fair. I was supposed to hold onto Momma's hand, but I let go, just for a second. When I turned to grab her hand again, she was gone. All I could see was a sea of legs. The crowd swept in so fast and chaotic, it pushed me away from Momma until I was completely alone standing on a grassy patch next to the main drag. Luckily, on that day, Momma found me within minutes. Momma's hand wouldn't lead me away from the nightmare that surrounded me in the jailhouse.

I left the jail and walked back toward the hotel with my head spinning. Daddy would be *arraigned* on Monday, a term I had learned from my novels. Daddy would enter his plea of *not guilty*, the judge would set his bail, I would pay the clerk, and then we would wait for the trial, at least that's what happened in my books. So, I would go to the courthouse on Monday and wait for him. I would get him back.

Around four o'clock, I snuck in through the back entrance to the hotel, cutting through the kitchen. I could smell that Henrietta already had the grease hot for the dinner service. We would have customers soon, so I ran the four flights of stairs up to my room to clean up before going to work. I splashed some water on my face and brushed my hair, re-pinning it back on the sides.

"Meg?" I called down the hall.

She responded with an annoyed, "Yeah, Hattie, what?" from the room we used as a parlor.

"Make sure the boys get dinner and washed up before bed. We've got church tomorrow, and you kids have Sunday school," I told her, "Oh, and, Daddy's out. If you need me, I'll be downstairs." For this last part, I looked straight at her from the doorway of our makeshift parlor, "Make sure it's an emergency."

I didn't have time to tell Meg what happened. I planned to tell her later that night, after the boys were asleep and the customers had all come and gone. Meg would surely have made a huge scene and give some sort of tear-soaked monologue, but I had work to do, so I put off the inevitable, ran down the stairs, and gave the dining room a quick once-over. At four-thirty on the dot, I unlocked the front door and flipped the *Sorry, We're Closed* to *Yes, We're Open! Please come in.*

The café was crowded that night with a steady stream of hungry customers. When the place was empty and clean, and the front door securely locked, I sat down to a bowl of butter beans and ham. After devouring every bite, I carefully counted the register drawer. Between lunch and dinner that day, there was $46.25 in the register. Daddy always counted the drawer privately after every service, so I had no idea so much money would be in it. I also had no idea how much Daddy's bail would cost. I hoped the $46.25 would be enough.

The next morning, I awoke in a foggy haze. My muscles ached, and my mind immediately rushed to panic over Daddy being arrested. When I opened my eyes, I couldn't believe what I saw. Momma was sitting at the end of my bed, staring at me.

"Wake up, Hattie. We gotta get to church."

I sprang up and was about to wrap my arms around her neck, sure that the nightmare of the last nine months was over. However, as my eyes cleared, I realized that I wasn't looking at my mother's, but rather her twin's.

"Aunt Mittie, what are you doing here?" I whispered as I glanced at Meg's bed.

"I already sent Meg downstairs with the boys for some breakfast," Mittie answered, "I figured we needed to have ourselves a little talk, just us ladies."

I couldn't believe how much Mittie looked like Momma, even if she did look a bit older. Momma's skin was always so smooth, but Mittie had the beginnings of lines around her eyes and more of a tan than Momma ever let herself get. "A wide brim hat is a lady's best friend," Momma would say every time we headed to the garden to dig around in the dirt. Still, Mittie had my mother's eyes, cobalt blue, with the power to convince anyone of anything. I hadn't looked into those eyes for months.

"So, I guess you heard about Daddy?" I asked.

"Yes, Honey. Melvin and I heard last night. You should have sent word. We're your family."

"Aunt Mittie, I haven't seen you since before Momma..."

"I know. I'm sorry. I just couldn't...but you need me now more than ever. Now, have you heard anything? About your Daddy?"

"All I know is that he's been arrested for killin' Momma. His arraignment is on Monday. I'm going."

"Oh."

"Yes, and nobody else knows yet, and I think that's best. I thought about tellin' Meg, but decided not to. I'll go on Monday and get this all straightened out. He'll come home, and there won't be nothin' more to talk about."

With that, I hopped out of bed and went to my wardrobe. I chose my blue floral dress and cream slip. From the top shelf, I pulled down my straw hat with a lily-of-the-valley detail on the side that I thought complimented the little flowers on the dress. I also pulled out my cream gloves that matched the hat.

"That's a pretty dress," Mittie said.

"Thanks, Daddy gave it to me for my birthday," I said. I may have emphasized the word *Daddy* too hard. I saw Mittie flinch in the reflection of the little mirror on my vanity.

"Hattie, Honey, we don't know what's gonna happen with your daddy. I know you want him to come home, but just in case..."

"You don't want him to come home?" I snapped back at her.

"Hattie, I didn't say that. What I meant is that we must have a plan. You kids cannot stay here by yourselves if Hubbard doesn't get out."

"I'm not a kid. I did just fine yesterday. And we're not by ourselves. Henrietta and Ruthie are here to help out."

"You're barely fourteen years old. Working to the bone in a café is no place for a young lady. You'll be old and withered before you know it! And who do you think is going to take care of Meg and the boys?" Mittie's refined façade started to crack.

"I will! I have been doin' this for months and will keep doin' it!"

I stopped myself from saying that I was taking care of this family long before Daddy went to jail. By the look on Mittie's face, I could tell she had her reservations regarding Daddy. I slipped my dress over my head and turned to the little mirror. I looked tired. My hair desperately needed to be washed. My dress was much looser than it was a month ago. Nine months ago, my face was full, and my cheeks had a rosy tint. Sure, I was a little plump then, but I was pretty. Now, my face was a sallow mess. Maybe Aunt Mittie was right; maybe I did need some help.

Mittie stood up and looked at me in the mirror, "We'll talk more about this after church. Hurry downstairs and get some food before it gets cold." She kissed the top of my head and left me alone in my bedroom.

After church, while Meg and the boys were in Sunday school, I convinced Mittie not to tell them what was going on with Daddy. We told Meg that we had some business to attend to with the café, prior instructions from Daddy. We told her, in support of our lie, and that she would have to miss school to help Uncle Melvin and Henrietta out with the breakfast and lunch service. Needless to say, she shared a few choice words with me about the injustices of her life once we were alone in our bedroom. As hard as it was, I didn't snap back at her with the truth. There was no need for both our lives to be turned upside down.

Early Monday morning, Mittie and I headed to the courthouse. Each man we passed tipped the brim of his hat at Mittie, and would then try to slyly look her up and down. Unlike Momma, Mittie either didn't like attention from men or didn't notice their admiration. Depending on her mood, Momma would have offered a coy smile or a "Morning, Handsome!"

Momma found the effect she had on men delightful, even hysterical at times, but not Aunt Mittie. Mittie stoically stared straight ahead, her hand tightly grasped around mine.

As we walked, hand in hand, I feared that every man, woman and child on the streets of Grove Hill that morning knew that secretly hidden in my purse was $46.25, the money I had taken from the register and hid under my mattress Saturday night. I had never in my life seen, held, much less walked around in public with that kind of money. I kept expecting someone to snatch my purse and flee down the street so fast that I would never catch up with the thief. I wriggled out of Mittie's grasp and wrapped both hands tightly around the handles of my purse, holding it close to me. When we reached the courthouse, walked up the stairs, and crossed into the foyer, I breathed a sigh of relief that I wasn't robbed on the street and, therefore, wouldn't have to explain to Daddy how all of the money earned on Saturday was stolen from me.

My relief was short lived. On a large placard next to the courtroom's entrance was the docket for the day. Fourth on the list was Daddy's name and, next to it, the words *Murder 1st Degree.* I stared at his name for probably a full minute, still unable to believe what happened in our dining room Saturday afternoon. Mittie tugged on my arm, pulling from my stupor.

We took our seats in the courtroom, fifth row from the front on the left side. I had hoped to be on the front row so that Daddy could see me clearly, but the room had already begun to fill. I saw reporters from the Clarke County Democrat, Sheriff's Deputies, and dozens others I assumed were concerned family members of other men and women on the day's docket. Aunt Mittie pointed out the prosecuting attorneys seated at the table on the right, directly in front of the judge's bench. Mr. Frank Poole and County Solicitor A. S. Johnson represented the state of Alabama. Daddy knew these men! They ate at our café at least twice a week, if not more often. How could they think Daddy was guilty of such a crime? For God's sake, Mr. Johnson came in for lunch three times the week before Daddy was arrested!

I was so surprised at the sight of these men who, until that moment, acted as if they were friends with Daddy, that I nearly missed the man seated three rows in front of us. Grandpa Andrews, Daddy's father, must have arrived very early to get such a good seat. I couldn't imagine what he felt when he learned his youngest child was handcuffed and thrown in jail like some common criminal. I don't even know how Grandpa Andrews learned that Daddy was arrested, but I was thrilled that he was there. Judge Bedsole would see General Jackson Andrews; named so not for any military service, but because he completely deserved such a distinguished name; sitting there, and realize that no son of his could possibly be a murderous letch. I wanted to force my way into his row so that Daddy would see us seated together in solidarity for him, but I decided to sit tight and concentrate on protecting the $46.25 that would buy Daddy's freedom.

Finally, after listening to the attorneys' arguments over charges, preliminary motions, and bail amounts of other accused criminals, Daddy's case was introduced. The sight of him with shackles on both his wrists and ankles nearly brought tears to my eyes, but I forced myself to smile at him, and gave a small wave so that he knew I was on his side. I marveled at the fact that even in shackles, he was the most handsome man in the room.

When Daddy was seated behind the left table next to Paul Jones, his appointed attorney and another frequent diner at the café, the bailiff began, "Next up, Hubbard Andrews, alias Herbert Andrews, alias Hubbard Anders, alias Herbert Anders, unlawfully and with malice aforethought killed Addie Andrews, alias Addie Anders, by shooting her with a gun. The charge is murder in the first degree as held over by the Grand Jury on September 15, 1934."

"Mister Andrews," Judge Bedsole began, "how do you plead?"

"Not guilty, Your Honor." Daddy's voice sounded sure and strong.

"Your Honor, we request this charge be dismissed based on the circumstantial nature of the evidence in this case," said Mr. Jones on Daddy's behalf. "Mister Andrews is an upstanding member of this community, the successful proprietor of the Andrews Hotel and Café, and a loving father of four children. He grieves the great tragedy of his dear wife's death every day."

"I know all about Mister Andrews, Paul," said Judge Bedsole.

"Your Honor, considering the gruesome and egregious nature of this crime, this charge must stand," Mr. Poole said from behind the prosecution's table.

"I agree, Frank. What do you propose in the matter of bail?"

"Well, Your Honor, the state requests bail be refused and that Mister Andrews is remanded to Kilby while awaiting trial."

When I heard the prosecutor's request, I immediately started to panic. Why would they refuse to dismiss the charges? Could they refuse Daddy bail? Kilby State Prison was all the way in Montgomery. That had to be at least a hundred miles away. I would never see him!

Mr. Jones jumped in, "Your Honor, if the charge of murder must stand, then we ask that Mister Andrews be released on his own recognizance. His four children, left motherless by this tragic accident, need their father. Please do not make these babies orphans."

"No need for the dramatic, Paul," said Judge Bedsole.

"And, Your Honor, I have in my possession, a letter of bond from several upstanding citizens of Crenshaw County, including the Crenshaw County Sheriff and General Jackson Andrews. If I may, Your Honor?"

"Go ahead, Paul," instructed the judge.

"The letter states, 'I, Sam W. Ewing, Sheriff of Crenshaw County, Alabama, hereby certify that the within is a good and sufficient bond in the sum of $5000'..."

The crowd gasped at such a large sum of money. So much chatter erupted that Judge Bedsole rapped his gavel, "Settle down, everyone. Paul, continue."

Mr. Jones, continued reading the letter, "That the within is a good and sufficient bond in the sum of $5000 and if the same were presented to me in my county, I would approve the same.' And then it is signed at the bottom in his own hand as well as General Andrews and several others." Mr. Jones handed the letter to Judge Bedsole for examination.

"Your Honor," said Mr. Poole from the prosecution's desk, "this ain't Crenshaw County. And here in Clarke County, we all know that Mister Andrews has the means to pay whatever bail we set, and now, thanks to that letter, we know that he has friends all over the state ready to help him in any way he wants. I fear that if we release Mister Andrews today, that all his buddies over in Crenshaw will help him disappear into the night. We owe it to Addie Andrews and to her babies that this does not happen."

"I tend to agree with you, Frank," said Judge Bedsole and then turned to Daddy and said, "Mister Andrews, bail is denied. You are hereby remanded to Kilby State Prison until your trial, which we'll set after preliminary."

The judge shuffled through some papers on his desk for a minute. "Preliminary hearing is set for December 3. And we'll call that lunch, boys. Dismissed."

Judge Bedsole banged his gavel once more before exiting the courtroom. The deputy walked over to Daddy and led him toward the door near the front of the courtroom. My heart sank as Daddy looked at me over his shoulder.

"Hattie, Sweetie, we'll figure this out," then he disappeared through the door.

I sat there feeling confused and foolish. The litany of everything I didn't know raced through my head. How could I think $46.25 would be enough to save him when $5000 wasn't enough? When would I see him again? How would I get from Grove Hill to Montgomery? Why didn't I let Momma teach me how to drive? Why was I always too scared to try? When would Daddy's trial be? What's a preliminary hearing? And why, on God's green Earth, does Mr. Poole think Daddy killed Momma?

"What am I going to do?"

My voice sounded so small and frail amidst the chaos of the courtroom. I couldn't stop the tears that time. They fell from my cheeks and splashed on the purse that I was still clutching tightly to my chest.

"Well," Mittie responded, "You'll come home with me." She squeezed my hand again. This time, I didn't let go until we reached the hotel.

chapter ten

September 1934
Grove Hill, Alabama

After leaving the courthouse, Aunt Mittie and I entered the hotel through the alley behind Main Street. Actually, Aunt Mittie led me around the hotel and through the alley to the staff entrance.

Before opening the door, she gently held my hand in hers, "The best place for you is with me. I know I'm not your Momma, but she was part of me."

I mumbled a faint agreement, still wounded from failing at the courthouse.

"Go on upstairs and start packing...just your clothes and valuables. We have everything else you would need in Luverne."

"Yes, Ma'am. And what about ... ?"

"Don't worry with them. I'll tell 'em what's happened. Go on now."

I know I should have been panicked by the thoughts of Daddy going to jail, having to face a murder trial, and us moving again after barely being settled into the hotel, but for the first time in months, I actually felt like I could breathe. Aunt Mittie was not my mother, but she would help me.

Truth be known, Daddy was always busy with the hotel and had little time left in the day to care for us. He still disappeared at night now and then, with no explanation of where he was running off to or what he was doing. Sometimes, I heard him come back in through the staff entrance long after everyone else, including me, should have been sound asleep, and he didn't even try to creep around. He would come barreling through the door, gulp water directly from the kitchen tap, then saunter up the stairs. To my knowledge, he never saw my candle burning in the dining room, or me crouched near the front counter, peering into the kitchen. I might as well have been a ghost as much as he noticed me hiding in the shadows with my finger marking my place in my latest novel from the Bookmobile. Maybe, Aunt Mittie would pay more attention.

* * * * *

Luverne, Alabama, lies three counties over from Grove Hill in Crenshaw County. A lot of our people lived there, so I was pretty familiar with it. Momma grew up in Searight at the south end of the county. Papa Lowman, Momma's daddy, still lived there with his two youngest daughters. Momma's mother passed away a few years before all of this happened, and was buried there in the family cemetery. If you travel north a few miles, you'll reach Brantley, where Grandpa and Grandma Andrews live on a big, sprawling farm, with mostly cotton, corn, and soybeans, but it's beautiful with gentle hills and lots of surrounding woods to explore. In the center is Luverne, the county seat. Every six months or so, Momma would get a hankering to drive to Luverne and sit in the little Methodist church where she and Daddy first met. I wonder if she still thinks of that little church. Maybe, from time to time, she leaves heaven for a bit and pays the wooden chapel a visit.

Aunt Mittie and Uncle Melvin owned a farm on the outskirts of Luverne and grew, of course, cotton, corn, and soybeans. They also had stables with four riding horses, and a big garden out back where any type of vegetable I could imagine was found. They also had strawberry patches, scuppernong vines, peach trees, and lemon trees. In the summer, if we were hungry and supper was too far off, we could sneak through the patches and trees for a snack. We just needed to make sure to check for bugs first and brush off the dust and dirt.

Aunt Mittie and Uncle Melvin had three children of their own: Lawmon, Mariah, and Malley who were close in age to Meg, Billy and Albert. As I packed my belongings from the wardrobe into my suitcase, I prayed that Meg would keep her spoiled mouth closed and the boys would knock their shoes off before tracking mud through Aunt Mittie's kitchen. I was afraid that Aunt Mittie's house was going to be too crowded and that we would wear out our welcome quickly. I don't remember Mittie's house being any bigger than ours in Frisco City. I assumed Meg and I would share a room with Mariah, and the boys would tuck in with Lawmon and Malley. I would have completely understood if our cousins resented us for taking up so much space, but no matter how crowded it would be, I refused to complain. Aunt Mittie was right. I was too young to be a mother to three kids. I needed help.

Up in my soon-to-be former bedroom in the hotel, I packed the contents of my wardrobe into a suitcase. In the bottom of the case, I placed my under-things and snugly tucked my nightgown around them just in case one of the boys started digging through my case. Next to those, I placed the old pair of work pants and shirt that Momma used to wear. Next in the case were my church shoes (I was wearing my everyday pair), three cotton frocks, my blue floral dress from Daddy, two silk church dresses, my straw hat, and two hats that used to be Momma's, including the straw hat with the lily-of-the-valley detail on the side, then, finally, my two pairs of gloves. I laid my hairbrush, hand mirror, and toothbrush carefully on top, and wrapped the few pieces of jewelry that I owned (a brooch from Momma, the tiny cross pendant and chain given to me on my twelfth birthday, and the birthstone pendant I only wore on very special occasions) in my silk scarf, and tucked the bundle down in one side of the case. I carefully folded the dark winter coat I had barely worn since Momma insisted to Daddy two Christmases ago that, "a young lady needs a proper coat and one with some style!"

I placed it on top, then closed the case with a good shove.

I ran my fingers along the monogram near the clasp: AAL. The first big A was for Addie. The second big A was for Andrews. The L was for Lowman. I would have given all the contents of the suitcase away, everything I owned, just to have her back.

I was finished packing and sitting on my bed reading when Meg walked in our room. Her face was flushed and swollen from crying.

"You should have told me," was all she said before pulling her suitcase from under her bed and turning toward her wardrobe.

We didn't say another word while she packed. Down the hall, I could hear Aunt Mittie packing the boys' belongings. I wondered if they would ever understand why I chose not to tell them about Daddy. I wondered if Meg would ever forgive me for not telling her the truth.

chapter eleven

September 1934

During lunch on Monday, Aunt Mittie and Uncle Melvin announced their decision to close the hotel and café while Daddy was away. They informed all of the guests and helped them make arrangements to leave. Henrietta and I fixed one last supper for our guests, the kids, and Mittie and Melvin. Fried chicken, butter beans, white rice with gravy, and peach cobbler made for a delicious, albeit quiet, meal. I don't think anyone knew what to say. Silence seemed more appropriate than the usual dinner pleasantries. After supper, we covered the furniture with sheets from the beds while Melvin and Billy boarded up the front street level windows, making sure to prominently display the closed sign. When we were finished, I hugged Henrietta goodbye and gave her the note I had written for Ruthie. In it, I apologized for the abrupt decision to close and promised to hire her back as soon as Daddy cleared up the mess.

Early Tuesday morning, just as the sun was coming up on Main Street, we loaded our suitcases into the back of Uncle Melvin's truck. The hundred-mile haul to Luverne would take most of the day, so Uncle Melvin wanted to get an early start. Aunt Mittie and I packed a picnic lunch of leftover fried chicken and cobbler for the road. I locked the front door behind us and gave the key to Uncle Melvin for safekeeping. Melvin, Mittie, Meg, and I squeezed in the front seat. Billy and Albert climbed in the back of the truck. Two small suitcases served as their seats for the ride to Crenshaw County. By eight a.m. the sun beat down on us and promised to make it a sweltering drive. As we pulled away in Uncle Melvin's truck, I closed my eyes and tried to imagine the wind blowing in my face while we hurtled down the road in Momma's Model T.

We reached Luverne around two o'clock, after trudging along behind all means of farm equipment, letting the boys run around in an open field sometime around noon, and giving Uncle Melvin some time to "close my ol' eyes for a spell" somewhere in the middle of Butler County. The road to Mittie and Melvin's place took us right through downtown Luverne. I couldn't believe how busy downtown was in the middle of a Tuesday afternoon! There must have been thousands of people in Luverne. By that September in Grove Hill, I practically knew every face on the streets downtown if not the right name to go with each. As we drove through Luverne, I stared at the strangers, wondering how many I would meet before I got to go back to the hotel with Daddy. I wondered what the people were like; if they were nice like Aunt Mittie, or nasty gossips like old Mrs. Williams back in Frisco City. I wondered if they knew about Daddy. I wondered if they knew that Addie Andrews was my mother and that the four ratty kids in this truck were her "motherless babes."

Melvin and Mittie's place was even smaller than I remembered. The little wooden two-story house sat on the corner of several acres of cotton, corn, and soybean plots. It had four steps that led to a really nice front porch with two rockers and a big swing. There was plenty of room on the porch for the whole family, including the four of us if we sat on the stairs, to all be together. The inside of the house, however, was a different story. All seven of the children shared two small bedrooms on the second floor. I silently thanked the Lord that only three girls had to share the tiny room that Mariah, Mittie's daughter, showed Meg and me when we first arrived. Mariah seemed thrilled at the prospect of having two sisters. I was sure her excitement wouldn't last long once the cramped quarters began to take effect. I swear Meg's and my suitcases took up half the room. I bet if I stood in the middle of that room and stretched out my arms, that my fingertips would touch opposite walls. But the room did have a window, which was good, because it felt like it was 100 degrees up there.

Billy and Albert's room was identical to ours, only with one more body to contend with. Luckily, I don't think they noticed or cared. As soon as they were allowed, the boys ran off behind the house to explore the farm. We didn't see them again that day until it was time to eat supper.

Aunt Mittie and Uncle Melvin shared the larger room across the hall. According to Mariah, we were not allowed to go in there under any circumstances.

"Momma and Daddy's room is strictly off limits," warned Mariah when she noticed me peek inside the room through the open door. Wallpaper covered the walls and surrounded the perfectly made bed in a sea of pink and yellow flowers. "Want some lemonade? I just made some," Mariah said as she pulled the door to Aunt Mittie and Uncle Melvin's bedroom closed.

The rest of the house was a simple foursquare design with a tiny kitchen and attached dining room in the back of the house. A foyer and small parlor greeted visitors in front. A small, primitive-looking bathroom with a shower was set off the kitchen next to the pantry. I reminded myself that things could be worse: The bathroom could have been outside.

During supper that night, Mittie explained our chores and her expectations, or "House Rules" as she put it. Schoolwork must be completed precisely and energetically. She cautioned Meg, Billy, and Albert that she would give the school her blessing to use the rod if necessary, but warned the three of them that they better not need it or they would receive double in her house. Before school each morning and after school each afternoon, the boys would help Melvin with farm work. Even little Albert would be expected to do his share. Meg was given a list of household chores, which she and Mariah were instructed to complete each afternoon. The list included sweeping the house and porch, dusting all the furniture and fixtures, mopping the floors every other day, cleaning the bathroom, and helping Aunt Mittie and me fix supper. I wanted to chime in that I was used to feeding a crowd and, therefore, would not need their help. Four people would never fit in that tiny kitchen.

"And, Hattie," Aunt Mittie said, "you'll help me with the laundry and cooking until you start Thorsby in a few weeks."

"Until I start what?" I asked.

"Well, a young lady should have a proper education. I'll send word tomorrow to the headmistress and request that you be admitted as soon as possible. I'll explain your situation. I'm sure she will understand the need for discretion. If the Good

Lord allows it, the school will show us a little sympathy and allow you to start the term late."

"Ma'am, what is Thorsby?" I asked.

"Oh, Hattie dear, Thorsby Institute is one of the best high schools in the state. It's up in Thorsby, in Chilton County. I think a secretarial curriculum will be best for you, as well as the social graces. You'll live there, of course, but I hear they have a fine boarding house on the grounds." Mittie misinterpreted the shocked look on my face for opposition rather than elation.

She continued without letting me get a word in, "Hattie, I'll have no arguments. You need this."

I would have never dreamed of arguing with such a wonderful and completely unexpected privilege!

For the first time in months, I was excited, truly excited. School would be a real adventure. I had read about boarding schools and fantasized about being sent to one. I thought my education was done and that I would spend the rest of my life in a kitchen or dining room somewhere feeding the hungry masses. Secretarial classes meant I could work in an office building, maybe in Mobile or Birmingham, far away from the dusty dirt roads of the farms and good ol' boys of Alabama. I would rent a room in a ladies' boarding house and eat in cafes rather than serve in one. Now, I got to go to the Thorsby Institute. The name sounded so prestigious. I won't have to share a tiny bed in a tiny room with my cousin and my sister. But, a terrifying thought came to mind. It was the same thought that was at the heart of so many of Momma and Daddy's arguments, and it had plagued Daddy since the rumors surrounding Momma's death drove us out of Frisco City. I was sure this delightful fantasy was about to come to a fast end.

"Aunt Mittie, how will I pay for a school like that?"

"Your Papa Lowman will pay your tuition, and we'll help out, too, however we can, right, Melvin?"

"Oh, um, yes, Mittie," said Uncle Melvin, looking up from his plate for the first time since saying grace.

chapter twelve

October 1934
Luverne, Alabama

Every night after Aunt Mittie told me about the Thorsby Institute, I went to sleep praying that the school would accept me, and that Papa Lowman could afford the tuition. One night, I suggested to Aunt Mittie that Grandpa Andrews might be able to help with the tuition, too.

"The Lowmans do not need any assistance from the Andrews family," Mittie answered and quickly left the room to fetch another load for ironing.

Mittie was a laundress in Luverne which meant nearly every day, customers dropped off their dirty bedding, dresses, work shirts and britches, even their underwear, for Mittie to wash, dry, iron, and fold. The laundry was back-breaking work and seemed endless. Every day, Mittie and I would build a fire out back for the wash water, one bucket for the soapy water, one for rinsing and wringing the clothes out, and one for the starch. The starch was made from mixing flour with cool water, then slowly thinning it with boiling water from the bucket over the fire. We would take turns scrubbing the clothes on Mittie's old washboard; wringing them out; dipping them in the starch water; and then hanging them on the line to dry. After only two weeks, the lye soap had caused my hands to dry out and crack. I needed to get away from the laundry. Thorsby became my dream escape.

Thankfully, Aunt Mittie had an electric iron rather than one made from actual iron that had to be heated over a fire. I think it was the only modern appliance in the whole house. For hours, I stood over the hot iron in the small front room of the house, ironing the linens and clothing of Luverne's finest residents. Some days, I would find myself praying for a hurricane to blow in through the window to cool my face off and carry the stacks of laundry to kingdom come.

Three weeks after Aunt Mittie sent the admission request to Thorsby Institute, my salvation arrived in the afternoon post. We received word that I was accepted and, even though starting so late in the semester was frowned upon, the headmistress, Ms. Helen Jenkins, understood my unique and unfortunate situation, and agreed to allow me to start as soon as I could arrive in Thorsby.

Along with the acceptance letter was a catalogue that detailed the curriculum, supply list for my classes and living quarters, the student code of conduct, and the precise requirements of the dress code for young ladies enrolled at Thorsby Institute. Day dresses, stockings, gloves, and a hat were to be worn every day on and off campus. Violation of the dress code would result in privileges being revoked and possible expulsion. Mittie and I read through the entire catalogue, word for word, after all of the laundry was completely washed, dried, and ironed for the day.

"Well, I guess us ladies will be spending the day in town tomorrow," Mittie said after neatly returning the catalogue to its linen envelope. "No niece of mine is gonna walk around Thorsby with grease-stained dresses and threadbare gloves. No ma'am!"

The next day, Mittie bought me two new day dresses, two pairs of stockings, new gloves, a new hat, and the most beautiful lavender party dress with tiny pearl buttons down the bodice. Well, the buttons were fake pearls, but I could barely tell. She decided that these items, combined with my two church dresses, winter coat, and the hats I brought from the hotel, would make a proper wardrobe for a young lady. She also agreed to help me take in the blue floral dress from Daddy so that it would fit me properly again. I had lost quite a bit of weight over the last several months. Between my responsibilities at the hotel and ironing in the heat, I was thin as a rail. In return for her generosity, I promised Mittie that I would make her proud at Thorsby.

That afternoon when we got back to the farm, I was so excited to show Meg my new things, especially the party dress. I ran upstairs and showed her the delicate buttons and pretty flutter sleeves. I never considered that she would be anything but happy for me. I was wrong. Meg was furious and stormed out of the tiny room.

When I tried to chase after her, Aunt Mittie stopped me, "Let her go, Honey. She'll get her turn soon enough."

That Sunday, Papa Lowman came home with us after church. After a very lengthy discussion with Uncle Melvin and Aunt Mittie, they all agreed that I would start Thorsby Institute a week from that Monday. Aunt Mittie and Uncle Melvin would drive me the two counties north to Chilton County on the following Saturday. They would help me get settled in my room at the boarding house, and drive back on Sunday. So, over the span of barely six months, I left my childhood home in Frisco City, lived in a hotel in Grove Hill, scrubbed laundry on a farm in Luverne, and would soon reside in a boarding house as the newest student at Thorsby Institute. Momma was right. A new adventure could be found around any corner. I just had to take the turn.

chapter thirteen

November 1934
Thorsby, Alabama

As Uncle Melvin's truck turned onto Main Street in Thorsby, Alabama, I could barely hide my excitement. My nervousness actually made Mittie smile.

"Hattie, Dear, you are allowed to be happy," Mittie said and patted my knee.

Happy was an understatement. My face might not have shown it, but I was thrilled. Inside, I danced, leaped. I was going back to school! This was an adventure I actually wanted rather than one I was forced to endure. For three weeks, I had done nothing but dream of the possibilities. Maybe Thorsby Institute would have a real library like the ones mentioned in my mystery novels. Maybe I would have my own room and a window with sun dancing through sheer, white curtains. Maybe, across the hall from my little piece of heaven, a high-spirited girl with an infectious laugh would live and be as desperate for a best friend as I had become since leaving Frisco City.

Above all, I was excited about a fresh start. I prayed that no one in Chilton County had ever met a Lowman or Andrews. This was my opportunity to be someone other than poor, pitiful Hattie Andrews: Girl without a mother, and daughter of an accused murderer. I didn't know anyone who lived in Chilton County, so how could they know of my now infamous parents or me? And thanks to Aunt Mittie and Uncle Melvin's generosity of a new wardrobe, I could dress the part of carefree debutant or serious academic, whichever I chose to be. A month earlier, the hundred miles of old stage coach roads and Indian paths between Crenshaw and Chilton Counties might as well have been a million miles long. Before Aunt Mittie mentioned Thorsby, the thought of traveling those roads had never crossed my mind. As we rode closer and closer to Thorsby, I decided the six hours of roads that serpentine between Luverne and Crenshaw County were just enough time and distance to deliver my rebirth as smart, chic Hattie Andrews, Thorsby Institute student.

When we pulled up to Thorsby Institute, I was overwhelmed by its size. A huge stone building stood before me, with five large steps that led to heavy, dark wooden doors. Above the doors was a large stone archway with the words *Thorsby Institute* carved in the stone. The building was inviting and terrifying at the same time. I stood at the bottom of the steps and marveled at my new world.

"Well, come on now, get on up there," said Melvin as he dusted off his hat and ushered Aunt Mittie and me up the stairs.

Through the large double doors was an impressive foyer with marble floors and a gigantic portrait of Theodore T. Thorson, founder of Thorsby, Alabama, as stated on the small plaque at the bottom of the ornately carved frame. The foyer led to a long hallway with dark, wooden floors and several closed doors. The first door had a sign on it that read *Administrative Offices.*

"This way, you two. Quickly now," said Mittie, motioning for Uncle Melvin to open the door.

"Go on now," Mittie said, giving me a gentle nudge through the door.

"May I help you, Miss?" a woman seated behind a dark, wooden desk asked me without raising her face from her typewriter. Rather, she gazed at me over the top rims of the glasses resting on her sharply angled nose. Her hair was slicked back in a tight bun, reminiscent of the horrible witches found in nursery rhymes. I stiffened as she glared at me.

"Um, I'm Hattie Andrews," I said and hoped my voice sounded stronger than I felt as I stood before her. Thankfully, Aunt Mittie intervened.

"We are here to see Ms. Jenkins," said Mittie. "Miss Andrews, my niece, is a new student."

"Yes, of course," the secretary said. "Ms. Jenkins has been expecting you." She rose from her desk and crossed to a closed door on the rear wall. Her skirt, which skimmed her legs just above the ankles, barely shifted at all with each stride. "Wait here," she commanded, and, after rapping on the door twice, she slipped into the room and silently closed the door behind her. I decided right then that I would always do exactly what she instructed.

"Well," said Uncle Melvin, "she's about as icy as they come, huh?"

"Melvin," Mittie snapped, her voice a low whisper. "Not another word." Mittie cut her gaze at Uncle Melvin, then she turned to me and pinched my cheeks. She looked into my eyes and smoothed the shoulders of my blouse with her gloved hands. "Now remember, when we meet Ms. Jenkins, stand up straight and look her in the eye. Speak up, but not too loudly. Show her the graceful young lady you are."

The secretary opened the door and glided out, "Ms. Jenkins will be with you shortly." She floated back to her desk and, without a sound, sat in her chair. For several moments, the only noise I heard was the sound of her fingers clicking the keys of her black typewriter.

Then, Ms. Helen Jenkins, Headmistress of Thorsby Institute, appeared in the doorway. She looked to be about fifty years old and wore a navy suit with a white blouse buttoned to the base of her neck. Her hair was also slicked back in a low bun. The name Helen suggested a sweet, gentle nature, but her nose was nearly as sharp as the secretary's nose. I feared all the women of Thorsby carried the same serious countenance.

"I am pleased you arrived safely, Miss Andrews," began Ms. Jenkins. She spoke with a low pitch and strong, precise articulation. "Mister and Miz Franklin, I have no doubt that you will find Thorsby Institute an exemplary and beneficial environment for Miss Andrews. We pride ourselves on producing the finest young men and women in the state of Alabama. Now, if you will follow me."

Ms. Jenkins turned, left the office, and continued without hesitation down the long hallway. Aunt Mittie gestured for me to keep up with Ms. Jenkins, but her pace, both feet and tongue, made it quite difficult. I must admit that I remember only half of what Ms. Jenkins said on that first day. She had the strangest accent I had ever heard. I was used to the Alabama drawl of slow vowels and forgotten consonants, feminine voices that rose and fell in a delicate rhythm, and male voices that bellowed from church pulpits, but Ms. Jenkins's voice was unlike anything

I had heard. Really, she had no accent. Her words were flat, almost emotionless, except for the select times when she spoke in swift, razor-like tones.

"This is the main academic building. On this floor, you will find four classrooms and the library. At the end of this hallway is the faculty lounge. Students are not permitted to enter the lounge under any circumstances."

As we hurried past the door, Ms. Jenkins motioned to the library. I tried to peek inside and must have paused too long.

"Miss Andrews, do try to keep up," said Ms. Jenkins, then opened one of the doors to reveal a well-lit stairway.

The three of us hurried up the stairs behind Ms. Jenkins. I could tell from Aunt Mittie's pursed lips, that she was having a little trouble climbing the stairs so quickly.

The landing led to another flight of stairs, but we followed Ms. Jenkins into the second floor hallway. The building, nearly deserted on a Saturday, was even quieter on the second floor. The only sounds I heard were Ms. Jenkins's voice, the rapping of her heels on the wooden floor, and Aunt Mittie's breathing.

"On this floor, you will find eight classrooms and the ladies' lavatory. As you have been enrolled in our secretarial curriculum as well as household arts and the social graces, you will spend a large portion of your school day on this floor."

After a quick glance at the second floor, we were back in the stairwell, climbing the last flight to the third floor. The third floor seemed a little smaller than the others and, according to Ms. Jenkins, contained a laboratory used by the students enrolled in the Teacher's College, the music room, a small art studio, and one more unidentified classroom. After showing the third floor, Ms. Jenkins turned and descended the three flights of the stairs at a pace rare for a woman of her age. I tucked my chin to my chest so I could see each step clearly and avoid tumbling down the stairs.

"Posture, Miss Andrews, posture," Ms. Jenkins warned as she turned to witness my last few steps down the stairs.

After the main building, Ms. Jenkins showed us the Congregational Church to the right. The church was used for assembly every Friday morning at 8:30 a.m.

"On the dot," said Ms. Jenkins. At this point, she reminded me of the student handbook: Tardiness was not permitted. The church was also used for student organizations and Sunday morning services.

We left the church and cut across the courtyard behind the main building. The courtyard was artfully designed with stone paths, iron benches, and peach trees. On the far side of the courtyard was the dormitory. A very sturdy woman named Lois Leach, Matron of the Thorsby Institute Dormitory, greeted us.

"Miss Andrews," Ms. Jenkins said and handed me the folded card she had been carrying, "this is your course schedule. Individual room numbers for each class are included. Ms. Fairbank, the librarian, will issue you textbooks on Monday. I pray that you are a fast learner and devoted student, Miss Andrews. I suggest that you request tutorial sessions from your teachers in order to catch up on the lessons you have missed. You will find the faculty here at Thorsby to be very generous with their time. Now, Ms. Leach will show you to your room and review the dormitory rules and schedule."

"Thank you, Ms. Jenkins," I said as I tried to make a mental note of the names, places, and instructions I had just received.

"Well then, welcome to Thorsby Institute, Miss Andrews. Mister and Miz Franklin, rest assured your niece is in good hands. Ms. Leach, I leave you to it." With that, Ms. Jenkins disappeared into the dormitory.

"Hattie, is it?" Ms. Leach asked. Her rosy cheeks plumped around her bright, slightly crooked smile.

"Yes, Ma'am," I answered.

"Hattie, your room is on the third floor, eh. Grab your bags and we'll head up. Mister Franklin, you'll wait on the landing, eh. No gents on the ladies' floor, right." Every sentence this woman spoke sounded like a question. Was she asking us or telling us?

The whole way from the dormitory to the truck and back, then all the way up the three flights of stairs to my assigned room, Ms. Leach talked nonstop.

"Thorsby is a gift, eh, a real gift. No place like it," she said, wheezing between sentences. "I never had the opportunity for such a fine education when I was a girl. So, I hope you don't squander this opportunity, Miss Hattie Andrews." She said my name as if she was introducing a delightful storybook character.

"Back home in South Dakota," she continued, "I dreamt of going to a place like this, but never got the chance, eh. But at least I'm here now. The cold back home was too hard on my respiratory system." She leaned against the wall of the second floor landing for a moment, causing Aunt Mittie and me to pause, each with a suitcase in our hands.

"Now, where was I?" she asked, blotting her forehead with a handkerchief.

"South Dakota," I said.

"Oh, yes," she said. "Well that was a long time ago," she dismissed the thought with a wave of her handkerchief. "A few housekeeping matters: Three meals are served per day in the dining hall. Otherwise, stay out of there unless you're scheduled to work kitchen duty. You'll rotate shifts with the other household arts students. Secondly, don't let me catch you trying to sneak back in here after curfew. I'm not as fast as I used to be, but I hear all and see all."

"You will not have to worry about that," said Mittie. "Hattie is here for an education, nothing more."

"Oh, now, we have plenty of social gatherings for the students. That's part of the education, of course," said Ms. Leach. "And all of 'em are properly chaperoned by Ms. Jenkins herself."

"Of course," I said.

Using the wooden railing, Ms. Leach practically dragged herself up the last flight of stairs to the third floor, my new home.

"Washrooms are located on the ends," Ms. Leach said, pointing down the hallway, first right and then left. "I suggest you wake up early to wash up. You don't want to get caught behind all the other young ladies. Ms. Jenkins does not allow tardiness for any reason."

"Yes, Ma'am, she mentioned that," I said.

"Well, here we are," she said, and opened the door to my room. "Home, sweet, home!" She stepped out of the way so that I could see inside.

I was assigned a room near the center of the hallway. It was one of about twenty rooms on the floor, all occupied according to Ms. Leach. There was a single bed along one wall, a small wardrobe and vanity on the opposite wall, and just enough space to walk between the wardrobe and bed. A modest desk under a bright window finished off the room. I was elated. I had never had my own room before. *My own space,* I thought and smiled at Aunt Mittie.

"I'll leave you to it, eh. Go on and get settled. Dinner is at six sharp."

Ms. Leach smiled again, then headed down the stairs. I heard her chatting away to someone, but couldn't make out exactly what she was saying.

Aunt Mittie and I unpacked the two suitcases I had brought with me. Aunt Mittie carefully hung my clothes in the wardrobe while I arranged my toiletries on the vanity.

"Hattie, Dear, sit for a minute," Aunt Mittie said, and patted the bed next to her. "I need to tell you something."

I sat next to her on the thin mattress. She took my hand again, the same way she did in the alley behind the hotel. "This is your chance, Dear, and I don't want you to spoil it. I expect you to keep up with your studies and do as Ms. Jenkins and the other teachers tell ya to. This is a great opportunity, one your momma and I didn't get. So, you make her proud. Make me proud." Mittie kissed my forehead and stood to leave.

Down by the truck, I hugged Aunt Mittie tightly. Uncle Melvin, always hesitant to show any kind of affection, tipped his hat and mumbled something that sounded like "good luck" before hopping behind the wheel. He seemed anxious to get on the road back to Crenshaw. I waved to Aunt Mittie until the truck was out of sight. Then, I mustered up every bit of courage I had and walked back into the dormitory alone.

chapter fourteen

January 1935
Thorsby Institute, Thorsby, Alabama

My first weeks at Thorsby passed quickly. The cool days of November and December flew by as I worked to catch up on my classes and adapt to my new academic life. Before I could settle into a routine, Mittie and Melvin sent me a train ticket home for the holidays. I packed the hand-stitched gifts I had made for Meg, Mittie, and the rest of my now-large family in my suitcase, monogrammed linen handkerchiefs for each of them, navy stitches for the boys, mauve stitches for the girls. The gifts were a project for my household arts class and provided my first "A" for the term. With my gifts neatly packed, I rode the L&N by myself from Thorsby to Luverne for the two-week Christmas break.

Right after New Year's, I took the train back to Thorsby. I had only been back in my dormitory for a few minutes and had just unpacked my suitcase when Ms. Leach started banging on my door. I came back from winter break a day early so I could get settled and hopefully have the library and courtyard to myself for the day. Quiet time to read at Thorsby was as scarce as it was at the hotel, but sneaking down to the kitchen after curfew was strictly prohibited. Judging from the excitement in Ms. Leach's banging, I wouldn't find much quiet that day.

"Hattie, Dear, open up," Ms. Leach said. She must have run up the stairs, because she sounded winded.

"Come in, Ms. Leach."

"Hattie, thank Jehovah you came back early. I wanted to give you this while the other girls weren't around. I didn't think you'd want them in your private family affairs, eh." Ms. Leach handed me a letter. I turned it over to reveal the Kilby State Penitentiary postmark, dated December 18, 1934. I recognized Daddy's handwriting immediately. He had addressed the letter to *Miss Hattie Andrews*. It must have arrived right after I left for Luverne. I was dying to see Meg, Billy, Albert, Aunt Mittie, and even quiet Uncle Melvin, so I had left as soon as I was released for the semester break. When none of us heard from Daddy over the holidays, I thought he had forgotten Christmas.

"I hid it under my mattress so no one would see it," Ms. Leach continued, still breathing hard from the three flights of stairs.

I had almost convinced myself that Daddy had forgotten about us entirely. I hadn't heard a word from him since we left Grove Hill. Aunt Mittie kept track of any developments regarding his trial, and sent him regular updates on all of us, but we never received word back from him. His attorney, Mr. Jones, provided routine updates, but we never heard directly from Daddy. So, when I saw the letter, I was honestly shocked that he had written me. I felt my face flush and couldn't imagine what the letter contained.

Staring at the envelope in my hand, I felt incredibly exposed. Although Ms. Jenkins and Ms. Leach knew about my situation, no one else at Thorsby Institute did, and I intended to keep it that way. They knew nothing of gunshots and handcuffs. As far as my friends here knew, Momma died in a tragic accident, end of story, no details, no embellishments, and no lies.

"Thank you, Ms. Leach. I appreciate your discretion."

Ms. Leach stood in my doorway and looked at the letter, waiting for me to invite her in so that we could read it together, as if we were going to have story time. I, unlike a few of the young women enrolled in my Poise and Grace class, didn't need lessons to politely ask for privacy.

"Was there something else, Ms. Leach?" I asked while gently placing the letter in my pocket.

"Well, no, I just..."

"Ms. Leach, thank you again for delivering the letter. And thank you for taking such care with it. Now, if you will excuse me, I am just plum exhausted from my trip. I really must lie down." With that, I quietly closed the door.

I sat on the foot of my bed and opened the letter, careful not to tear the envelope or smudge the writing. The letter itself appeared to be written on some kind of paper napkin. Couldn't he find real stationary? As a man awaiting trial, shouldn't he be given the necessary supplies needed to write a proper letter to his family? I had convinced myself that Daddy would be all right inside the windowless walls and metal bars of Kilby. For several nights after his arraignment, I prayed that he would be assigned one of the private cells with a private bathroom. I had read about the privileged wing in the paper when the facility was first built. I was sure that he would be placed on that wing. After all, he wasn't a convicted criminal. No one had pronounced him guilty of the heinous crime he was accused of committing. He was an innocent man awaiting trial at Kilby because there was nowhere to keep him in Clarke County. Daddy was only there because the judge hadn't given any thought to his guilt or innocence. Judge Bedsole threw him away like a piece of trash left over from his lunch.

I unfolded the napkin to see only a few lines scribbled in Daddy's fluid handwriting. The ink had bled into the napkin in places.

Dear Sweetie,

I am so sorry I had to leave you. I know this has been a difficult time for you, and I am so sorry to have made it worse. I am in a private room at Kilby, and spend most of my days missing all of you. I wish we could celebrate Christmas and ring in the New Year together. Please do not worry. I am fine and will be home very soon. I am sure all of this will be worked out. Hattie, Dear, I would never hurt your mother. She meant the world to me. I am heartbroken without her.

Mittie sends me regular updates. I am so proud of my children, but mostly you, Sweetie. I hope you are enjoying your time at school and are learning all your subjects. The Lowmans are good people. They are good to take care of all of you while I am away. Please do not hold this against them.

I love you, Sweetie.
Daddy

I read the letter over and over again, obsessing over every word. *I would never hurt your mother.* Daddy didn't do what the pathetic gossips of Frisco City couldn't stop yammering on about. He didn't hurt Momma. He never would. His love for her and me was there in black and white. What did he mean by *please do not hold this against them*? Were the Lowmans responsible for Daddy being arrested? Did they think Daddy killed Momma? Is that why it took Aunt Mittie so long to come check on us, to be the mother we needed? Did Aunt Mittie think he's guilty, too?

I couldn't sit there any longer. Any dream I had on the train ride back to school of taking an afternoon nap was dashed. I felt confused. I needed to ask Aunt Mittie what she thought of my father. I needed to tell Daddy that I believed him. I needed Momma. Frustrated by my inability to do anything about the situation, I went for a chilly walk through the streets of Thorsby trying to distract myself with the Christmas decorations still hanging on the doorways of the Scandinavian style homes. Finding no comfort, I stopped in the Lutheran Chapel in the center of town. I sat on the back pew and prayed to God. I prayed that Daddy would be freed. I prayed that his trial would be soon and quick. I prayed that the family I had left would remain intact through this whole ordeal. I prayed for Momma and implored for God, Jesus, anyone, to let me feel her presence. After nearly an hour of praying alone in the chapel, all I felt in return was the draft from the crack under the heavy chapel door, and the sun setting behind me.

chapter fifteen

September 1935
Thorsby Institute, Thorsby, Alabama

After spending summer break standing over the hot iron in Aunt Mittie's steamy parlor, I returned to Thorsby Institute ready to begin my new classes and thankful that the salve Uncle Melvin gave me for my birthday healed the cracks in my hands before I returned to school. The lye soap that was so effective in removing stains of all sorts from the laundry had wreaked havoc on my skin. I didn't want my classmates at Thorsby to see what I really did over my summer vacation. I would happily allow them to assume I spent a leisurely summer riding horses, picking blackberries, reading on the sunny porch, and perfecting my peach cobbler recipe. Truth be known, those activities were reserved for Sunday alone. Most of my summer days were spent hunched over the iron in Aunt Mittie's parlor. Ironing, however, was a small price to pay for another term at Thorsby.

I thoroughly enjoyed most of my new classes, if not for their entertainment value then for the benefit they could serve later in my life. My Advanced Stenography and Dictation class was fast-paced and competitive. The girls and I enjoyed weekly competitions to see who was most thorough or fastest in taking dictation. I excelled in Culinary Arts, which was far beyond the fried pork chops of our café in Grove Hill. Miss Stoddard, our Culinary Arts and Home Economics Instructor, started the semester off with a bang, or rather a flame, by teaching us how to caramelize sugar on the top of a Crème Brule. By the second week of our home economics class, I had already completed a lovely set of organza curtains that hung above the little window in my room.

The only class I didn't enjoy was my poetry class. I understood the purpose of the class. Studying the art form aided in our transformation from country farm girls to socially graceful and educated young women, but the poetic drivel bored me to tears. As far as I could tell, poetry was nothing but a bunch of syrupy rhymes that didn't tell much of a story at all. The class featured a collection of whiny writers who could probably stand a bit of hard labor with Aunt Mittie's iron. But there was promise on the horizon. Ms. Klingenhoefer, our poetry instructor, promised to introduce us to Edgar Allan Poe. I read several of his sinister short stories during my sleepless nights in Grove Hill, so I was curious to see what he did with rhyme. My third term at Thorsby promised to be filled with new, exciting experiences.

Shortly before Parent's Weekend in September, I received word that Aunt Mittie and Uncle Melvin would attend the event. I had only been back at school for a few weeks, so I didn't think that Uncle Melvin would be willing to make the trip so soon. I feared that I would spend the weekend alone while the other girls on my floor enjoyed time with their families. Aunt Mittie's news of their trip proved that I did have a family, even if mine wasn't the traditional mother and father anymore.

Ms. Jenkins, our fearless leader, had planned an exciting weekend for all of us. The weekend would kick off with a welcome assembly and chorale performance in the Congregational Church. I hadn't inherited Momma's gift for song, so I didn't enroll in the music classes. I would participate in the welcome portion of the festivities as a spectator only. After that, a lavish lunch would be served in the dormitory dining hall. The Culinary Arts students didn't have to prepare the meal, but we did have to report to the dining hall at 8:00 a.m. to dress the tables in white linens, fresh cut flowers, and full table settings. Rumor had it that Ms. Jenkins was watching and judging all of us to see whose table manners still needed polishing, including the parents' knowledge of etiquette. That night, a light supper was planned and a dance to follow. At the time, square dancing was the only dance I knew Aunt Mittie and Uncle Melvin to take part in, so I wasn't sure how that part of Parents' Weekend would play out. The weekend was to conclude with breakfast and chapel services Sunday morning.

On the first morning of Parents' Weekend, after setting the tables in the dining hall, I ran up to my room to freshen up before Mittie and Melvin were scheduled to arrive. I had just finished re-pinning the sides of my hair and securing my small hat at a very smart angle when I heard the bell on our floor ring. Immediately, the quiet hall sprang to life. All of us hurried out of our rooms and to the stairwell to see whose family was the first to arrive.

"Miss Andrews, your Auntie and Uncle are here, eh!" Ms. Leach called. I found it hysterical when Ms. Leach tried to be proper. She used our surnames rather than first names. She tried her best to use a demure tone. She forced herself to move at a slower pace, but in the end, she always yelled up the stairs. I think she could have used a few more lessons on grace from Ms. Jenkins.

In the foyer, I hugged Aunt Mittie and tried to hug Uncle Melvin, but he offered me his hand instead.

"Hattie, Dear, you look well," said Aunt Mittie with a smile. "Thorsby seems to agree with you."

"Thank you, Ma'am," I said trying to remember all that Ms. Jenkins had taught me so far. I feared that she was lurking behind one of the antiques in the parlor, ready to chastise the first of us girls who crossed one of her sacred boundaries. "Perhaps, you and Uncle Melvin would care to take a walk with me in the courtyard?"

"That would be lovely, Hattie. Melvin will you join us?" Aunt Mittie asked Melvin.

"Uh, um, sure. Guess so," agreed Melvin, as if he had other choices. I found Melvin's devotion and obedience to Mittie endearing. I bet Momma found him boring.

I was pleasantly surprised at Aunt Mittie's ability to immediately adapt to Ms. Jenkins's version of polite society. Uncle Melvin, on the other hand, needed a little warm up, but by the time we saw Ms. Jenkins at the assembly, he had remembered the training of his youth. As soon as we were out of sight of the parlor though, my excitement for the weekend took over. I squeezed Mittie's hand, delighted that she had come to visit.

I missed Aunt Mittie so much, even though her home represented backbreaking work that I detested. Unfortunately, over the summer, I had let my suspicion of her grow into anger. Daddy's letter had made me suspicious of all the Lowmans, even Aunt Mittie, but by the end of the summer, I had decided that even if the Lowmans were responsible for Daddy's arrest, Aunt Mittie could not be involved. She was tough on us and her expectations were high, but her love for us was obvious. There was no way that she could love me that much and be responsible for one of the worst days of my life. Unfortunately, this epiphany took weeks to come. I wasted day after day in silence, refusing to speak to her and trying my best to avoid her, even if that meant volunteering to iron inside alone while she and Meg washed, wrung, and hung the laundry outside together. I never told Aunt Mittie why I was so angry, and she never asked. She just let me be angry. I felt awful for the way I treated her and needed to make it up to her this weekend.

We had about an hour before the assembly, so we found a bench tucked under a massive oak tree in the far corner of the courtyard. The branches of the oak provided some much needed shade as the temperature climbed into the nineties. Mittie and I sat on the bench while Uncle Melvin leaned against the tree, fanning himself with his hat. Just as I was about to tell Aunt Mittie about my new class schedule and catch her up on the goings on of the other girls on my floor, she interrupted my thoughts.

"Hattie, Honey, we aren't just here for Parents' Weekend," Mittie began.

"Oh?" I asked.

"No. Your Daddy's trial starts this comin' Monday."

"Oh," I said.

The words hung heavy over the little bench. I hadn't heard from Daddy since the one letter in January and had finally been able to put him out of my mind over the last few weeks. I had foolishly started to let myself believe that my life in Thorsby was my real life, but news of the trial brought me abruptly back to reality. No amount of crème brule, sheer curtains, or dark poetry could change the fact that Daddy was still sitting in Kilby awaiting trial.

"I spoke with Ms. Jenkins, and she has agreed to a leave of absence for you. Would you like to attend the trial?"

"Of course!" I answered without hesitation.

My hasty response surprised and irritated me a little. I hadn't heard from Daddy since January, although I had written eight months' worth of letters to him inquiring about his health and trial; telling him about school and my life in Thorsby; and mailing a letter to Daddy took extra effort and careful planning. I never put my letters to him in the regular post at my dormitory. Any envelope marked with the Kilby State Prison address was carefully placed in my purse and carried to the post office in downtown Thorsby. I would stick the stamp on the corner of the envelope myself and place the letter directly in the outgoing mail. Daddy never wrote me back, not even once.

My face flushed. Why, after all those months of silence from him, should I still care? But the fact of the matter was that I did care. He was still *Daddy* to me, and I had a responsibility to be there for him.

"Are ya sure?" asked Uncle Melvin, "You don't got to."

"Yes, Sir, I'm sure," and turning to Aunt Mittie, "Will you be there?"

"Yes, Dear, from start to finish."

"Will we stay at our hotel?"

"Yes, Dear, but it doesn't belong to your daddy no more. He had to sell it for the lawyer bills. This trial's been real expensive," said Aunt Mittie.

"Oh... um, when will we leave for Grove Hill?" I asked.

"Bright n' early, I s'pose. If we wanna make to Grove Hill before dark," said Uncle Melvin.

"But I am doing a scripture reading at Chapel Service tomorrow morning! I don't want to tell them that I can't do it."

Mittie squeezed my hand tightly, "Well, then we'll leave right after the service, right Melvin? We would love to see you read."

Thankfully, and as usual, Melvin agreed with Mittie.

chapter sixteen

September 1935
Grove Hill, Alabama

Parents' Weekend passed in a fog. My one persistent thought was that I was going to see Daddy. A weird mixture of excitement, fear, and pure dread came over me. I'm not sure what songs were sung at the welcome assembly, or if I used the right forks during lunch. Fortunately, Uncle Melvin remembered how to waltz, and I had practically memorized my scripture reading, so I was able to get through the after-dinner dance and Sunday chapel services without any embarrassing spectacle. By this time, packing my suitcase had become routine and required little thought or consideration. Every inch of my mind belonged to Daddy.

My classmates and dormitory neighbors were no more the wiser about my scandal-ridden family than they were before. Aunt Mittie and Ms. Leach provided my alibi for my absence from school to Rose and Lily, my two closest friends at Thorsby. The pug-nosed sisters from Birmingham were told that I was needed in Luverne to care for a sick relative and would be back as soon as possible.

"Hattie is her favorite niece and no one could care for her better. I'm so thankful Ms. Jenkins is permitting her to go," said Aunt Mittie as Ms. Leach added more *bless her hearts* and *Godspeeds* than necessary. Rose and Lily were both extremely chatty, so I knew the lie would be passed around school before any rumors had time to begin. Aunt Mittie's willingness to lie surprised me. She always seemed like such an honest, forthright woman. Protecting my reputation had become a group effort and required actions I never thought possible.

As promised and agreed to, we left right after chapel services on Sunday morning. Halfway to Grove Hill, in the cab of Melvin's truck, I fell asleep on Mittie's shoulder. When I opened my eyes again, we were in front of what used to be our hotel and café. I swear the place had shrunk. It had been renamed *The Grove Hotel.* That made no sense to me. Naming the hotel after the town required no originality, and there was no grove anywhere in the hotel. We didn't even have a courtyard or patio out back, just an alleyway to carry the kitchen garbage through. I personally felt that *The Andrews* had a much more dignified ring to it. Of course, maybe *Andrews* wasn't such a dignified name in these parts any more.

When we walked into the hotel lobby, I half expected to see Daddy behind the registration desk, and was completely disappointed when a short, round little woman handed Uncle Melvin a room key.

"We'll be needin' a cot for the girl," said Melvin.

"Yes, Sir, we'll bring one up. You're on the second floor. After ya get settled and freshen up, come on down for supper. Henrietta's got some deee-licious pot roast on the stove. Bathroom's at the end of the hall."

I smiled when I heard Henrietta's name, not only because her name meant supper would be fantastic, but also because she was here. Not everything had to change constantly.

As promised, a cot was placed in the room for me. The rest of the furniture in the room was the same as it had been a year ago when we draped sheets over it and boarded up the windows. Back then, the room I shared with Meg seemed plenty spacious for the two of us, but now, between the suitcases, vanity, double bed, and my cot, we could barely move around in the room. The three of us were crammed in there like sardines, and after the long, hot drive, Uncle Melvin kind of smelled like a bony fish. I hung my dress for court as quickly as I could, and ran downstairs to the café, partly to see Henrietta, partly out of hunger, but mostly to protect my nose from Uncle Melvin's stench.

"Miss Hattie, you come give me a hug!" Henrietta said as she saw me walk through the café. She hugged me so tightly that she nearly squeezed the wind out of me. "You must be in town fo' your Daddy's trial. I's hopin' to see you."

"Yes, Ma'am. The trial starts tomorrow."

"Oh, I know, Child. Ain't nobody talking 'bout nothin' else. Just yo' Daddy. Did he or didn't he and all that." Henrietta must have seen me flinch at the mention of Daddy's possible guilt, because she went on to say, "Oh, Honey, but I believe the good Lord knows he didn't hurt your momma. He'll make sure he goes free. Don't you worry none."

Henrietta always believed that enough faith in the Lord could move mountains. I knew God could move mountains, but I didn't know if he wanted to move this particular heap.

"Thank you, Henrietta," I said and, "Aunt Mittie and Uncle Melvin are on their way down. I think we just want to get a bite of supper before we go to bed."

The strangeness of the situation had started to sink in. For the first time, I was going to eat in the café as a customer, and then sleep on the second floor, rather than the fourth, as if this building was never my home. The sun had already set outside. I was hoping a good meal and the cool, moonless sky would cause me to drift off to sleep quickly. I had a feeling I would need every bit of strength I had once I sat down in the courtroom.

The next day, the trial was to begin at 9:00 a.m., but Aunt Mittie insisted we be there by eight. By 8:30, the place was packed. Every seat was filled, and reporters covered nearly every bit of floor space, apparently waiting for the trial of the century to start. As I looked around the room, I wondered if any of the businesses in Grove Hill opened their doors that day, as I'm pretty sure every shopkeeper, salesman, and clerk from Main Street, Jackson Road, and Court Road was crammed in the pews. The First Methodist Church Ladies' Auxiliary had filled the last row on the left side, and were busy fanning themselves and running their mouths when the bailiff first entered. I guess they opted to watch a courtroom drama rather than listen to their tawdry radio stories that day.

L.V. Thompkins had been appointed bailiff for Daddy's trial, and he did his best to silence the excited audience. He looked over the crowd for a minute, loudly cleared his throat, and then, "Listen up! Now, Judge Bedsole has seen this here crowd and gave me permission to clear the room if ya'll cain't keep quiet."

The crowd immediately went silent at the threat of missing out on the spectacle. After that, the prosecuting attorneys, Mr. Frank Poole and County Solicitor A. S. Johnson, took their seats. Then Mr. Jones and Daddy's team came into the courtroom. The crowd immediately started whispering about who was smarter, who was more charming, and who came from which long-suffering Alabama family.

A collective gasp, as if everyone sucked in air at the exact same time, came from the crowd when two sheriff's deputies led Daddy into the room and seated him next to his attorneys. The sight of Daddy stunned me. Someone had gotten him a nice suit for the event, and he looked freshly shaven, but he was thinner than I had ever seen him. It had only been a year since I was last seated here, but now he looked much, much older. His hair had begun to gray at the temples. Fine lines had formed near his eyes and connected his nose to the corners of his mouth. Still, his natural charm and timeless good looks were undeniable. He gave a half smile to the crowd and a wink to me, which triggered an audible sigh from the Ladies' Auxiliary and a throaty warning from the bailiff.

"All rise! The honorable Judge Bedsole presiding..."

As the bailiff continued to hail in Judge Bedsole and the jury, a reporter seated next to me whispered to a man with a camera crouching on the floor, "Well, Bob, here we go. Off to the circus."

My stomach apparently agreed and started turning somersaults.

chapter seventeen

September 23, 1935
Grove Hill, Alabama

After an hour of formalities, most of which I didn't understand, the *good part,* according to the reporter next to me, was set to begin. I don't think he knew who I was or why I was there. To the strangers in the crowd, I must have looked like just another spectator hoping to have a juicy story by suppertime. Surely, if he knew who I was, he would have stopped making his tacky comments within earshot of me.

I wanted to grab him by the shoulders and say, "Listen! I'm that man's daughter. The victim was my mother!" But I didn't. Rather, I sat on the hard pew in a complete state of confusion. I didn't know whether to ignore or memorize everything and everyone around me. Unfortunately, my terror and curiosity got the best of me, so I listened to every word.

The *good part,* as the reporter mentioned, was opening statements. The lead prosecutor, Mr. Frank Poole, took his place behind a large podium facing Judge Bedsole. I heard the pencils of every reporter in the room working like mad as soon as Mr. Poole stood. He was a tall rail of a man. I had always been surprised by how thin he was, considering the ample portions he would consume in the café. Small, round glasses perched on the tip of his nose, and his shoulders created sharp points under his suit jacket. He seemed to tower over the room as he began his opening statement. I wondered if the reporters would cast Mr. Poole as a beacon for justice or a cobra rising for his attack in their daily commentary.

"Ladies and Gentlemen of the Jury," Mr. Poole said as he began to read from the notebook he had placed on the podium, "the State of Alabama will prove to you through the use of expert testimony and accounts from reputable citizens who know Mister Hubbard Andrews best, that he, Mister Hubbard Andrews, shot his wife, Addie Andrews, in cold blood on the morning of January 31, 1934. We will prove beyond a shadow of a doubt that this was no accident, as Mister Andrews would have you believe, but that it was in fact a cold, calculated murder." Mr. Poole glanced up, momentarily interrupted by the crowd's reaction to the word *murder.*

"Settle down," said Judge Bedsole. Daddy's trial had barely begun, and the judge already looked annoyed. "Continue, Mister Poole." At the arraignment, everything was "all right, Frank," and "Not yet, John," but today, Judge Bedsole ruled in a much more formal fashion. Every syllable sounded so serious.

Reading again from his notebook, Mr. Poole started up again, "Facing divorce and financial ruin, driven by desperation and lust, Mister Andrews led his unsuspecting wife into the woods of Barlow Bend under the guise of a weekend hunting trip. Hidden by the thick pine, darkness, and fog, Mister Hubbard Andrews took the shotgun given to him by his father-in-law and, at nearly point-blank range, shot the beautiful Addie Andrews to death, blowing the top of her head off. Mister Andrews has taken a mother away from her children and a child and sister away from her loving family. It is your job, ladies and gentlemen, to see that justice prevails. We will prove Mister Andrews's crime. You must make him pay for his heinous actions." Mr. Poole looked up from his paper again, stared at the jury for what seemed to be an uncomfortably long time, and finally took his seat.

A medley of *oh my, goodness gracious,* unintelligible sighs, and chest thumping erupted from the galley. Whether their sighs and noises were in agreement with Mr. Poole, or a display of their amusement at his remarks and odd stare, I'll never know. I forced myself to move past the mental picture of Momma's fatal wound. I squeezed my eyes shut and pictured her shiny hair and bright eyes instead.

"Opening statement for the defense?" asked Judge Bedsole.

"Thank you, Your Honor," said Mr. Jones, rising from his seat. Unlike Mr. Poole, who remained behind the podium, Mr. Jones put his hands in his pockets and began to walk around the courtroom a bit, finally stopping to lean against the front of the podium. I was struck by how relaxed he appeared in his seersucker suit. The room was hot, and everyone in the place was starting to drip, but not Mr. Jones. He looked cool as a cucumber, as if he had ice cubes hidden in his pockets. Facing the jury directly, Mr. Jones began.

"Ladies and gentlemen, what we've got here is a tragedy, a terrible tragedy. Mister Andrews is not the cold-blooded killer that the prosecution would like to trick you into believing with all their fancy experts. Rather, Mister Andrews was the unfortunate witness to an accident that took his beautiful Addie. Mister Andrews is a family man and a grieving widower. The simple truth is that Addie Andrews loved to hunt, and Hubbard loved Addie, so as any devoted husband would, he did whatever he could to make her happy. That's the only crime he's guilty of—trying to make his wife happy." Then, walking toward three male jurors on the front row, "Hard work, am I right, boys? Something we should all try to do—make the missus happy," he paused for just a second. Mr. Jones's voice was syrupy with empathy. "We shouldn't punish him for that. We can't blame him for what he did not do. We can't convict him of a crime that never happened." As he leaned in closer toward the jury, both hands on the railing that fenced the box, each member of the jury seemed to hang on Mr. Jones's every word. His voice softened as he said, "Addie's death was a tragic accident. Convicting Hubbard Andrews of a crime he didn't commit would be just as tragic. Don't let Mister Prosecutin' Attorney over there fool ya. You are all God-fearing, good, Christian citizens of the great state of Alabama. I know without a shadow of a doubt, ya'll know what's right, and will do what's right. Thank yew." Mr. Jones bowed his head toward the jury, then turned away from them to cross to his seat, giving Mr. Poole a sly smile.

Mr. Poole called Mr. Dave McCord to the stand as the first witness for the prosecution. Mr. McCord looked about eighty years old. His black skin was as wrinkled as the cotton sheets at Aunt Mittie's before the hot iron flattened them out. Like a lot of the men in the room, he was wearing what was more than likely the only suit in his thinly stocked wardrobe.

Mr. McCord used a cane to walk down the aisle, leaning hard on his left side with every step. Steadying himself against the witness chair, he propped his cane on the armrest and placed one hand on the bible balanced in the bailiff's hand. After Mr. McCord promised to tell the truth, he sat in the wooden chair, removed a handkerchief from his pocket, and blotted his forehead. His labored breathing created a rhythmic hum over the captivated crowd.

"Please state your full name and profession," said Mr. Poole from behind the center podium.

"Dave McCord, and I is a farmer mostly."

"And where is your farm?"

"I rents a plot in Barlow Bend." Mr. McCord's voice was deeper and stronger than I expected it to be, considering his apparent health issues. Even with his head bowed, his voice reflected strength his body no longer possessed.

"And are you familiar with Mister Hubbard Andrews?"

"Yes, Sir, I is."

"How well do you know Mister Andrews?"

"I used to porter for Mister Andrews and Miz Addie. Back before my fingers got so twisted."

"Yes," said Mr. Poole, and then consulted his notes again. "Mister McCord, you testified to the Grand Jury that on January 31, 1934, you witnessed Mister and Miz Andrews enter the woods near your farm in Barlow Bend. Do you stand by this statement?"

"Yessa, I do."

"You also testified that approximately three hours later, you witnessed Mister Andrews emerge alone from the woods."

"Yes."

"And you are positive the man you saw was Hubbard Andrews?"

"Yessa. He's carryin' sumpin big and walked straight back to his car."

Whispers of "that musta been Addie" rushed through the crowd. Mr. Poole glanced over his shoulder and looked over his glasses perched on his rigid nose to the gallery until silence returned.

Turning back to the witness, Mr. Poole continued his questioning. "Did Mister Andrews appear to be in a hurry when you witnessed him emerge from the woods and walk to his car with the bundle?"

"Nossah. He looked like he was just walkin'. But he look awful tired."

"Uh huh. And in the three hours between Mister Andrews and Miz Andrews entering the woods and Mister Andrews emerging alone, did you hear anything from the woods?"

"Just the usual for that time of year," said Mr. McCord.

"Did you hear a gunshot?" Mr. Poole's teeth clacked on the word "shot".

"Yessa," said Mr. McCord.

"Thank you."

"I heard several shots that morning. I guess one of 'em mighta been the one that got Miz Addie."

"Thank you, Mister McCord," Mr. Poole said, although his tone didn't sound grateful. "That will be all."

"Your witness, Mister Jones," announced Judge Bedsole.

Daddy's attorney rose from his seat. Walking toward the front of the room, he placed a notebook on the podium, and then took two more steps toward Mr. McCord.

"Mister McCord," Jones began, "you're a sharecropper in Barlow Bend, right?"

"Yessa."

"You don't own the land you farm, do you?"

"No," said Mr. McCord, his pride unfaltering at the mention of renting rather than owning. In Alabama, the only difference between the *haves* and the *have-nots* at that time, was land. Other than that, we were all pretty much the same.

"And just to clarify, did you witness Mister Andrews shoot Miz Addie Andrews on January 31, 1934?"

"No, Sir."

"So, you didn't porter for them that morning?"

"No, Sir, my hands don't do so good in the cold air."

"Did Mister Andrews ask you to porter for them that morning?"

"Yessa."

"But you refused on account of your condition?"

"I didn't feel good 'bout taken Mister Andrews's money if I couldn't do the work."

"And you spoke to Mister and Miz Andrews before they entered the woods that morning?"

"Yessa."

"And do recall anything strange regarding Mister Andrews's behavior on that morning?"

"No, Sir. They seemed ready to get to it, get in them woods before the sun come up." Mr. McCord wiped his forehead again, and then, "Miss Addie brought me a pumpkin pie that morning. She was always real sweet to me. Treated me real good." Mr. McCord raised his head on that last statement. For a second, his gaze met mine, as if he knew I was Momma's eldest child. Until Mr. McCord mentioned the pie, I had completely forgotten about helping Momma make it a few days before she walked into the woods with Daddy.

"Did Mister Andrews appear angry or upset in any way?"

"No, Sir."

"Did he seem like the murderin' type?"

Mr. Poole jumped to his feet. "Objection! Speculation. Mister McCord is in no way qualified to judge Mister Andrews' mental or emotional state on that morning."

"Sustained. Agreed," said Judge Bedsole. "Stick to the facts, Jones."

"Certainly," said Mr. Jones to the judge. "Mister McCord, how far from Mister Andrews were you when you saw him emerge from the woods that morning?"

"Well, that's hard to say."

"Approximately, then."

"Guess a couple hundred yards away."

"Where were you exactly?"

"I's in the field, checkin' for freeze."

"So, from that distance, would it be fair to assume that you couldn't *really* see what state Mister Andrews was in? Whether he was hurrying or not, upset or not, or even what or who he was carrying?"

"Objection!" Mr. Poole snapped, jumping to his feet again. "We have already determined that the bundle Mister Andrews carried from the woods that morning was Miz Addie Andrews."

"Actually, Your Honor," said Mr. Jones, "we have not established that yet. And if Mister McCord is supposed to be some sort of eye-witness to the account, I think the jury should know exactly where Mister McCord was and exactly what he thinks he witnessed."

"Overruled," said Judge Bedsole, siding that time with Daddy's team.

"Mister McCord," said Mr. Jones, turning back to the old man, "I want to thank you for coming here today. It couldn't have been an easy trip in your condition."

"No, Sir, but I does my duty."

"Yes, you have. But considering your health, I do wonder, how is your eyesight?"

"Well, I s'pose it ain't as good as it used be neither."

"Thank you, Mister McCord. That's all, Your Honor," and Mr. Jones returned to his seat.

"You're dismissed," Judge Bedsole said to Mr. McCord, and then, "Poole, call your next witness."

The rustling crowd watched Mr. McCord limp down the center aisle and waited to see whom the State would call to the stand next.

"The State calls Stephen Andrews," said Mr. Poole.

"But," I whispered to Aunt Mittie seated next to me, "he's Daddy's cousin!" I didn't understand why Daddy's own flesh and blood would take the stand for Mr. Poole.

"Shhh," Aunt Mittie whispered back, lightly patting my knee. "We'll just have to listen to what he has to say, Hattie."

The heavy, rear doors of the courtroom opened. I craned my neck and head around just as Cousin Stephen walked through the doors. Two steps into the courtroom, he stopped short and examined the crowd for a moment. By the expression on his face, I guessed he didn't expect such a full house.

Nearly a year and a half had passed since I last saw Cousin Stephen, a shorter, slightly less handsome version of Daddy, but he looked exactly the same as he did on the April afternoon he appeared with the tall stranger and Marshal Brooks back in Frisco City. If only I could have predicted then where their questions would lead.

After the bailiff motioned him forward with a few flicks of his fingers, Cousin Stephen marched to the witness stand, took the oath, and sat down. I wish I could have seen Daddy's face as he looked upon his cousin, now batting for the other team. I hope he gave Cousin Stephen a nasty glare.

"Please state your full name and profession for the record," Mr. Poole said, looking down at the podium rather than at his new witness. After scribbling something on his trusty notebook, he finally lifted his head and stared forward. I had to assume he looked at Cousin Stephen, although my view was a bit skewed because his back turned to me.

"Uh . . . I'm Stephen Andrews. A deputy in Jackson."

"And how do you know the defendant?"

"He's my cousin."

"And did you see the defendant at any point on the morning of January 31, 1934?"

"Yes."

"Did you see the victim that morning?"

"Objection!" Mr. Jones snapped to his feet, abandoning his casual behavior for the first time. The crowd reacted to the outburst with an appreciative gasp, but I feared they approved Mr. Jones's dramatic flair rather than the possibility of his pointing out an infraction. "Miz Andrews has not been established as a *victim*. I move that word be struck from the record."

Judge Bedsole offered Mr. Jones an irritated glance. "Mister Jones," said Judge Bedsole. "We are engaged in a murder trial. Therefore, we have established Miz Addie Andrews as the victim in the alleged murder of which we are presently adjudicatin'. Overruled."

Mr. Jones, a bit deflated, sat.

With a nod to Mr. Jones, Mr. Poole continued, "Deputy Andrews, did you see Miz Addie Andrews at any point on the morning in question."

"Frank, you know I did. I wouldn't be here otherwise." Cousin Stephen's sarcastic tone garnered a few muffled guffaws from the audience.

"*Deputy Andrews*," Mr. Poole said, stressing each part of Cousin Stephen's official title, a subtle yet effective way of chastising Cousin Stephen for his use of Mr. Poole's first name, "at what time did you see Hubbard and Addie Andrews that morning?"

"I guess it was around 9 a.m."

"Please describe for the jury your interaction with the defendant that morning."

"Well, I had stepped outside the station for a smoke when Hubbard pulled up out front."

"Was he alone?"

"Not exactly." Cousin Stephen shifted in his seat and leaned on the right armrest.

"Who was with the defendant?"

"Well, he had Addie with him."

"And what condition was Addie in when you saw her?"

Leaning forward a bit, Cousin Stephen lowered his voice, "You know what condition she was in, Frank."

"Describe for the record, Deputy Andrews, Addie Andrews's physical condition."

Cousin Stephen hesitated and stared straight at me. With a pained expression, he nearly whispered, "She was dead. Addie Andrews was dead."

"Please speak up, Deputy Andrews."

"She was dead," Cousin Stephen repeated, loud enough for the pigeons out front hear.

"Were you able to determine what killed Miz Andrews?"

"Yes," Cousin Stephen said, and then coughed into his hand. "She had been shot."

"And how did you determine that?"

"How did I determine what?"

"That Addie Andrews had been shot. Did you view any wounds that would lead you to believe she had been shot?"

"Yes. Of course." Agitation grew on Cousin Stephen's face as he answered the prosecutor's questions through clenched teeth.

"So, what wound did you see? Describe the effect of the gunshot," Mr. Poole ordered.

"The top of her head was gone!" Cousin Stephen shifted in his seat again, and then, "Frank, man, her family is here! There's no need for this. For Christ's sake, her daughter's right there!" As Cousin Stephen pointed at me, the entire audience twisted in their seats to gaze upon the poor, grieving daughter. "Hattie don't need to hear this," Cousin Stephen pleaded to Judge Bedsole.

The courtroom erupted as the crowd struggled to look at me, their mouths gaping open as they practically drooled at the new-found excitement in the room. Reporters closed in around me.

"She's right here, Bob," the reporter nearest me, crouched on the floor next to my seat, yelled. "It's Hattie! It's Hattie!"

Several flash bulbs popped around me as Judge Bedsole pounded his gavel, the sound thundering over the crowd. The next several seconds were a blur of commotion. Uncle Melvin shoved a couple of the reporters, forcing them to keep their distance. Aunt Mittie tried to shield me from the photographers, first holding her pocketbook in front of my face, and then pulling me to her bosom, her arms wrapped tightly around me.

"Order," yelled Judge Bedsole. "Order! This courtroom will be silent!" He hammered his gavel on his desk until, at last, the frenzy died down. "You will remain quiet, or I will clear this room!"

The crowd fell silent, but the air around me remained charged, almost electrified. I squeezed Aunt Mittie's hand as I resisted the urge to run from the courtroom and all the way back to Thorsby, where I could live unnoticed. At Thorsby, I was merely Hattie, a good student with a delicate hand for needlepoint and an ear for dictation. Here, I was Hattie, child of the dead woman, and daughter of the accused. Remaining in that room required every ounce of strength I had.

"Now, Frank, get aholt of your witness," said Judge Bedsole, pointing his gavel at the long-nosed prosecutor. "I'll stand for no more foolishness. From any of ya!"

"Absolutely, Your Honor." Mr. Poole consulted his notebook once again, and then raised his head toward the witness stand. "Please describe your interaction with Mister Hubbard Andrews on the morning of January 31, 1934."

"Well," Cousin Stephen began, "as I said, I had just stepped out for a smoke when Hub, I mean Hubbard Andrews, pult up in his car."

"Was he driving fast? Did he appear to be in a hurry?"

"I don't recall. Guess not."

"Go on. What happened after Mister Andrews pulled his car in front of the police station?"

"Well, Hubbard jumps out and yells to me that Addie's in the backseat. That she'd been shot. I runned over and looked in, and there she was. Wrapped up in a blanket. I could see a little bit of her hair stickin' out from under a blanket."

"And why did Mister Andrews bring Miz Andrews to you rather than to a doctor?"

"She didn't need a doctor. She was already gone."

"By the time he drove thirty miles from Barlow Bend to his family confidant in Jackson, she no longer needed a doctor?"

"No. She didn't need no doctor. It looked like she was killed instantly," snapped Cousin Stephen, "and I don't like your tone!"

"Permission to treat the witness as hostile," Mr. Poole said.

"You're the one makin' me hostile!" Cousin Stephen shot back.

"Granted," ordered Judge Bedsole, "and I'd recommend you calm down right now, Deputy. I'm not afraid to hold you in contempt and toss your behind in a cell of your own."

Cousin Stephen sunk in his chair, letting out a deep sigh. With a shrug of his shoulders, he appeared to slough off Mr. Poole's accusations.

"Now, Deputy Andrews," continued Mr. Poole, "why did Mister Andrews come to you, all the way over in Jackson, rather than the authorities in Barlow Bend?"

"I'm not sure."

"Was it because you are his cousin?"

"Maybe so."

"Was it because the defendant knew that you, his cousin, his trusted flesh and blood, would help him cover up his crime rather than hold him responsible for his heinous act?"

"Absolutely not!" Cousin Stephen smacked the wooden armrest of his chair hard with his hand. "I already told you that ain't true!"

Before the judge could reach for his gavel, Mr. Jones was on his feet again, protesting Mr. Poole's line of questions. "He answered the question, now order him to move on!"

Mr. Poole yelled back at Daddy's attorney, but the two men's voices jumbled together in an angry, distorted mess.

Judge Bedsole rapped his gavel hard against his desk, rattling the windows that lined either side of the courtroom. "That's it! The next man that raises his voice will find his butt on the curb!"

The entire courtroom froze. Mr. Poole, Cousin Stephen, and Mr. Jones all turned toward Judge Bedsole. I held my breath and waited for someone, anyone to speak, terrified of how the judge would react.

Finally, after several tense seconds ticked by, Mr. Poole asked his next question, "After viewing Miz Andrews's body in the defendant's car, what did you and the defendant discuss?"

"I told Hubbard that her body would have to be taken to the coroner in Grove Hill and that an investigation would be conducted. Standard procedure for any gunshot related fatality."

"And what did Mister Andrews do next?"

"Well, we decided that I would take Addie's body to Grove Hill and Hubbard would go home. So, I guess he went home."

"So, you let him leave?"

"He had to go tell the children what happened. He had to plan Addie's fun'ral."

"And did Mister Andrews tell you when he wanted the funeral to be?"

"Yes."

"When was that?"

"Hubbard said he wanted it to be as soon as possible," Cousin Stephen said. Then, with a frustrated sigh, he added, "He wanted her buried the next day."

"So, knowing a full investigation should be mounted into the death of Addie Andrews, you assisted Mister Andrews, your cousin, the only witness to the supposed *accident*, bury the body the very next day rather than insist proper time for an investigation be allotted *before* the burial? Would you give a stranger such assistance? Such allowances?"

"Objection!" Mr. Jones sprang to his feet again and brought with him the gasps and cheers of the crowd.

"Withdrawn, Your Honor," Mr. Poole said, and pointed a smirk in Mr. Jones's direction, in full view of the pleased crowd.

"Very well," said Judge Bedsole. "We're gonna take a ten minute recess. When we return, Mister Jones, you'll get your chance at Deputy Andrews." Then he waved his gavel over the expanse of the crowd and said, "As for the rest of you, I expect you to cool off and clam up!"

I remained in my seat, my hand clutched in Aunt Mittie's, through the recess. After the bulk of the crowd rushed out the door, desperate to get a breath of fresh air and empty their lungs of new gossip I assumed, Daddy turned in his chair and looked at me.

"Sweetie," Daddy said, "don't worry 'bout a thing. This is all just a little courtroom drama. It don't mean anything."

"Hubbard," Aunt Mittie warned, as she wrapped her arm around me again, "please don't." After her plea, Daddy turned back around in his seat, consulting in whispers with his team of attorneys.

* * * * *

"Deputy Andrews," Mr. Jones began once the judge and gallery were seated again, "did Mister Andrews offer an explanation for Addie Andrews's injuries when you saw him that morning in Jackson?"

"Yes," answered Cousin Stephen, much calmer than before the recess. "Hubbard said Addie was moving around a big oak, trying to tree a squirrel, when her gun went off."

"So, Mister Andrews, Hubbard, told you that Addie's death was an accident?"

"Yes."

"Do you have any reason to doubt his story?"

"No."

"Why not?"

"He was in shock. Covered in Addie's blood. Just in shock. I felt so bad for him. Having to see her die, right in front of him. And then he wrapped her in that blanket and carried her through the woods. If it were my Louise ... I just can't imagine it." Cousin Stephen shook his head and let out another deep sigh. "I just can't imagine it."

"Just a couple more questions, Deputy Andrews. I know you've been raked over the coals this morning," said Mr. Jones. He paused as the audience collectively snorted in agreement. "How well do you know Hubbard Andrews?"

"I've known him my whole life. We grew up together."

"And have you ever known Hubbard Andrews to be a violent man?"

"Absolutely not," Cousin Stephen answered. "There ain't a violent bone in his body."

"'Ain't a violent bone in his body.' Thank you, Deputy Andrews. That will be all."

"Deputy Andrews," Judge Bedsole said, with an air of exhaustion in his deep baritone, "you're dismissed."

Cousin Stephen nodded at Daddy as he passed the defendant's table and walked down the aisle. Several reporters followed Stephen out of the courtroom before Judge Bedsole ordered the prosecutor to proceed.

"Call your next witness, Frank."

"The State calls Reverend J.T. Mathis."

J.T. Mathis was the preacher at the Baptist Church in Searight. Momma talked about Reverend Mathis a lot during our visits with Papa Lowman and her sisters. She called Reverend

Mathis a childhood chum. I never met him on our trips, so I was surprised by his boyish good looks. He had shiny blonde hair, thick and kind of wavy on top. He was sharply dressed in a freshly-pressed suit and crisp, white shirt. I could see the quick twinkle of shiny cufflinks as he walked to the witness stand. He was shorter than Daddy and a little thinner, but still handsome. Ever since the trial, I have always wondered why Momma never mentioned his good looks. As the good preacher repeated the bailiff's oath, I thought how silly it seemed to swear in a preacher. Shouldn't preachers be honest with or without an oath?

"Mister Mathis, please state for the record your full name and profession," requested Mr. Poole.

"My name is Jacob Thomas Mathis, and I am the pastor of the First Baptist Church in Searight."

"And did you know Miz Addie Andrews?"

"Yes, Sir, I did."

"How well did you know the victim?"

"Very well. We grew up together in Searight and remained friends over the years."

"Did you and Miz Andrews communicate on a regular basis?"

"Yes, Miz Andrews would come see me when she visited her family in Searight. She often sought my counsel, and we prayed together during her visits."

"Miz Andrews sought your counsel?" asked Mr. Poole.

"Yes, Sir."

"Regarding what?"

"Objection, Your Honor!" said Mr. Jones, springing to his feet. "Surely, the conversations between a pastor and a member of his flock should be considered confidential."

"I'll allow it, Mister Jones. Reverend Mathis, please answer the question."

"Addie, I mean Miz Andrews, sought my counsel regarding her marriage."

"And what concerns did Miz Andrews have about her marriage?" asked Mr. Poole.

"Well, she had reason to believe that Mister Andrews was not faithful to their weddin' vows." The crowd perked up at that accusation. I could hear the gossip wheels starting to turn again.

"And what was your advice to Miz Andrews?"

"I suggested that she speak to her husband regarding the rumors of infidelity and her suspicions."

"Did she take your advice?"

"Yes, she confronted Mister Andrews last summer. She told him that the affairs were hurtful and that they must stop."

"Objection!" Mr. Jones said, "We have no proof that these rumors were actually affairs!"

"The jury will disregard Reverend Mathis's use of the word *affair,*" ordered Judge Bedsole. I didn't see the point, though. The word turned my stomach and seemed to hang in the air. Even if I tried, and believe me I did, I couldn't disregard the word. Did Momma really tell this man that Daddy had affairs? Did Daddy betray her?

"Please go on, Reverend Mathis. Miz Andrews confronted the defendant, and then what happened?" said Mr. Poole, trying to get back on track.

"Well, nothing changed."

"And how do you know this?"

"Because Miz Andrews told me. She told me about confronting Mister Andrews in July and then of an incident in the fall before she died. I... I think in October."

"And what did Miz Andrews tell you happened in October?"

"That they attended a dance at the Methodist church in Frisco City. Apparently, one of Mister Andrews's mistresses was there, too. Addie was humiliated." Reverend Mathis glared at Daddy with hurtful disgust. Mr. Poole, seeing his witness agitated, crossed from behind the podium and stood in front of Daddy, blocking Reverend Mathis's view.

"So, he humiliated her!" Mr. Poole pointed at Daddy with an arm so long and thin, it seemed to go on for miles.

"Yes." Reverend Mathis agreed, but Mathis's voice started to deflate. He dropped his gaze and gripped the wooden railing in front of the witness chair with one hand. His boyish face fell into a deep, sad expression. Until then, I had never considered the possibility that others out there in Nowhere, Alabama, may be missing Momma, too. Perhaps, she was loved by many, not just Daddy, Billy, Meg, Albert, Aunt Mittie, and me. Reverend Mathis obviously missed her, too.

"When did Miz Andrews tell you about this incident?"

"During Christmastime. She was in Searight to visit her family. We talked and prayed about her marriage for a long time that day."

"And what was the outcome of your conversation?"

"Well, Miz Andrews decided that she had no choice but to ask her husband for a divorce." At that, a gasp came from the Ladies Auxiliary, and pain hit me as if I'd been punched in the gut, but Reverend Mathis continued without pause, "She decided she would tell Mister Andrews after the holiday celebrations were over."

"Did she?"

"I don't know. That was the last time I talked to her. She was dead a few weeks later."

"Thank you, Reverend Mathis. That will be all."

Divorce? I had heard the word and had heard rumors of people far removed from my world getting divorced, but no one in my family had ever been divorced. *Divorce* happened to other people, not my momma and daddy!

“Cross, Mister Jones?” asked Judge Bedsole.

“Yes, Your Honor,” said Mr. Jones as he stood and quickly referenced his notes. “Reverend Mathis, you have testified that you and Miz Andrews were childhood friends?”

“Yes,” Mathis responded.

“Wouldn’t childhood sweethearts be a more accurate description?”

“Well, we were sweethearts at one time, but that was ages ago.”

“Ages ago? Are ya sure ya’ll didn’t start back up again?”

“No, Sir. Absolutely not!” Reverend Mathis protested.

“Weren’t ya’ll doin’ a lot more than prayin’ in that little church?” asked Mr. Jones.

“No, Sir, and I take great offense at the suggestion that I would…”

“Didn’t you care for her?”

“Well, of course, but I wouldn’t…”

“And weren’t you supportive of Addie leaving Hubbard?”

“I didn’t see any other way for her…”

“So you were pushing for the divorce?”

“I would never push someone towards…”

“And weren’t you prepared to leave your own wife for Miz Andrews?” Mr. Jones fired away at Reverend Mathis without hesitation until he finally broke the good preacher.

“Hubbard humiliated her! You ruined her!” shouted Reverend Mathis, who stood in the witness stand and pointed at Daddy. Reverend Mathis leaned toward Daddy’s table and glared at him with more hatred than I have ever seen on one man’s face. The crowd erupted again.

“Reverend Mathis!” Judge Bedsole banged his gavel to silence the room, “Remain seated, Sir!”

Reverend Mathis quickly sat, visibly embarrassed by his outburst and flustered by the line of questioning.

"So," said Mr. Jones after the crowd fell silent, "You feel quite passionate about this woman, your beautiful childhood sweetheart, the one that got away but returned to you to cry on your shoulder about her supposed unhappy marriage. An unhappy marriage to a man you obviously don't like. A man that I am sure you would say anything about to *ruin*. You hate the fact that Miz Andrews chose to marry Mister Andrews instead of you, don't you? But you want all of us to believe ya'll were just prayin'? Just doin' the Lord's work in that chapel, huh?"

"Objection!" shouted Mr. Poole.

"Withdrawn. Good to see you, Reverend. My best to Ruth. That's it, Your Honor," said Mr. Jones and took his seat again looking no worse for the wear for the heated exchange. The crowd smirked at Jones's mention of Reverend Mathis's wife by her first name. Mr. Jones's moxy in the courtroom would dominate the dinner conversations all over Clarke County that night.

"Your Honor, I have a follow up for the Reverend," said Mr. Poole.

"Go on," said Judge Bedsole.

"Reverend Mathis, was Miz Andrews eager to ask Mister Andrews for a divorce?" asked Mr. Poole.

"No, Sir."

"And why not?"

"She was afraid of what his reaction would be," answered Reverend Mathis. His face fell again with the words. This time his expression had a hint of guilt. He looked like a sad little boy, like Billy did in the weeks following Momma's death.

"Thank you. Nothing further."

"Thank you, Reverend Mathis. You're dismissed. We'll take a short recess. Be ready in fifteen." With that, Judge Bedsole rapped his gavel again and disappeared through a door behind his bench.

chapter eighteen

September 23, 1935
Grove Hill, Alabama

Uncle Melvin offered to hold our seats during the recess so that Aunt Mittie and I could get a bit of fresh air. The temperature in the courtroom had risen quickly once the mid-morning sun poured in the windows and mixed with the dozens of spectators. The thoughts that Momma might have been as unhappy as Reverend Mathis described, and that Daddy could betray her in such a way, combined with the hot and humid air of the courtroom and swirled around my stomach. I jumped at Uncle Melvin's offer to escape for a few minutes.

Unfortunately, in my haste to leave the room, I nearly ran smack dab into Mrs. Williams in the hallway. I was completely shocked to see her, and even more so, that I didn't hear her first before laying eyes on her. She was standing in the middle of the foyer holding court for the Ladies Auxiliary. Of course, in her courtroom, she acted as both judge and queen. *Why on Earth is that old gossip here?* I thought to myself. Never having to hear Mrs. Williams's obnoxious pecking again was supposed to be the one good thing about leaving Frisco City.

"I should be testifying next. I'm just as nervous as a wet cat," Mrs. Williams told her adoring fans. "I just pray to the good Lord for strength. I have heard that Mister Jones is a bulldog with his cross-examination. Well, I'll just remind him that I know his momma quite well, and I'm sure she wouldn't mind a 'tall if I were to bend him over my knee and remind him of his manners!" Mrs. Williams's shrieking laughter bounced off every hard surface in the foyer.

If it had been possible for Mrs. Williams to speak at a remotely polite volume, I would have questioned what I heard, but there was no point. Every word was crystal clear. Mrs. Williams was a witness for the prosecution. She wasn't there to support Daddy, but rather to assist in my losing both of my parents over the course of two years.

"Hattie, Honey," I heard Mrs. Williams call after me as I rushed by her. "Hattie, you must meet the Ladies' Auxiliary!"

I know it is rude to ignore your elders, but thankfully, Aunt Mittie abetted my transgression and helped me move quickly, without stopping, through the river of onlookers. We swiftly walked around the group and out the front doors of the courthouse before having to speak to Mrs. Williams or her adoring fans, and before I gave in to the temptation to point out the old crow's hypocrisy. How she could accept help from Daddy for years and then stab him in the back was beyond my comprehension. "Hubbard, Dear, the front latch is fussin' with me again," and "Hattie, Honey, when your daddy gets home, would you send him over, please?" *Disgusting.*

Those were just two of the seemingly endless requests that came out of that uppity hag's mouth over the years. Mrs. Williams had conveniently forgotten the good things Daddy had done for her, and just in time for her to be a star witness. Standing in the courthouse foyer, I heard Momma telling me in one ear to tell the old cow exactly what I thought of her, and then Ms. Jenkins's reminders of poise, grace, and dignity in my other ear. Ms. Jenkins won that day, but I promised myself that I would never forgive Mrs. Williams. Were I an old lady from Sicily, I would have spat three times on her grave.

Back inside the courtroom, Mrs. Williams tottered to the witness stand. Her round hips shifted up and down as if independent from the rest of her body. Between her crooked back and her considerable derrière, the skirt of her pale blue suit was at least three inches shorter in the back than in the front. Still, she managed to sit as if she was the Queen of England and the wooden chair was her throne.

"Miz Williams, please tell the court how you know the defendant, Mister Andrews," said Mr. Poole.

"Mister and Miz Andrews, bless her soul, lived across the street from me for nearly fourteen years in Frisco City."

"So, you knew the family well?"

"Oh yes. You see...I try to keep an eye out for everyone in town. Make sure everyone is safe. These are troublin' times, ya know."

As Mrs. Williams spoke, I couldn't help but notice the juror's faces strain as she got louder and louder. Throughout her testimony, she fanned herself with a fan from a revival two summers ago, and kept dabbing her forehead with a handkerchief. I knew it was wrong, but I asked God to make her faint from the heat right there on the stand. He refused my request, of course, but I think a few of the jurors wished her testimony to be short as well, if for no other reason than to protect their ears.

"Did Mister and Miz Andrews appear to have a good marriage?"

"Oh, they were quite smitten with each other, at first," said Mrs. Williams.

"At first?" asked Mr. Poole.

"Objection," said Mr. Jones, "Miz Williams is by no means qualified to cast judgment on my client's marriage, Your Honor."

"I disagree," said Mr. Poole, "Miz Williams was witness to the marriage for nearly its entirety."

"Well, I also object to this line of questioning. My client's marriage is not on trial," said Mr. Jones.

"The state of the marriage speaks directly to motive, Your Honor," said Mr. Poole.

"Agreed, Mister Poole," said Judge Bedsole, "overruled."

"Go on, please, Miz Williams, you said the two seemed 'smitten at first.' Did the marriage appear to change?" asked Mr. Poole, picking up the line of questioning again.

"Over the last few years, their marriage seemed to change quite a lot, I'd say."

"Really? How so?"

"Well, at first, they were perfectly in love and were quickly blessed with four beautiful youngins. But a few years ago, things started to change. I would hear them argue all the time, day and night. I mean, I tried not to listen, seems unchristian to eavesdrop on them, but sometimes you just hear what you hear."

"And what did you hear?"

"Oh, you know, they'd be yellin' about this and that." Mrs. Williams began to wave the fan even more energetically. "I can't repeat those words with a Christian tongue, Mister Poole!"

"Of course, Miz Williams," answered Mr. Poole.

"I felt so bad for the babies havin' to hear their foul words," continued Mrs. Williams, trying desperately to appear sympathetic to the four of us. "And Mister Andrews would come and go at such strange hours."

"Strange hours, Miz Williams?"

"Yes, Sir. Ever since my dear husband died, bless his soul, I just don't sleep too well. So, at night, I sit up with my bible. Do you know I have seen Mister Andrews leave his home well after dark and not return till nearly dawn? Now, you just got to be up to no good stayin' out all night. And with poor Addie and those babies all alone at home. Just no good."

"In your recollection, how often would Mister Andrews leave his home in the evenings?"

"At least twiced a week, sir. Only the Lord knows what he was up to."

"Did he leave the night of October 30, 1933?"

"Well, now, let me think. That was a long time ago."

"Do you remember the night of October 30, 1933? Do recall anything from that night?"

"Oh, of course! That's the day that *The Romance of Helen Trent* premiered on CBS. Do you listen to the radio much, Mister Poole?"

"Um, can't say that I do."

"Oh, you should. After my dear Thomas passed on, bless his soul, I bought a real nice one. You can hear programs from all over the country!"

"Well, that sounds nice..."

"Makes good company for an old widow like me. And you should listen to Helen Trent. It's a wonderful program, very exciting."

"I'm sure it is," said Mr. Poole as he tried to get Mrs. Williams back on track.

"It is! I never miss an episode, that is, until today."

"Well, I apologize that you're missing your program. Now, Miz Williams, do you recall anything else from October 30, 1933, from that evening?"

"Well, I do recall there being a dance at the church that night. I still try to go, even though I'm not much for the dance floors anymore, I get terrible pains sometimes. Doc Stallsmith calls it arth-a-ri-tus. Well, my artharitus was flarin' up real bad, so I went home early. I sat up soaking my feet in the parlor most of the night..."

"Miz Williams," said Mr. Poole sharply and then paused, rolling his shoulders back and wrapping his long fingers around both sides of the podium. "Do you recall anything from the *Andrews* residence on the evening of October 30, 1933?"

"Oh, yes! Mister and Miz Andrews came home a little while after I did. I had just sat down with my soak and my bible when I heard Addie yellin' at Hubbard as they come up the street. They went in the house pretty quick, so I couldn't hear as good once the door shut, but then, not even a minute later, Mister Andrews stormed back out. He stomped down the front steps and started headin' downtown."

"Thank you, Miz Williams."

"I don't know where he was off to in such a state," said Mrs. Williams, unable to stop herself, "but I betch you he was in search of that devil whiskey."

"Miz Williams..."

"You know how you men get when you're all rowed up!"

"Miz Williams..."

"Even my own sweet Thomas was tempted now and then. You men can be awful weak creatures. Full o' sin."

"Thank you, Miz Williams. That will be all."

"You are most welcome, Mister Poole," said Mrs. Williams in a nauseatingly sweet tone.

As Mr. Jones rose from his seat for his turn, I said a quick prayer in my head. *Please, Lord, please. Let Mr. Jones rip that old hag apart.*

"Miz Williams, how are you today?" asked Mr. Jones "I am so sorry to hear about Mister Williams. He was a good man."

"Thank you, Paul. I mean *Mister Jones.*"

"And how is your health, Miz Williams? Are you getting on all right on your own?"

"Oh, yes, just a little artharitus. I guess I have slowed down a little bit."

"But it sounds like you keep up with the world with that radio of yours?"

"Oh, absolutely. I listen as much as I can. Singers and sermons and news stories and, of course, Helen Trent."

"Miz Williams," said Mr. Jones as he turned away from the old woman and walked toward the door, "what volume do you set your radio to?"

Mrs. Williams did not answer.

"Miz Williams?" asked Mr. Jones still turned away from her. She still did not answer. Turning back to face her, Mr. Jones asked, "Miz Williams, are you going to answer the question?"

"I'm not gonna speak to your back, young man."

"I apologize. Now," as Mr. Jones walked back toward the witness stand, "please answer the question."

"I already did. I listen to singers and sermons and news stories and my dramas."

"No, Ma'am, not that question. I asked you what volume do you set your radio to?" The crowd gave a knowing and sympathetic sigh. Mrs. Williams crossed her arms and pursed her lips.

Mr. Jones continued the cross examination without forcing Mrs. Williams to admit she was hard of hearing.

"Miz Williams, do you still live on Bowden Street in Frisco City?"

"Yes."

"And you have a pretty good view of the Andrews home from your house?"

"Yes, from my parlor window there's a straight shot to their porch."

"Nothing obstructs your view, like say, a large oak tree?"

"Well, yes, there's that big oak."

"I bet that provides some nice shade," said Mr. Jones, leaning once again on the jury box.

"Oh, yes, keeps their porch nice and cool in the summer."

"That must be nice. And to the left of their house, what's over there?"

"An old barn."

"And more trees?"

"Well, yes, Mister Jones, more trees."

"So, on the night of October 30, 1933, as you soaked your feet and read your Bible and listened to your radio, you looked up from your Bible just in time to see Mister Andrews clearly leave his home, turn left, and walk all the way downtown? You saw him walk all the way downtown?"

"Well, I..."

"Was it a full moon?"

"I don't recall whether it was or wasn't."

"Was there light comin' from the surrounding homes?"

"Well, I don't know... it was very late."

"Is it possible that you did not see exactly where Mister Andrews went?"

"I suppose."

"Is it possible that Mister Andrews exited his home, turned left, and then went in that barn, not downtown?"

"I guess he could have."

"Miz Williams, with all due respect, I think your soap opera programs have heightened your imagination. Would you agree that it is possible that Mister Andrews was, shall we say, sleepin' in the dawg house that night, as many of us men have had to do from time to time when we tick off the missus? Only, in my client's case, the dawg house is that old barn next to his home?"

Folding her arms, Mrs. Williams looked directly at Daddy as she said, "I saw what I saw, Paul!"

"Miz Williams, did you and your dear Thomas, God rest his soul, ever argue?"

"Of course, we disagreed sometimes."

"Did you ever send him out to the dog house?"

"Well, I'm sure ..."

"Did you ever yell so loud that the neighbors might hear ya?"

"Well, Mister Jones, I'm sure we had our moments, but ..."

"As all married couples do, Miz Williams, as all couples do. Thank you, Miz Williams. I'll tell Momma you said 'hi'," and Mr. Jones took his seat.

Judge Bedsole ordered a lunch break after Mrs. Williams's testimony, allowing her an opportunity to hear the reviews and sympathies of the Ladies Auxiliary and other adoring fans crowded in the hallway. I had hoped that I would get to see Daddy during the break, but his attorneys rushed him off to a back room before anyone could get to him. Aunt Mittie explained that they were probably trying to avoid the reporters and photographers, but Daddy's quick exit without even a look at me, still hurt. At the café, I tried to eat the chicken salad sandwich Aunt Mittie ordered for me, but the act of chewing only increased my nausea. I was pleased with the way Mr. Jones had handled Mrs. Williams. Maybe she'd be more careful in her future assumptions and accusations, but one big question still hung over my head. Did Daddy betray Momma? Did Momma cheat on Daddy in return? I always thought their fighting was just part of their personalities, too strong-willed to be defeated. Was I wrong? Mr. Jones didn't answer that question. He examined the question. He momentarily distracted all of us from the question. He provided plausible theories and more than enough tit-for-tat, but no one answered the question with any degree of certainty. And Daddy ran off before I could ask him directly. Did Daddy betray Momma? Did Momma have her own secrets to hide?

Back at the courthouse, Aunt Mittie ordered a few reporters out of our seats, demanding that they have a little respect for family members. As Uncle Melvin and I moved to join Mittie, I saw John Howard leaning over Mr. Poole. Uncle John wore a very serious, desperate expression, and Mr. Poole's shoulders looked stiffer than ever. If Uncle John had any pride at all, he should have been embarrassed by what he did that afternoon. He stood there and begged Mr. Poole to let him take the stand.

"Come on, I can help. I got plenty to say about ol' Hubbard and a few choice ones about Addie," said Uncle John.

"Mister Howard, I have already told you. Your assistance is not needed," Mr. Poole answered.

"Come on, you wouldn't be here if it weren't for me. You were ready to let him get away with it. I deserve my turn!" Uncle John desperately wanted his moment in the spotlight.

"Mister Howard, leave now or I will have you removed."

"Fine, I'm goin.'"

Uncle John barreled down the aisle and slammed the door shut behind him. He looked just as angry as he did the night Momma poured out his whiskey. I bet Momma would have been just as pleased by his banishment from the courtroom as she was when he stormed out of the kitchen that night. When he passed my pew, the familiar stench of stale liquor floated by me. Whatever Aunt Audrey saw in him that made her marry the man must be a secret between her and God, because I sure couldn't see any redeeming qualities.

Momma was certainly right about him. Uncle John was a pathetic excuse for a man, and he apparently considered himself responsible for Daddy being accused of murder. Surely, these educated men had more reason than the rantings of a drunk to drag my family through all of this. It really didn't matter what reasons actually existed. Regardless of what truly prompted Mr. Poole to accuse Daddy of something so awful and drag his name through the mud, from that moment on, I no longer considered John Howard family. If Uncle John considered himself a proud member of Daddy's lynching party, he had officially lost the privilege to be treated as family. I should spit on Uncle John's grave one day, too.

The last witness of the day was Mr. Dominic Lavender, Alabama License Inspector. Aunt Mittie and Uncle Melvin had to explain his testimony to me during supper that evening. According to Mittie and Melvin, all the highly-technical and confusing mumbo jumbo from Mr. Lavender boiled down to motive. He testified that the hotel in Grove Hill had been licensed under several names including Hubbard Andrews, Herbert Andrews, Hubbard Anders, and, for the two years leading to Momma's death, Addie Andrews. Mr. Poole then tried to convey to the jury that the frequent name changes on the business license were highly suspicious and typical of someone trying to scoot around the law. Mr. Poole suggested that Daddy killed Momma before she could divorce him, and take the hotel, his livelihood, away.

"But Aunt Mittie, that sounds awful," I said, unable again to enjoy the plate of food in front of me. I didn't understand why Daddy would change the license so often. Why did he change his name back and forth? His actions did seem terribly suspicious, at least to me.

"I know, I know, it was damaging, but Mister Jones smoothed things over a little," said Mittie. She was trying her best to calm me, and I pretended as best I could, but inside, I was a wreck. Yes, Mr. Jones had pointed out that at the time of Momma's death, Daddy was a successful Raleigh Man in Monroe County and didn't need the hotel to support his family, but I was afraid the damage was done. Between the rumors of broken marriage vows, loud arguments, suspicious business dealings, and Momma's supposed unhappiness, would anyone on the jury believe that Momma's death was an accident? Would anyone in that room believe Daddy's story? Did I still believe his story? That last question washed over me, soured my stomach, and created a clammy feeling that I couldn't ignore. Before I got sick at the table, I asked to be excused, and rushed up the stairs.

chapter nineteen

September 24, 1935
Grove Hill, Alabama

The next day, Uncle Melvin, Aunt Mittie, and I arrived back at the courthouse bright and early. I was feeling much stronger than the day before, at least physically. I had decided to concentrate on supporting Daddy and was determined to stick with my new plan. Momma detested the idle gossip that ran rampant through the streets of Frisco City, so in her honor, I intended to ignore all of it. I also reminded myself that Mr. Poole, no matter how completely wrong he was, had a job to do. I desperately needed Mr. Jones, Daddy's attorney, to keep doing his job, and for the jury to believe the Clarke County native. Daddy's fate, and mine, rested in the clever hands of the hometown boy.

Mr. Poole, still trying to provide enough evidence for a conviction, called William Murray, the strange large man in the dark jacket who I first saw in Frisco City, then later witnessed handcuffing Daddy in the café, to the stand as the first witness of the day. According to Mr. Murray, he was a detective with the Clarke County Sheriff's Department, and the lead detective investigating Momma's death.

"Detective Murray," Mr. Poole began, "what was assumed to be the original cause of death for Addie Andrews?"

"Hunting accident," answered Detective Murray.

"So, what made you investigate Addie Andrews's death further?"

"The County Coroner said a few things that got me thinkin'."

"What did the coroner say?"

"Well, he told me that Miz Andrews was supposedly squirrel hunting with her husband, but, according to the coroner, her husband's cousin, Stephen Andrews, not Hubbard Andrews, brought the body in. Hubbard Andrews had dropped off Miz Andrews's body to Stephen at the police station in Jackson."

"What was suspicious about that?"

"I found it odd that Mister Andrews would drive from Barlow Bend to Jackson, the opposite direction of the Andrews home in Frisco City."

"Well," said Mr. Poole, "Mister Andrews may not have been thinking clearly. Maybe he was in shock. Is that possible?"

"Maybe, but I was also suspicious of the wound the coroner described. It didn't sound like somethin' that would happen while squirrel huntin'."

"Uh huh, so that was why you began a criminal investigation?"

"I had my suspicions, and then I started hearing all these rumors, wild stories about the two of them, Mister and Miz Andrews, and then Miz Andrews's father, Malachi Lowman, and her brother-in-law, John Howard, came to see me. Drove all the way from Searight to Grove Hill. They also had their suspicions about the way Addie died and Hubbard's involvement in the whole thing. I figured I should at least look around a bit."

"And what did you find?"

"Well I went back to the doc, uh… the coroner. He said 'the top of her head was blown off.' Said it was one of the most gruesome things he had ever seen, especially from squirrel hunting."

"For those of us who are not experienced hunters, explain why you found that to be suspicious."

"Well, you hunt squirrel with a .22 or somethin' like it. Somethin' small enough so that the meat will still be intact once you shoot the animal. Somethin' small enough for a squirrel isn't gonna blow a woman's head off. It just didn't make sense."

"Uh huh. In your opinion, what type of gun would be necessary to inflict a wound such as the one described by the coroner?"

"Somethin' big and solid, like a shotgun. I figure the shot entered under her chin and came out the top of her head."

Mr. Poole walked back to his table. His assistant handed him a long, slender box. Mr. Poole opened the box and unveiled a shotgun. "You're saying the wound had to be caused by a shotgun. Like this one?" He waved the gun around so that the jury and audience could see the weapon.

"Yes, Sir."

"But, you wouldn't hunt squirrel with a gun like this?"

"No, Sir, you'd blow the vermin to bits!"

"So, you absolutely would not use this gun to shoot a squirrel?"

"No, Sir, absolutely not."

"Mister Murray, did you interview Mister Andrews during your investigation?"

"Yes."

"And when you questioned Mister Andrews, did you ask him what kind of gun they were using that day out at Barlow Bend?"

"Yes, Sir. He told me they had two guns with them. He had a .22 rifle, and he claimed that Miz Andrews was carrying a shotgun."

"And did the defendant tell you how Miz Andrews came to be shot that morning?"

"Yes, Sir. Hubbard Andrews said that it was an accident. He claimed that Miz Andrews was turning a squirrel around a tree for him to shoot when her gun snagged a branch or somethin' and went off."

"Didn't that seem plausible to you?"

"No, it did not."

"Why not?"

"May I, Your Honor," Murray asked as he stood, "I'd like to show ya'll somethin'."

"Go ahead, Detective," said Judge Bedsole.

The detective walked to the center of the room, taking the shotgun from Mr. Poole.

"Mister Poole, would you stand here, uh, like a tree?"

The crowd giggled as Mr. Poole took his position. Mr. Poole was less amused, but cooperated. He stood very still in the middle of the room.

"Now," said Murray, "if I was tryin' to turn a squirrel for my huntin' partner around a tree, I would hold the gun like this." The detective held the butt of the gun with the barrel pointed down toward the floor and slowly walked in a circle around Mr. Poole. "I would try to scare or shuffle that squirrel in the right direction. How am I gonna shoot my own head off if the gun ain't pointed at me?"

"Good question, Detective."

"Thank you, Sir," Murray handed the gun back to Mr. Poole. Back on the stand, Murray continued, "That's when I determined that Mister Andrews was lying. He had to be the one carrying the shotgun. The shot had to come from his gun."

"Thank you, Detective Murray. Nothing further."

"I just have a couple of questions for this witness, Your Honor," said Mr. Jones from behind his table.

"Proceed, Mister Jones," said Judge Bedsole.

"Detective Murray, how much would you say a shotgun weighs? On average?" asked Mr. Jones.

"Oh, probably 'round ten pounds."

"Okay." said Mr. Jones, then turned toward Mr. Poole, "May I borrow that shotgun, Sir? Promise to be real careful." The jury laughed as Mr. Poole handed over the shotgun. "Now, if I could get a volunteer from the audience, maybe a lovely member of the Ladies Auxiliary? Good to see you joined us again today, ladies." Mr. Jones tipped a little bow to the Ladies Auxiliary as giggles erupted once again from the enraptured women.

"I'll help you, Mister Jones!" a tiny woman squealed and nearly jumped from her seat.

"Oh, I am much obliged, Miz?"

"Miz Timmons," answered the spirited volunteer as she hurried to the front.

"Now, Miz Timmons, I promise this won't hurt a bit." Mrs. Timmons found it difficult to control her giggles. "I just need you to hold this shotgun." Mr. Jones went to hand her the gun, then paused as Mrs. Timmons held out both hands, "One-handed, please," instructed Mr. Jones.

"Oooh," said Mrs. Timmons as she struggled to hold the gun in one hand, "that's heavy." Mrs. Timmons's hand was too small to grasp the butt of the gun. Instead, she held the barrel, just above the trigger. This made the butt drop and the barrel point up toward the ceiling.

"Now, walk from this table to Judge Bedsole's bench and back, please," said Mr. Jones.

Mrs. Timmons did as instructed. As she walked, the barrel bobbed back and forth like a buoy floating on the water.

"Detective Murray, is it possible that Miz Andrews would carry the shotgun like Miz Timmons here?"

"Well, maybe, but..."

"Detective Murray, we just witnessed a woman very near Miz Andrews's size and weight carry this shotgun with the barrel up, bouncin' back and forth, without any suggestion or coaching from me. So, yes or no, would it be possible that Miz Andrews was carrying a shotgun like this one in the same fashion as Miz Timmons just did?"

"Yes," answered Detective Murray.

"Is it possible that Miz Andrews would struggle to carry a shotgun steady if she was using only one hand to hold the gun and the other to feel around the tree?"

"Yes, I guess she might have."

Mr. Jones turned to Mrs. Timmons, "Thank you, Miz Timmons. That was lovely and right helpful."

"Oh, you are so welcome," said Mrs. Timmons. She giggled all the way to her seat.

"Now, Detective Williams," Mr. Jones said as he held the shotgun, "it is my understanding that the trigger of a shotgun is pretty delicate, easily pulled. Yes or no, Mister Williams?"

"Yes, the triggers are easy."

"Do you admit that it is possible as Miz Andrews moved around a tree in the shadows of early morning, that the trigger caught on a twig or branch and pulled, resulting in Miz Andrews shooting herself? Is that possible, yes or no?"

"I...uh...I suppose it could be possible, but I think that would be highly unlikely."

"So, yes, it would be possible?"

"Yes," resigned Detective Murray.

"Is it possible that Addie Andrews lost her footing in the twilight, causing her gun to fire?"

"I guess that might be possible?"

"So, isn't it true that the theory that Hubbard Andrews shot Addie Andrews is only one of several plausible theories?"

"To my mind, it is the *only* plausible theory!"

"One last question, Detective Murray," said Mr. Jones, "who was the original source of these rumors you spoke of? Who came to visit you?"

"Well, Miz Andrews's daddy came to me."

"Who was with him, Detective Murray?"

"Oh, you mean John Howard."

"Yes, Sir, I mean John Howard. Have you ever picked up Mister Howard for anything?"

"Objection, Your Honor!" snapped Mr. Poole, "Mister Howard is not on trial."

"If John Howard convinced Detective Murray that an accident was a murder, I think we should know what kind of man John Howard is."

"Overruled. I'll allow it," said Judge Bedsole.

"So, Detective Murray, have you ever detained Mister Howard for anything?" Mr. Jones picked up where he was interrupted.

"Yes, I have."

"What did you detain him for?"

"Public intoxication."

"Hmmm... and how many times, roughly, would you say you've detained him for public intoxication?"

"Probably five or six times."

"So, you began this investigation on the word of a drunk?"

"Sir, I..." Murray protested.

"No need, Detective Murray. I think we all know the nature of your *evidence*." Mr. Jones winked at the jury. Before Mr. Poole had the chance to object, Mr. Jones said, "Nothing further," and took his seat again.

"Your Honor, redirect?" Mr. Poole requested.

"Go on," ordered Judge Bedsole.

"Detective Murray, in your expert opinion, would an experienced hunter carry her weapon as Miz Timmons just carried this shotgun?" asked Mr. Poole.

"Objection, Your Honor, Murray is a detective, not a lady hunter expert," said Mr. Jones.

"Sustained, rephrase the question, Mister Poole," said Judge Bedsole.

"Okay. In your *opinion*, would an experienced hunter carry a gun with the barrel pointed at herself?"

"No, Sir, in my *opinion*, she would not."

Detective Murray left the courtroom after this last response. As he walked past the jury, I noticed a few of them exchange some very skeptical looks. For the first time since testimony began, I felt a glimmer of hope that maybe some of them were on Daddy's side.

During the recess that followed Detective Murray's testimony, Mr. Jones's aid approached me in the hallway.

"Are you Miss Hattie Andrews?" the young man asked. He spoke so softly I had to strain to hear him.

"Yes, I'm Hattie Andrews."

"Your father would like to have dinner with you tonight, and Judge Bedsole has agreed to allow it. Mister Jones has made all the arrangements. Are you available at six this evening?" The young man spoke in such a strange, formal tone. He must have graduated with honors from Thorsby Institute.

"Oh, um, of course, of course I'm available."

"Wonderful, we will meet here at six."

With that, he turned and walked away, his shoulders and back straight as a board. I could almost see the outline of a book balanced on his head.

I can barely describe exactly how I felt in that moment. I was excited to see and talk with Daddy. I hadn't talked to him in over a year. I missed him terribly. I missed my family as I once knew them, but I was nervous that Daddy wouldn't like the woman I was becoming. I was stronger than I was a year ago, more mature and determined. I was definitely more refined, thanks to Ms. Jenkins's teachings and Aunt Mittie's example. I was never wild, but now, I was more in control of my emotions, with the exception of last night. Even with all the training I had received, however, my mother's spirit had begun to flourish inside me. I knew my capabilities and knew that I had value all on my own. Would Daddy appreciate these changes? Would he see that I was no longer a child, or would he continue to make the rules and dictate every situation, even in his current predicament? Maybe, he was scared and lonely and just wanted to be with family. Six o'clock seemed days away.

After the recess, Mr. Poole called Papa Lowman to the stand. Before then, I didn't even know Papa Lowman was in town, much less in the courthouse. I felt a weight pressing on my chest as Papa Lowman settled into the witness chair.

Papa Lowman was the proud father of seven children. He had buried two beloved wives in his life and had farmed countless seasons of cotton, corn, and soybeans. The years had started to take their toll on his face, wrinkled skin, and ailing body. He had used every muscle in his body to provide a good life for his family. I knew that, but I also knew that by taking that witness stand, he was trying to destroy what was left of my family.

"Please state your name and relation to the deceased," said Mr. Poole.

"I am James Malachi Lowman," he said, "and Addie Andrews was my daughter."

"And did you know your daughter to be a hunter?"

"Yes. We loved to hunt. Taught her myself as soon as she was strong enough to carry a gun."

"Was she a good hunter?"

"She was a fine hunter, right good indeed. Best shot in Crenshaw County two years runnin' at the Spring Shoot. Juvenile division, but a real good shot. She had the touch."

"What did she prefer to hunt?"

"Anything really, but squirrel was her favorite."

"What type of gun did she shoot?"

"She preferred a .22 rifle. First, she had one that belonged to her momma. And then I gave her one as a weddin' present."

"That's a nice gift. What did you give your son-in-law as a wedding present?"

"Objection," said Mr. Jones, "Is this a trial or a review of the Sears and Roebuck catalogue?"

"Your Honor, I assure you this line of questioning is relevant," Mr. Poole said.

"Alright then, overruled. Get on with it, Mister Poole," ordered Judge Bedsole.

"Go ahead, Mister Lowman. What did you give your new son-in-law as a wedding gift?"

"Well, I gave him my daughter, first and foremost." Papa Lowman's voice cracked a bit. He cleared his throat and continued, "I gave him a shotgun. A shotgun."

"Once last question, if given the choice between her .22 and her husband's shotgun, which gun do you think your daughter would choose?"

"Always the .22, her .22."

After Mr. Poole took his seat, Mr. Jones stood and walked to the front of the defense table. He rested against the edge of the table during his entire cross-examination of Papa Lowman. Mr. Jones first offered his condolences and then began his questions.

"Would you consider your daughter to be a selfish woman?" Mr. Jones asked.

"No, Sir."

"So in your opinion, Addie was a generous woman?"

"Yes, most gen'rous. She'd give you everything she could. I raised my children to be good people and good Christians."

"Was she generous with her children?"

"Of course."

"And her husband?"

"She gave Hubbard whatever he wanted."

"Even her gun to shoot a squirrel?"

"I don't know that."

"No, you don't, Mister Lowman, because you weren't there. You weren't there." Mr. Jones walked around the table to his seat, and then looked at Papa Lowman, "Again, I am so sorry for your loss. That's it, Your Honor."

"Mister Poole," Judge Bedsole said, "Call your next witness."

"Mister Lowman was our last witness, Your Honor. The State rests."

"Alright then, let's call it a day. Mister Jones, be ready to go at 9 a.m. tomorrow. Court dismissed."

Judge Bedsole rapped his gavel. The courtroom went from silent to chaotic almost immediately. The reporters and photographers surrounded Mr. Poole and Mr. Jones, shouting questions and snapping pictures as fast as they could. Uncle Melvin escorted Aunt Mittie and me through the crowd. Luckily, the reporters were too fascinated by the attorneys to worry with us, and we were able to scoot out of the room without much delay. I needed to get back to the hotel in time to fix myself up a little before dinner with Daddy.

chapter twenty

September 24, 1935
Grove Hill, Alabama

I arrived back at the courthouse a few minutes before six. I chose my blue floral dress with matching gloves and hat. The dress had held up well over the last year since Daddy gave it to me, and Mittie's alterations made it fit perfectly. Alone in the hallway, I listened to the heels of my shoes tapping the floor as I paced back and forth in front of a long bench for several minutes. At six sharp, Mr. Jones's assistant met me in the lobby as promised. Even after court, he had his tie perfectly positioned, along with his jacket and vest, and walked just as stiffly as he did earlier that day.

The assistant led me down a long hallway toward the rear of the building. Two deputies sat outside the last door on the right. The assistant showed me into the room, and then left Daddy and me to dine alone, or whatever this strange meeting was going to be. I couldn't believe how nervous I was. Daddy looked nervous, too. He stood up from a cot against the far wall when Mr. Jones's assistant had opened the door.

I stood in the doorway and looked at the meager furnishings of the small room, not really knowing what I was supposed to do. The cot with a flat pillow and blanket was pushed against one wall. In the center of the room, a small table with two chairs had been set for dinner with two plates of fried chicken, okra, and white rice with brown gravy. Two slices of strawberry cake and two glasses of iced tea finished off the meal. Daddy had somehow arranged for all my favorites. I recognized the china pattern on the plates from the café, and Henrietta's skilled hand with the fried chicken.

After a moment, Daddy crossed the room and gave me a quick hug, "Would you like to sit down, Hattie?" He pulled a chair out for me.

I sat down and placed the napkin in my lap as Momma had tried and Ms. Jenkins finally succeeded in teaching me to do. Daddy stared at me for a long time while I fidgeted with my napkin, silverware, and tea glass.

"You've grown up, Hattie."

"Yes, Sir."

"You look well. How have you been?"

"Fine. And you?"

This was all very odd. I felt like I was speaking with an acquaintance, not my father. Had he been gone so long that we forgot how to interact with each other?

Daddy continued the idle, uncomfortable chitchat for a while longer. "How are Meg and the boys?"

"They're alright, I guess. I haven't seen them for a few weeks. I'm back at Thorsby for the fall term."

"Oh, yeah. How's school going for you?"

"I love it."

"Oh, that's good," Daddy said as he unwrapped his silverware and awkwardly placed his napkin in his lap. "Well, dig in. I asked Peetie to get all your favorites. Of course, maybe I should have asked you first. Do you still like this stuff?"

"Who's Peetie?" I asked.

"He works for Mister Jones. The young man who set this up... well, do you, like it, I mean?"

"Yes, Daddy, of course I do."

I couldn't believe how nervous he was. Even though I wasn't really hungry, I took a bite of the chicken just to try to put him at ease.

"Good," said Daddy and smiled, "so, how have the Lowmans been treating you?"

"Good. Meg and the boys seem happy, even though Aunt Mittie and Uncle Melvin's house is a little crowded."

"I bet it is."

"Mittie, Melvin, and Papa Lowman are paying for my school, you know."

"Yes, Hattie, I know."

Daddy seemed to flinch at the mention of Papa Lowman. I stared at him for a second while he looked down at his plate.

"Are you mad at him?" I asked.

"At who?"

"Papa Lowman. I'm mad at him, too. He shouldn't have done that today. He should be on..."

"Hattie, he just did what he thought was right. That's all anybody's doin'."

"But, how can you let them trash you like that? And Momma!"

"Hattie, I didn't ask you here to talk about the trial."

"But, I don't understand how you can let..."

"Hattie, I don't want to discuss this with you."

"Well, I do!"

"Hattie, drop it, damn it!"

My breath caught in my throat as Daddy cut his gaze at me. In the past, arguing with Daddy usually resulted in a pop on the behind, or worse, his belt, but now, he just turned his attention to his fried okra, "Eat your dinner before it gets cold, Hattie."

"I didn't mean to upset you," I told him, not knowing why I felt badly or why I felt compelled to apologize to him, but I did.

After several moments, Daddy broke the silence. "Sweetie, I wanted to talk to you about what's gonna happen once this is all done. I think I need to make a fresh start. I think we all do."

"But what about the jury?"

"Oh, I'm sure they're gonna go with me. Don't you worry 'bout that."

"Oh... oh, okay."

Daddy seemed so confident about how the trial would end, but after hearing the last two days of testimony, I didn't know how he could feel that way. In my mind, the jury could go either way. Discussing what kind of *fresh start* he may or may not need seemed pointless without knowing the jury's decision first.

"I've arranged a place for us in Uriah. We can go there, me and you and Meg and the boys and start over. Forget all about this mess."

"Uriah?"

"Yeah, it's real nice and nobody down there has heard about any of this. They don't care about being an Andrews or a Lowman or anything. We can just start over."

"Start over?"

"Yeah, I've got a few connections down there from my Raleigh days, so we should be able to get set up pretty easy."

"And I'm gonna go with you?"

"Of course, Sweetie. I'm gonna need your help with the boys. I'm sure Meg is old enough now that she won't need much, but the boys are still growin'. I'm gonna need your help, Hattie."

"But what about school?" I asked. Thorsby Institute was *my* fresh start. I had plans. I had a plan for my future. My fresh start had already begun. "Papa Lowman and Mittie already paid my tuition, and I promised Ms. Jenkins that I'd be back!"

I felt myself getting hysterical, but I couldn't stop. Every part of his fresh start became crystal clear. It would be the hotel and café all over again. I would quit school again and become housekeeper to four people and mother to two boys. Daddy would go to work, and I would do the rest.

"Sweetie, you'll finish school, just in Uriah. You don't need that school and those people. You need your family."

"But, what will I tell Aunt Mittie?"

"Hattie, this is my decision. Mittie's been real good to you, but she ain't part of this."

I couldn't believe Daddy could dismiss Mittie so easily. She loved me like I was her own. Momma was a part of her. How could Daddy just push Aunt Mittie aside as if he owed her nothing for the last year? Couldn't he see that I needed her? Couldn't he hear the arrogance in his words, his tone? Daddy didn't know it, but he flipped a switch in me during that dinner. Momma's voice was screaming in my ears.

"Daddy," I said looking right at him, "did you do it?"

"Hattie, of course not. How many times do I have to tell you that?"

"No, Daddy, not kill her. Did you betray her?"

Daddy didn't answer, but I didn't really let him. With the question just hanging there sucking all the air out of the room, I left. I rushed out without saying goodbye or anything else. At that moment, with him trashing my plans and dismissing Aunt

Mittie, I couldn't stand to look at him. Before saying something I couldn't or wouldn't take back, I left. I walked back to the hotel slowly, trying to digest everything that Daddy had just said, and the fact that I had actually asked him if he ran around on Momma. I tried to figure out what I was going to say to Aunt Mittie. I didn't want to use her and throw her away. I didn't want to be like Daddy.

chapter twenty-one

September 25, 1935
Grove Hill, Alabama

The next day, Aunt Mittie, Uncle Melvin, and I headed back to the courthouse. Mr. Poole had rested the prosecution's case the day before, so I was anxious to hear what Mr. Jones had in store for Daddy's defense. With no witnesses to Momma's death other than Daddy, his case rested on the jury believing that Momma accidentally shot herself in the woods near Barlow Bend and that Daddy was too good a man to commit murder. Unfortunately, Mr. Poole had painted the story of an unhappy marriage and desperate circumstances quite well. I had begun to understand why Mr. Poole, Detective Murray, and Papa Lowman thought he killed her. I didn't agree with them, but I could understand the theory.

Waiting in the hallway of the courthouse that morning, was a parade of familiar faces: Grandpa Andrews, Leroy Andrews, Mr. Hendrix from Frisco City, and several of Daddy's siblings. According to Aunt Mittie, they were all here to testify on Daddy's behalf. Aunt Mittie called them character witnesses.

As soon as we arrived, Uncle Melvin found us a couple of seats near the front, but when I moved toward the row, Aunt Mittie grabbed my hand and pulled me back into the hallway.

"Hattie, Honey, I need to talk to you," said Aunt Mittie, as she moved toward a corner, tucked away from the crowd.

"Are you alright?" I asked.

"Oh, fine, dear, just a little nervous is all." Aunt Mittie seemed to struggle with the words, but finally continued, "Hattie, I'm taking the stand for your daddy today."

"Oh, okay," I said, still reeling from Daddy's plan for a fresh start. I had tossed and turned the whole night before trying to come up with a way to tell Aunt Mittie about Daddy's plan without disappointing her. In my heart, I knew she would never approve of me leaving school to take on the role of mother and housekeeper at fifteen, even if Daddy did mention a high school in Uriah. I didn't want to leave Thorsby or turn my back on everything Mittie had done for me, but I didn't know if or how I could turn my back on Daddy. He was my Father. *Honor thy father and mother,* right? But I knew Mittie and Melvin had sacrificed so much in the last year. Now, Aunt Mittie was going to stand up for him. What would she have done if she knew how easily Daddy had dismissed her? What would she have done if she knew he was ready to throw her away?

"I just needed to tell you ... well, you've heard some horrible things about your momma and daddy over the last couple of days, and I just wanted to tell you something before Mr. Jones starts. I don't want you to feel ambushed again."

"Well, thank you, Aunt Mittie, but you don't have to explain anything to me. You can testify for Daddy if you want to, if you think that's best."

"I don't think your daddy killed my sister, and I know your momma and daddy loved each other. That's what Mr. Jones has asked me to testify to."

"Well, then I guess that's what you'll say. But won't Papa Lowman be upset with you if you tell the judge that?"

"Probably, well, very. He's not gonna like it. But I don't think your daddy should pay for sins he didn't commit."

"I'm sorry you're caught in the middle of this."

"Hattie, Honey, I'm sorry you've had to hear all these awful things 'bout your parents. I am."

"That's not your fault, Aunt Mittie."

"Well, I'm afraid something else might come out still. Somethin' no child should have to know about their daddy, but I can't let you hear about it first in front of a crowd o' people." Aunt Mittie rubbed her palms on the hem of her dress, tucking it around her knees and took a deep breath. "I hope I'm doing the right thing. I just don't know what else to do…"

"Aunt Mittie, just tell me. Nothing could be worse than all the things I've already heard."

I was wrong, so wrong. Aunt Mittie was about to answer the question I had asked the night before. My heart sank when I learned from Aunt Mittie on that hard courthouse bench that the answer was yes. On March 30, 1933, ten months before Momma died, Daddy buried a stillborn infant, named only Baby Andrews. The baby's mother was a woman named Elsie Zona Lawrence. Momma and that baby, that symbol and proof of Daddy's betrayal, were buried in the same cemetery in Frisco City, Alabama. Only the baby's grave had no headstone. It was marked by a blank stone outlining the tiny coffin. My mind raced back to Momma's funeral and the small infant grave a few feet from hers.

"Hattie, I think your daddy tries to be a good man, but he falls short. I think he loved your momma, but failed her in many ways. That's why it took me so long to come to you, Hattie, after she died. I couldn't stand to see him knowing how much he hurt her."

"Why are you telling me this?"

"Well, I'm not going to lie on the stand, under oath to God. If Mister Poole asks me about Elsie or the baby, I will have to tell him what I know. I don't want you to feel lied to or that we were hiding stuff from you."

"But you have lied ... he did, too."

"No, Honey, we didn't lie to you."

"But ya'll kept this from me. Why didn't Momma tell me?"

"Now, Hattie Andrews, why on Earth would your mother tell you 'bout somethin' like this? As far as your momma was concerned, that baby was dead and buried, and that trash Elsie Lawrence was long gone."

I sat on the bench stunned into silence. I thought Momma and I were so close. I thought she told me all her secrets.

"Is she here?" I asked Mittie.

"Who?"

"The woman. Elsie." I wiped a tear off my face before it had a chance to find more and puddle under my eyes.

"No, she isn't. Nobody knows where she is."

"Good." Two more tears wet the fingertip of my glove.

"Hattie, Honey, I did try to hide this and I'm sorry. I never wanted you to think anything less of your daddy. But I think you are old enough now to know the whole truth. Your daddy loves you. I know he does. And I know he loved your momma, too. Yes, he's made some big mistakes, no denying it. But no matter what you might hear today, no matter what mistakes he's made, I want you to remember that he loves you."

"Why are you doing this?" I asked, "Tell Mister Jones that you won't take the stand."

"Hattie, Honey, I'm afraid if I don't, the jury will think your Daddy's guilty. He's guilty of plenty, but not this. Having me stand up for him will go a long way with the jury. You can't lose both your parents. You just can't."

"But I..." I tried to protest again, but Mittie stopped me.

"Hattie," Mittie said as she motioned toward the line of character witnesses in the hallway, "at least half the people in that line know about Elsie and that baby. If Mister Poole doesn't ask me about it, he'll ask somebody else, so whether I take the stand or not, the jury will find out. Mister Poole's not gonna keep this secret. I wish he would, but I know he won't." Mittie paused and brushed a tear off her own cheek. "Addie was my sister. My twin. I've known her and loved her since before I took my first breath. And I miss her every day. I wouldn't testify for your daddy if I thought for a second he coulda killed her. So, if I don't think he killed her, nobody else should. Hopefully, the jury will see that."

Throughout the day, the line of family and friends from the hallway took the stand. Each one told of a good man with excellent character and Christian morals. Mister Hendrix told the court of his prosperous sales business in Monroe County and said that Daddy "always gave ya a fair deal" with the Raleigh products he sold door-to-door throughout Monroe County. Grandpa Andrews told of Daddy's Christian upbringing. Several of Daddy's siblings told us how devoted Daddy was to Momma and that he was completely smitten with her from the moment they met in that church in Luverne.

All I could focus on was that Daddy probably cheated on Momma with tramps from all over the county and definitely did with one woman who lived in our town. He probably came home to Momma stinking of Elsie. Momma probably passed her on the street, probably wanted to scratch her eyes out, but didn't. At one time, Momma and Elsie may have even been friends, sharing recipes and gardening tips at Hendrix General Store. Then Momma watched Elsie's belly grow with Daddy's betrayal. Frisco City is a small town. I bet every single person in Frisco City knew, everyone but me.

During both of the nights following the prosecution's testimony of affairs, lies, and betrayals, I lay on my cot wondering which rooms in the hotel Daddy had chosen to break Momma's heart in. Now, I knew he didn't even have the courtesy to run around in another county. He chose to humiliate her just a few steps from her home. How could he do that to her? How could I be expected to go back to him if he was freed?

The story of Elsie and the baby came out during Leroy Andrews's testimony. Leroy was Daddy's cousin and had moved to Frisco City in 1931 with his wife Jewell. Leroy did odd jobs around town, earning enough money for a modest home and food on the table. Jewell and Momma became friends, and the four attended church socials and dances together. Leroy testified that Momma and Daddy had a good, solid marriage and that he never heard mention of a pending divorce. However, during the cross examination, Leroy admitted to the jury, judge, and captivated audience that in March of 1933 he helped Daddy bury a stillborn in Union Cemetery in Frisco City. No one in the room seemed shocked by the story except the jury and me.

Mittie was the last witness Mr. Jones called to the stand. I could tell by the way she clasped her hands tightly together in her lap, that she was still uneasy. I knew she risked angering her father and her sisters by testifying for the defense. I admired her courage though, not because her testimony could help Daddy, but because she was doing what she believed was right regardless of the consequences or what other people told her to do. Aunt Mittie might not have ever admitted it, but she had more in common with Momma than just her face.

"Please state your name for the record," Mr. Jones began.

"My name is Mittie Lowman Franklin."

"And how do you know Hubbard Andrews?"

"He was married to my sister, Addie."

"You two were actually twins, right?"

"Yes, Sir, identical twins."

"So, would you say you knew your sister well?"

"As well as I know myself."

"And how well do you know Mister Andrews?"

"Very well."

"Miz Franklin, would you mind speakin' up a bit? Just so we can hear you clearly," asked Mr. Jones.

"Umm, okay," said Mittie, "Mister Andrews was married to my sister for over fifteen years. I spent a lot of time with her and her children and Hubbard. I saw Addie every chance I got."

Mittie's voice started to catch a bit, and, for the first time, I could really see her grief. I knew what it felt like to lose a mother. In that moment, I thought of Meg and prayed I would never have to learn the pain of losing a sister, especially the kind of sorrow shown on Aunt Mittie's face that afternoon on the witness stand.

"I'm sorry this is painful for you, Miz Franklin," said Mr. Jones and offered Aunt Mittie his handkerchief.

"No, thank you," she said, waving off the handkerchief, "I'd like to continue, please." Aunt Mittie seemed to swallow her pain and focused her attention on Mr. Jones.

"Miz Franklin, was your sister happy in her marriage to Hubbard Andrews?"

"For the most part, yes."

"What do you mean 'for the most part'?"

"Well, they had their problems, but at the root was love, undeniable love."

"Did she ever mention to you that she was planning on getting a divorce from Mister Andrews?"

"Never."

"In your opinion, what kind of man is Hubbard Andrews?"

"Well, I think he tries to be a good man, but sometimes, he fails. I think he does his best as a father, and I think he tried to be a good husband."

"When was the last time you saw your sister?"

"The weekend before she died."

"What type of mood was she in then?"

"Happy," said Mittie, then smiled a little, "she was happy. She was excited about their hunting trip. Addie loved to hunt, especially with Hubbard."

"What happened to your sister at Barlow Bend?" asked Mr. Jones.

"Objection!" yelled Mr. Poole, "Speculation! Miz Franklin was not witness to Miz Andrews's death."

"So, sorry, Your Honor. I'll rephrase. Mister Poole's right. The only witness to the accident was Mister Andrews," said Mr. Jones.

"Objection, Your Honor!" repeated Mr. Poole, "Mister Jones is ... uh ... he is ..."

"What's your objection, Mister Poole?" asked the judge.

"Well, I, umm ..."

"Your Honor, I apologize for gettin' Mister Poole all rattled. Why don't I just move on?"

"Good idea. Get on with it," said Judge Bedsole. A frazzled Mr. Poole sat back down, and a few of the jurors laughed for a second.

"Now, Miz Franklin," continued Mr. Jones, "do you believe that Hubbard Andrews killed your sister?"

"No, I do not."

"In your *opinion,* was your sister's death an accident?"

"Yes, I believe it was."

"And why do you believe that?"

"Because I believe that Hubbard Andrews really did love my sister. He carried her for two miles through the woods so that she could be given a Christian burial and her family could say goodbye. I think he really loved her."

"Thank you, Miz Franklin. Nothing more, Your Honor."

Mr. Poole, still appearing rattled by Mr. Jones's questions for Aunt Mittie, declined to cross-examine, so she was dismissed from the witness stand and joined me in my pew. With that, Mr. Jones declared the defense's case finished. Judge Bedsole gave his usual instructions to the jury (no speaking to the press or anyone else about the case), told Mr. Jones and Mr. Poole to be ready with closing arguments at 9 a.m. sharp, and rapped his gavel on his desk to signify the close of day three of Daddy's trial. After the bailiff dismissed all of us for the day, Mr. Jones's assistant, Peetie, approached me with another invitation for dinner with Daddy. I declined the invitation, politely, the way Ms. Jenkins had taught me.

"No thank you. Unfortunately, I will be unable to join him for dinner this evening. Please thank him for the invitation for me," I told Peetie, and then left the courthouse.

In truth, I couldn't stand the idea of sitting across a table from Daddy. I didn't know if I would ever be able to look him in the eyes again. Instead, I walked back to the hotel in silence with Aunt Mittie and Uncle Melvin, wondering if I had, in fact, lost both of my parents regardless of the jury's decision.

chapter twenty-two

September 26, 1935
Grove Hill, Alabama

Closing arguments started shortly after 9 a.m. on September 26, 1935. The courtroom was packed by eight that morning, and the temperature seemed to rise with every new spectator. I swear every person in Grove Hill was trying to squeeze into the room to hear Mr. Jones's last-ditch effort to save Daddy's life and Mr. Poole's final attempt to end it.

Mr. Poole was up first, and, from his usual rigid stance behind the center podium, he cleared his throat and began, "Ladies and gentlemen of the jury, what happened to Addie Andrews at Barlow Bend on January 31, 1934? Who ended her life?" He paused as he looked from his notes to the jury. "That is the question you have been tasked to answer. Mr. Hubbard Andrews would like you to believe that his wife's death was an accident, but, as you have learned over the last three days, Hubbard Andrews would like you to believe a mountain of untruths." With that line, I heard several agreeable mutters from the crowd, which were quickly met by the cautionary stares of Judge Bedsole and his bailiff.

"He would like you to believe he was a faithful husband, but you now know he was not," Mr. Poole continued and gained steam as he rolled through the next few lines of his meticulously planned speech. "He would like you to believe he was a devoted father and husband, but now you know he thought only of himself on that cold January morning. He would like you to believe he is an honest, hardworking businessman, but now you know him to be a cunning and desperate fraud. You now know that his fear of being exposed drove him to end his young wife's life." Mr. Poole paused again to let the full weight of his words press against the ears and rest on the shoulders of the jury.

"If we could expose the secrets of Barlow Bend, we would learn that Mister Hubbard Andrews drove his unsuspecting victim miles from the warmth and comfort of her home in Frisco City, to the thick, icy woods. He walked her two miles into those woods, and then, once so far into the woods that his crime would have no witness, he shot Addie Andrews at close range, ensuring a fatal wound." Mr. Poole took one last pause, waiting for a reaction, but his words seemed to muzzle the usually opinionated and frequently vocal crowd into silence.

Mr. Poole concluded his speech with an air of empathy, not for Daddy or Momma, us kids or the family that aches for her, but for the jury. "As if his crime was not heinous enough, he then enlisted the help of family and friends to quickly dispose of her body and all physical evidence of his crime and then coolly slipped into the role of grieving widower. He not only killed his own wife, but he wants you to offer him comfort, sympathy, and support. Ladies and gentlemen, a decision has been assigned to you. You must decide whether you will be fooled by his ruse and allow him to get away with robbing four children of their mother, and a family of their daughter and sister, or will you say, 'No more, Mister Andrews.' I believe your decision is clear. You must convict him of his crime, of what he truly is, a liar, a womanizer, and a calculated killer. You must return a verdict of guilty. Mister Hubbard Andrews is guilty of first degree murder."

Mr. Poole took one more look at the jury and then at the audience behind him. When he turned to the crowd, they broke into applause. I couldn't believe it. They actually applauded as if they were at a play. At that moment, the truth of why every seat was filled rang out. Sure, the reporters were doing their jobs, and a few family members were on hand to offer support for Momma or Daddy, whichever side their loyalties lay, but the crowd was there for themselves. To them, this wasn't the real trial that could lead a man to a life in a cell or, God forbid, the electric chair. This was some tacky soap opera come to life in their own pathetic town, right in front of their pathetic eyes. Momma would have been disgusted by the whole display, truly and completely disgusted. She would have narrowed her perfect blue eyes at them and then dismissed them from her life.

"They're just a trifle, Honey, just a trifle." Momma's voice floated around in my mind.

"Quiet down, everybody, hesh up," Judge Bedsole silenced the crowd again, "I'm not gonna warn you people again." Unfortunately, any sincere belief that future outbursts from this crowd wouldn't happen had left his voice. "Mister Jones, go on with your closin'. Get to it."

Mr. Jones had chosen a light grey suit with a pale blue tie today. He appeared well rested without a glimpse of worry as he rose and set his notebook on the podium. He smiled at the jury as he started to speak, "Ladies. Gentlemen. Mister Poole is right. We've come to decision time. You've listened to all the supposed expert testimony, solicited opinions, and wildly concocted theories that were brought forth by Mister Poole over the last three days. You've listened to all of this, but heard no real evidence of a crime. You've heard grief. You've heard rumors. You've heard suspicions. But you've heard no evidence. The State has a false hunch that Hubbard Andrews killed Addie Andrews, but they have no proof of that hunch. So that's all they've got, a hunch."

Moving toward the jury box, Mr. Jones motioned to Daddy and then to the two rows behind Daddy where Grandpa Andrews, cousins Stephen and Leroy, Leroy's wife Jewell, Aunt Mittie, Uncle Melvin, and I all sat. "What you have," Mr. Jones continued in his kind, gentle tone, "is evidence of a fifteen-year marriage that produced four children and a community of people who loved both Addie and Hubbard Andrews." Mr. Jones then turned to the jury and spoke directly to each one, trying to hold their gazes as long as possible.

"So now, let me tell you what really happened on January 31, 1934. Hubbard and Addie Andrews drove out to Barlow Bend before dawn. They were hoping to get a few squirrels, maybe even a turkey, on the last day of the rifle huntin' season. They hiked two miles into the woods looking for their prize. They crossed the Alabama River at Barlow Bend and finally heard some squirrels rustling the vines, climbing up a tree. Addie had the shotgun, Hubbard the .22. Addie tried to scare 'em around that tree so Hubbard could take the shot, and then tragedy struck. Addie's gun snagged on a twig and went off, killing her instantly. In shock at the site of his beautiful Addie dead in front of him, Hubbard did what any good man would do. He tenderly wrapped his beloved wife in a blanket, rowed her body across the river, and then carried her for two miles through the thick pine. The damp, cold air stung his fingers. The sharp branches slapped his face and snagged his clothes. As her body grew cold, his arms burned with the burden of his load, but he pushed on for the two-mile hike back to their car. Why? Not so he could fool you, not so he could get away with some imagined crime. He carried her so that he could give his Addie, the mother of his children, a Christian burial. He carried her so that everyone who loved her could say goodbye. He carried her because he couldn't stand the thought of leaving her, even for a moment, alone in those woods."

Mr. Jones paused for a moment, glancing at Daddy, and then strangely, at me, "Hubbard Andrews is not a perfect man. But you cannot deny his love for Addie Andrews. A love so strong that it would not allow him to harm her. Instead, that love propelled him to carry her home, to her children, to her family. You must honor that love with a verdict of not guilty. Thank you, ladies and gentlemen, I know you will make the right decision."

As Mr. Jones took his seat, applause did not arise from the audience. Rather, the unfolding of handkerchiefs and sniffles could be heard from both sides of the courtroom. Papa Lowman quietly walked out. Aunt Mittie quickly excused herself. I sat completely silent, stunned by the vision of Daddy carrying her. In my mind's eye, I saw Momma wrapped in a blanket, slumped lifeless in Daddy's arms. I tried to resurrect my anger, remember what I had learned over the three days, but in my mind, all I saw was Daddy carrying her, step after step through the cold, damp woods. All I felt for him was pity, a deep pity for Momma's *sweet-like-chocolate-candy Harry,* carrying his wild love to her grave. In that moment, his past sins didn't matter. My heart ached for him.

chapter twenty-three

September 18, 1935
Grove Hill, Alabama

The jury began deliberations around 10 a.m. on Thursday morning. By Friday evening, a verdict still wasn't back. The town buzzed with talk of *did he* or *didn't he.* At supper with Aunt Mittie and Uncle Melvin, every single person who walked into the café rushed over to our table to ask if we had heard anything. They, of course, offered some trite version of sympathy or encouragement, but I knew their game. They were all so terrified that they might have missed the big climax. A few of the tacky fans didn't even try to hide their relief of learning that they hadn't missed the grand finale.

After supper, I tried to read, but couldn't force my eyes to focus on the page, or my mind on the words. I told Aunt Mittie I was going on a walk and slipped out the staff entrance to the alley behind the hotel. The alley led to a field. Across the field was a small patch of pine trees. Lit by a full moon overhead, I walked into the woods until I found a fallen tree. I sat on the rotting trunk, looked up at the clear night sky, and tried to wrap my mind around everything I had learned during Daddy's trial.

I couldn't understand why Momma stayed with Daddy. She could have left him. She knew about the baby and Elsie. She probably knew about others, too. So why did she stay? It seemed unlike her to put up with his betrayal. She never put up with selfish or childish behavior from us, so why him? The whole thing seemed beneath her. Did she try to ignore it? Did she try to change him? Did she have her own sins to atone for? I couldn't make sense of any of it.

What I did know was that Momma stayed through all of it. I would have known if she intended to leave. I think I would've sensed that. I would have known if they were that unhappy with each other. So, if she stayed, there must have been love. Maybe she loved him in spite of his flaws. Maybe she loved him because he was flawed. Maybe she loved the fact that this perfectly handsome man with his perfectly wavy hair and perfect blue eyes and perfectly respectable family was flawed. Maybe she loved the chaos of it all.

I also knew Momma was not one to go back on her word. If she said she would do something, she did it. She wasn't afraid of things getting messy, and she was stubborn as all get-out. Maybe that was it. Momma was too stubborn to leave. She was so determined to love Daddy that she wouldn't let him off her hook. Maybe she was determined that he was a good man at heart, and she was going to force him to live by their marriage, by the promises they made sixteen years ago.

So where did all of this leave me? What would I do when the jury came back? What would I do if the jury came back with a guilty verdict? I decided I would keep fighting. That's what Momma would do. I believed in my heart that he didn't kill her. He was far from innocent, but he wasn't guilty of this crime. If the jury came back with a guilty verdict, I would conjure up all of Momma's stubbornness and determination and figure out how to mount an appeal. I had read about appeals in the newspaper and was sure Mr. Jones would know something about them, too.

I also realized then, sitting on that hard tree trunk and staring into the darkness of the woods, what I would do if the jury came back with a not guilty verdict. As much as I didn't want to, I would help Aunt Mittie pack our suitcases one more time and move to Uriah with Daddy. I didn't want to drop out of Thorsby or change my future plans, but what else could I do? I would pick up where Momma left off. I would force him to live a good life. I would show Meg, Billy, and Albert how much Momma loved them. I would show them that she did not live foolishly or naively. She was not a stupid woman. She was not a fool. She was determined. She loved him, flaws and all.

At 10:30 p.m., Saturday, September 28, 1935, we were summoned back to the courthouse. The jury had finally reached a decision. The whole town crammed in the courtroom and crowded around the doors of the Clarke County Courthouse awaiting the verdict.

"Not guilty," was all I heard before the room erupted in a frenzy of reporters swarming around Daddy and cheers from the Ladies Auxiliary. The hundreds of onlookers poured out of the room and down the steps of the courthouse, surely running home to tell whomever they could the big news. I stood still once again, just like I did on the day Daddy was taken away in handcuffs. I stood frozen, mouth gaping, while the reality of the verdict sunk in. Daddy would be free. My family, what was left of it, would be together again. A new life awaited me in Uriah, Alabama–my third new life in less than two years.

"Aunt Mittie, I need to talk to you," I said, standing with Aunt Mittie behind the throng of reporters. "Daddy wants us to move to Uriah."

"I know, Honey," Mittie answered without looking at me. "We'll get your things from school and get back to Luverne. I'll help you pack up Meg and the boys."

"Aunt Mittie, please let me explain."

"Don't need to, Honey," said Mittie, "Your momma wouldn't leave him and neither will you."

PART 3

exodus & afterlife

chapter twenty-four

November 1935
Uriah, Alabama

I stood near Daddy's truck, parked in front of a small, clapboard house in Uriah, Alabama, which according to Daddy, was pronounced "You-rye" not "You-rye-a," no matter how it was spelled. The white paint was peeling off the little house, and the front steps looked in need of serious repairs. The house had no front porch to speak of.

"Well, home sweet home, kids," Daddy said and walked toward the little house. "Go on and git those suitcases outta the back." He motioned toward me as he walked up the dirt path to the little house. Daddy seemed perfectly comfortable in our new surroundings, as if the house and town weren't new at all, at least not to him.

"Hub," said a thin woman as she rushed out of the front door and toward Daddy, "you made it already!"

"Yeah, we made it," said Daddy and kissed the woman right on the mouth, "Sarah Walker, I want you to meet my family." Daddy turned around with a grand, sweeping motion and pointed at each one of us while he ran through our names and ages, "That's Albert, he's my youngest at seven, and then there's Billy, who's eleven, Meg's thirteen, and Hattie's my oldest. She's fourteen." I wondered if he had mentioned Momma, the missing member of his *family,* to Sarah Walker.

"I'm fifteen, Daddy. I turned fifteen in August," I said without taking my eyes off Sarah Walker. My voice sounded far away, like it came from someone else's body.

I reached my hand out to the woman. "It's good to meet you," I said while shaking her hand, unsure how to greet this stranger, "Ms. Walker, how do you know my father?" I knew the question was blunt, but I thought it was justified. Daddy hadn't mentioned a woman in Uriah while we were making our plans to leave the security and comfort of Aunt Mittie's home.

"Um, well," answered Sarah as she looked from me to Daddy and back again, "we met a while back. And you can call me Sarah."

"Uh, huh..." I said, not wanting to call the woman anything at all.

"We'll git to all that in a little bit. Right now, let's git y'alls' stuff in the house and get settled in," said Daddy as he started to help Billy and Albert unload the truck.

Sarah grabbed two suitcases and carried them inside, "Come on, boys, follow me. I'll give ya'll the grand tour!" She flitted her gaze at me as if she was afraid to make eye contact.

Widowed several years before we moved to Uriah and into her house, everything about Sarah Walker was skinny. She had a wispy, honey-colored bob cut right at her skinny chin. She had a tall, skinny frame that fell down from her skinny shoulders.

Her skinny hand felt a little damp in mine when I greeted her by the truck. Other than her extremely cheerful and rather twitchy disposition, there was nothing remarkable about her. She was just skinny.

Once inside the tiny front room of the house, Sarah started chirping away again. "The house only has two bedrooms, so I set the boys up in here," Sarah motioned to a single bed pushed into the far corner, "Y'all can keep your suitcases under the bed." She then gave the fastest *grand tour* of any house ever given. "The kitchen is right through here." She rushed through what looked to be a dining room and pointed into a kitchen with floral wallpaper, one green corner cabinet, a white sink, and a gas stove. The kitchen was about eight feet by eight feet at most. "I keep the icebox on the back porch. It's real nice out there. It's got a swing and everything." Sarah Walker motioned toward the back door leading out of the kitchen, and to the porch. Next, she moved toward a short hallway. Even in November, her skin was shiny with sweat. But I guess, to be fair, it was an awfully warm November.

The hallway from the dining room led to the rest of the house, "The bathroom is right here next to the girl's room, and, Hub, you'll be in here with me." Sarah motioned inside the room at the end of the hall. I peeked around her and Daddy to see a dresser, small mirror and one double bed. From the looks of it, Daddy and Sarah would share the one double bed. Daddy agreed to this arrangement without even looking in the room.

Meg and I carried our suitcases into the room Sarah Walker indicated as ours. I put my case in the corner and sat on the edge of the double bed that Meg and I would share.

"Did Daddy marry that woman?" Meg whispered.

"I don't know. I don't think so," I whispered back.

"How does he know her?" she asked.

"I don't know."

"What are we doing here?"

"I don't know, Meg. I guess where we're gonna live here," I said, and hoped that my tone would put an end to Meg's questions. "He's sharing a bedroom with her. A bed with her. I wonder if she was one of them." For a second, Frank Poole's face flashed in my mind.

"One of who?" asked Meg.

"Oh... no one... never mind."

Sitting on the bed next to Meg, I ran through the blurred events of the last two weeks in my head. Maybe Daddy told me about Sarah Walker, and I missed mention of her in our conversations. I remembered that as soon as Daddy was released from jail after his trial, he rode with Melvin, Mittie, and me to Thorsby to pick up the rest of my things, and then to Mittie and Melvin's home in Luverne. We stayed with Mittie and Melvin for about two weeks while Daddy "got us set up" in Uriah. Maybe he mentioned Sarah Walker then, but I was too busy with the kids to hear him.

Mittie helped us pack our suitcases the same way she did back at the hotel in Grove Hill. She also packed up the few belongings of Daddy's that had not been sold to pay his lawyers. Daddy and Melvin put everything into the back of an old pickup truck Daddy had purchased in Luverne for a few dollars. Sitting on the bed in Sarah Walker's house, I remembered the hurt look in Mittie's eyes when the last piece of luggage was secured. That look told me that her heart was broken at the thought of us kids leaving Luverne.

I remembered trying to convince Daddy to look for work in Luverne, but he refused. "I got us all set up in You-rye, Hattie," Daddy said, ending my futile attempt to stay near Mittie. Maybe he mentioned a woman in a little white house then, but for the life of me, I didn't remember any talk of living with any woman named Sarah Walker. We rode in Daddy's truck for six hours from Luverne to Uriah with no talk of skinny, dirty blondes with skinny hands. By the time we arrived in front of Sarah Walker's house, my left arm and both my legs were asleep from being pressed against Meg and having Albert on my lap. I hadn't thought for a second that someone would be waiting to greet us. Before we arrived in Uriah and I witnessed her press her lips against his, I swear Daddy never mentioned Sarah Walker.

Back in Luverne with Mittie, Daddy only said that he found us a place to live. I assumed that meant the five of us, not the five of us plus some woman he met ... when? That's what I wanted to know first. When exactly did Daddy meet Sarah Walker? Did he meet her while he was in jail in Kilby all the way over in Montgomery County? That seemed unlikely. I had heard of women writing to prisoners; that the heinous actions somehow made the criminals desirable, but what kind of woman would meet a man while he was being held for the murder of his wife, and invite him and his four children into her home? Did he meet her while on trial for murder in Grove Hill? Was she among the crowd desperately trying to catch a glimpse of the potentially dangerous, yet undeniably charming Hubbard Andrews? Maybe Peetie, Mr. Jones's aide, arranged a supper meeting between the happy couple. Did Daddy know her before the trial? Did he meet Sarah Walker before Momma died and my life turned upside down? Was Sarah Walker one of the many women that Mr. Poole, Mr. Jones, every witness, every person in the galley except me, seemed to know about for years before Momma died and that damn trial ever took place?

I was far too angry to sit on the bed in that hot, tiny room, and couldn't stand to look at Daddy right then, so I grabbed Meg by the hand and led her out of the room and out of the house.

"Come on, let's get out of here," I told Meg. "Daddy, we're gonna walk through town. Be back later," I yelled toward the dining room with Meg in tow.

Walking as fast as I could down the street toward Uriah's main drag, I couldn't believe that Daddy had taken the four of us from Mittie's proper home to live in sin with some woman he had met God knows how and God knows when. Was this seriously the *fresh start* he told me about in the jail cell in Grove Hill? Was this really his intention, to shack up with some stranger, to have his sons sleep in the parlor while he shares a bed with some woman down the hall? Daddy still hadn't said what he was going to do for work or how he planned to afford rent or food or anything. At that moment, for all I knew, mooching off of Ms. Sarah Walker was his fresh start. The lack of a wedding ring on Sarah Walker's left hand answered my question of whether or not Daddy had married the woman before we moved into her house. That realization only worsened my humiliation. The most I could say for the situation was at least there was no vow that Daddy could break this time. What would Momma have done in this situation, if her father had pulled a stunt like this? How would Billy and Albert ever know that Daddy's actions were wrong? I hoped that the dust kicking up under my shoes would bring me some clarity.

"Hattie, slow down," Meg whined, "You're goin' too fast."

Somewhere between moving to Grove Hill and adjusting to life at Thorsby, I learned how to explore a new town. So, dragging Meg behind me, I stepped onto Pecan Lane, named so for the pecan trees that lined the dirt road, and headed, I hoped, in the direction of Main Street. Every little town in Alabama, and I assumed the world, had a Main Street, and I knew I would find everything that the town of Uriah, surrounded completely by cotton fields and the patches of pine trees regularly sacrificed to the Blacksher Lumber Company, had to offer if I found Main Street. A half-mile later, Meg and I stood in front of Main Street Fashions, the one dress store in Uriah, and looked right and left. To the right were a bank and a Baptist Church, which meant I had just become a Baptist. At the time, little towns like Uriah rarely had more than one church, so whatever the church was: Baptist, Pentecostal, Methodist, or Episcopalian, that's what we became. To the left were the Cotton Café, a farmers' co-op, the Blacksher Lumber Store, and the local law enforcement. That was it. That was all Uriah had to offer. I grabbed Meg's hand again and headed to the Blacksher Lumber Store. From the look of the *Coca Cola* sign out front, I guessed that the store sold all sorts of dry goods and supplies, along with cold Cokes.

I bought a Coke for Meg and me to share with money Aunt Mittie had given to me before we left Luverne that morning. I didn't want to take the money, because I knew Mittie really couldn't afford to give any, but she insisted. The look on Mittie's face as Daddy backed the truck away from her house was almost more than I could bear.

Meg and I sat down on the edge of the wooden porch in front of the store. Ms. Jenkins would have surely scolded me for sitting on the floor with my legs dangling over the edge, but Daddy had thrown propriety out the window as soon as he kissed Sarah Walker. The Coke was cold and crisp and tasted great on such a hot afternoon. That year, it stayed in the eighties right through November. I tried to let the drink cool me off, but nothing was going to help that afternoon. Daddy's fresh start had become pointedly clear. Alone in the woods near the hotel, I had promised Momma that I would love him no matter what, but I also knew she expected more out of us than to live like this. I decided right then to take my life into my own hands.

"Meg, let's find the school. Daddy said there was a school here," I said as I stood and headed to the door, "It shouldn't be hard to find."

Meg polished off the Coke, and we headed back inside the store. The proprietor told me that we needed to walk to the end of Main Street and then turn left on Route 21. Ten minutes later, we were standing at the intersection.

I knew if I turned right onto Route 21, I would eventually reach Frisco City. I could have probably hitchhiked the fifteen miles or so, but knew there wasn't much left for me there. I could visit Momma; bring her fresh wildflowers, and then what? Should I lie down next to the small marker and pray for the millionth time that she come back to me? Momma was dead. She wasn't coming back no matter how badly I wanted her. Should I try to figure out whose baby was buried in the unmarked grave near Momma? That baby was dead. I guess he or she didn't matter anymore. I couldn't bring Momma back to life or change Daddy. And I couldn't go back to the way things were before the trial, to a time before I learned that my supposedly happy family was anything but happy. I couldn't forget what I had learned during the trial. That version of my life was done.

I could, however, scratch out a life that would one day make me happy. I could have something of my own. Standing at that intersection, I decided to turn left toward the school, as the man at the general store had instructed. Not even two blocks later, Meg and I stood in front of Blacksher School, a large, white building named for what appeared to be the big fish of Uriah. It wasn't quite as impressive as Thorsby, but it would definitely do. Daddy could have his fresh start, but I was going to have mine, too. I was halfway up the walkway before Meg stopped me.

"Hattie, what are you doing?" Meg asked.

"I'm going to enroll us. Don't you want to go to school?" I asked, and then Momma's voice found life, "or maybe you'd like to spend your days cleaning Sarah Walker's house?" It took Meg about two seconds to catch up with me.

"But don't you think Daddy should do this?" Meg asked.

"I'm not leaving this up to him."

I gave Meg a stern look and grabbed her hand as we walked into Blacksher for the first time. I could see straight through the windows along the back wall of the foyer. The school was a series of corridors built in a square around an open-air garden, and it was lovely. The windows let in an abundance of sunshine, and the garden housed benches and picnic tables alongside flowers and shade trees. I quickly found the principal's office, smoothed my hair, squared my shoulders, and opened the door. A plump, cheerful secretary looked up from a dark wooden desk.

"May I help you, Miss?" the secretary asked.

"My name is Hattie Andrews, and this is my sister Meg. We would like to enroll," I said with all the confidence and poise I had gained from my short time at Thorsby. "Do you charge tuition?"

I didn't know if Blacksher was a public or private school, and in my haste to find something better than what was happening inside Sarah Walker's house, I hadn't even thought about the fact that I couldn't pay tuition until I was standing in front of the Blacksher School Secretary.

"Well, it's good to meet you both. I'm Miss Walker, School Secretary. And, no, dear, this is a public school. We don't charge tuition."

"Okay then, Meg is in the ninth grade, and I am in the eleventh grade. We would like to start classes as soon as possible."

"Well, that's good, Dear, but where are your parents? They should be here."

"I told you," whispered Meg, "Now, let's go."

Ignoring Meg's plea, I continued, "My father will come by tomorrow to sign anything if necessary, but our mother is dead, so I take care of everything now."

"Oh," Miss Walker shifted uncomfortably in her chair, "bless your heart. Now...um...do you live around here? I've never seen you before, Miss Andrews."

"Yes, Ma'am. We just moved here. I was at Thorsby, but Daddy thought..."

"Oh, wait, are you Hubbard Andrews's girls? My sister told me ya'll were comin' to town."

"Your sister?" I asked.

"Yes, Sarah Walker."

"Oh. Um, yes, Ma'am," I said, feeling my cheeks flush, "we just got here today." A rude version of an old nursery rhyme went through my head as I stared at Miss Walker: *Sarah Walker could eat no fat; her sister could eat no lean.* I couldn't believe the two were related.

"Well, then. How 'bout you get your Daddy to come see me tomorrow, and we'll get you girls set up. Does that sound good?" the squishy Miss Walker asked.

No, that did not sound good, but I didn't see any other option. I would have to convince Daddy to go to the school tomorrow and enroll us. I was determined that Meg and I would both receive our diplomas, and the boys did not need to have a long break in school either. They would need to be enrolled in the grammar school next to Blacksher High School. I had promised Aunt Mittie that I would earn my diploma. I also promised her I would be responsible for Meg, Billy, and Albert's education as well. On the way back to Sarah Walker's house, I told Meg to let me talk to Daddy about school. I was afraid that Meg would give in too easily if Daddy wanted to drag his feet for whatever reason.

"Well," Daddy said when we walked into the dining room, "did ya'll find anything excitin'?"

"We need you to go to the school tomorrow to sign our enrollment papers. It's not far from here, just down Route 21," I said and waited for the debate to start.

"All right, I think I can do that," Daddy said and smiled as he went back to his newspaper.

Daddy didn't protest or object in any way. He just smiled at me with a smile I hadn't seen in almost two years, relaxed and easy. Sitting at the table with a glass of iced tea and newspaper in front of him, he looked rested, almost happy. He looked like he used to in the kitchen of the little house in Frisco City before our lives shattered. Maybe he really loved us and hadn't become the grossly selfish man I feared he had. *Maybe this won't be so bad,* I thought to myself, still determined to honor the promise I made to Momma several weeks before: to love Daddy despite his weaknesses.

Who knows? Maybe I could even learn to love Sarah Walker. Maybe I could accept this stranger into my life. After all, I was standing in her house. Stranger things have happened than a man moving on with his life after his wife dies. Then, I caught a glimpse of Sarah Walker through the doorway of the kitchen. She was barefoot, standing at the stove with her back to me. I stood in the dining room and watched her slip a wooden spoon between her cotton dress and sweaty skin and start scratching away. Then, she stirred the contents of the pot on the stove with the same spoon. Disgusting. Maybe, if I offered to help her, I could make sure that supper was at least sanitary. Maybe, I could hide that spoon.

chapter twenty-five

Winter 1936
Uriah, Alabama

The truck Daddy bought in Luverne before we moved to Uriah turned out to be the heart of his new business venture. Officially, he called himself a *truck driver,* but that did not accurately describe what he did. He hired himself out to local businesses and Uriah residents for pick-ups and deliveries, but he spent most of time junk-dealing. Day in and day out, he drove around Monroe and the surrounding counties, from moving sales, to junkyards, to abandoned houses or buildings. He would rescue whatever copper, metal, or otherwise valuable objects he could salvage from the garbage and then sell the scraps to anyone who was buying. He had successfully found another career that required total autonomy and odd hours, qualities Daddy seemed to prefer in a job. He left the house early in the morning, and would often be out long after the supper dishes were washed and put away. The exact details of what he did with the many hours between breakfast and bedtime were a mystery to all of us, including Sarah Walker.

At first, Sarah made a real attempt to welcome all of us into her home. I imagine she was quite lonely before we showed up, being widowed before having any children of her own, but I think playing house with Hubbard Andrews and his brood was more than she bargained for. Daddy tried to run the household as he did the hotel. He dictated supper menus to Sarah and chore lists for us kids to me, but then disappeared until the sun was down. I think Daddy enjoyed the fact that he could control the people in his life better than when Momma's impulses ruled our home. I don't remember him dictating anything to Momma. Sarah honestly tried to live within Daddy's strange conditions, but when he stopped coming home for supper altogether, Sarah's loneliness returned. I knew that Daddy was running around again, but Sarah was unfamiliar with Daddy's bad habits. By the New Year, her patience was running thin.

"There's some ham hocks in the icebox. Put em in with some greens," Daddy said one morning in January as he buttoned his coat. "Hattie will make the corn bread."

"And do you plan on eating this meal?" Sarah asked.

"Of course, Sarah," Daddy answered, "I'll have some tonight when I git back."

"With me or should I eat alone again?"

"Sarah, you never eat alone," Daddy said sloughing off Sarah's question as if it were of no importance at all.

"I guess you're right," Sarah said gaining steam, "I eat supper every night with your kids! Your kids! Not mine! I deserve to know where the hell you go day and night!"

I realized then, as I sat at the table, that I was physically stuck in the middle of an argument that started long before I walked into the dining room, probably long before any of us woke up that morning. Sarah looked crazed. She definitely lacked Momma's dominance. Momma got wild sometimes, but never with anger. Momma's anger was controlled and effective, terrifying at times with its pointed assaults. Sarah, on the other hand, lost the argument as soon as she opened her mouth. Really, she screeched more than spoke. I wanted to laugh at her naivety, but didn't out of kindness. It wasn't her fault that she lost the argument. She had no idea how to handle Daddy. Sarah was far too honest for the subtlety and cunning that Daddy required in a mate. She didn't know how to choose her battles with him. She definitely didn't know that it was way too early in the game to show her hand. Daddy gave her a look of total and complete dismissal. If he hadn't started to before that argument, Daddy moved on from Sarah Walker in that moment. She was weak, and Daddy grew bored with weakness very quickly. I knew it wouldn't be long before we would be moving again. After all, we were just houseguests, not family. Family has to be honored. Houseguests can be kicked out on their rear ends.

The final straw for Sarah Walker came one afternoon in March. Sarah, Albert, and I were walking home from the co-op on Main Street. Daddy's truck was parked in front of the Cotton Café. Supper was only a couple of hours away, but I guess Daddy wanted an afternoon treat. I hoped that Sarah would just walk by without stopping, but, like I said before, she just didn't know the game or how to play it. She stood in the front window and peered inside. Pathetically, she stared at Daddy as he leaned over the counter and ran his thumb over the delicate fingers of the waitress standing between the soda machine and a sink. His boyish grin and clear blue eyes danced in the direction of the waitress, plain as day. After a couple of minutes, he glanced toward the window. I know he saw Sarah standing there, but

Daddy didn't react at all. He turned back to the waitress and took her small hand in both of his. Sarah didn't say a word, but her face changed. Her skinny features became even more pointed, and her skin looked feverish. She turned and walked, nearly running, back home. Our time in her house was done.

Sarah stormed through the front door. She went to the kitchen and threw the day's prescribed groceries on the stove-top. A head of cabbage fell out of the bag and rolled to the floor. She stared at the cabbage for a full minute before storming through the dining room and down the short hallway.

"Sarah," I said, standing a few feet from her in the hallway, "he's done this before."

"What?" Sarah asked.

"It's just who he is. There was nothing you could do," I said, and Sarah slammed the door to her bedroom.

For the next several minutes, I heard the sounds of clothes and shoes being thrown around on the other side of the door. I went to my room where Meg was sitting alert on the bed, the dress she was mending gripped in both hands.

"What's going on?" Meg whispered.

"You better start packing," I told her, not bothering to whisper, "I don't think we're gonna be here much longer."

chapter twenty-six

Spring 1936
Uriah, Alabama

In my opinion, Sarah Walker was nicer than she had to be after she witnessed Daddy holding hands with the waitress at the Cotton Café. She let Meg and I stay in our room and let Daddy sleep in the front room with Billy and Albert until he found us a new place to live. She could have kicked us all out immediately. I knew Daddy didn't have much money, and hotel rooms were expensive. I'm not sure what we would have done if Sarah had thrown us all out on the street. We couldn't go back to Aunt Mittie. I think Daddy had officially severed that relationship when he took us away from her after the trial. Of course, I was partly to blame for Aunt Mittie's heartache. I could have fought harder to stay with her, but I chose Daddy over Aunt Mittie. Unfortunately, I don't think Daddy thought about us or what might happen to us while he was flirting and doing God knows what with that waitress. In the end, what Sarah Walker lacked in beauty she made up for in generosity. It's a shame she wasted that generosity on Daddy.

Within a few weeks, Daddy saved enough money to move us to a little place on the north side of Uriah. Nine dollars a month got us two bedrooms, one bathroom, a tiny kitchen, and a front room that I guess was supposed to function as a living room, but had barely enough room to fit the love seat and single wing-backed chair that Daddy found during his daily junking.

We learned quickly that this particular fresh start, our own place with an indoor bathroom, meant that everyone had to pitch in to put a roof over our heads and food on the table. Across the street from our new home were cotton fields as far as the eye could see. So, Billy talked the owner of the fields into hiring him to work a few hours before and after school for a couple of dollars a week.

Just off Route 21 in Uriah sits the Blacksher Home, a grand antebellum home belonging to the founding family of Uriah. The place was huge with wrap around porches, multiple fireplaces, and enough staircases and bedrooms to require breadcrumbs to travel from one end of the house and back again. Within days of moving into our new place, Daddy struck a deal with the Blackshers. He would haul debris and trash away, and Meg would help the staff with the laundry in exchange for a few dollars a month. Meg was less than thrilled to be back in the laundry business, but she was still too young to work in any of the shops downtown, not that there were many shops to choose from in Uriah.

I became a shop girl at Main Street Fashions. I straightened the racks of clothing, swept the floors, and helped customers decide which dress to pick for church dances and town gatherings. Mr. Simpson, owner of Main Street Fashions, gave his shop girls a discount on the previous season's dresses, gloves, hats, and other accessories. I didn't understand why the older stuff was discounted because it was just as nice as the new stuff, but I didn't dare ask, just in case Mr. Simpson decided the practice was as silly as I thought it to be. I gave half of my earnings to Daddy every week to help with rent and food, as did Meg and Billy, but I always saved a dollar or two for myself.

Once a month, Mr. Simpson would have me drag the mannequins to the back of the shop and change them into my pick from the latest collection. Then, I would wrestle the mannequins back into the window. It was like playing with very heavy, life sized dress-up dolls. Even though I only changed the mannequins once a month, every afternoon I was to make sure the window displays looked neat and fresh. At 4:45p.m., fifteen minutes before the end of my shift, I crawled into the front window and spruced up the display.

It was there in the shop window that I first glanced Ray Gordon Riley. After a couple of weeks, I began to linger in the window to steal a peek at the handsome, young basketball player from Blacksher High School. Each afternoon, not long after I crawled into the window, I would see him walking down Main Street on his way home from basketball practice. After that first sighting from the window, I saw him in the hallways of the school and at pep rallies with the rest of his team, but I didn't have any classes with him and didn't have the guts to speak to him. I wanted to though. If I had Momma's nerve, I would have walked right up to him and said, "My name's Hattie Andrews, and you want to get to know me better."

Instead, I asked my friend and lifelong Uriah resident, Sandy Bramwell, what she knew about him. According to Sandy, who sat right behind me in most of my classes, the handsome young man was the point guard for the Blacksher High basketball team and was the same year in school as Sandy and me. He went by his middle name, Gordon, and was the youngest of five children. Sandy said that some distant relative of Gordon's had been governor of Alabama in the 1800s but that you would never know it by his modesty.

"Oh, yeah, the Rileys are pretty well known 'round here, what with an ex-gov'ner in the family, but they ain't uppity 'bout it." The words flew out of Sandy's mouth as she tried to give me Gordon's entire history between classes. "You see, Gordon's daddy was a mail carrier here in Uriah, actually mapped out the first route in this part of the county so he was pretty well known himself. The family owns a little farm on the north side. Oh, it was real sad. Years ago, when we was all real little, Gordon's daddy just dropped dead one day, right in the middle of the field. Must have been 'round 1929, '30, cause we was just in grammar school at the time. Supposedly, Gordon's momma found him just lying there, dead in the middle of the cotton."

Gordon and I had something in common. We both knew how it felt to lose a parent. I wondered how his mother told him about his father. I wonder if she brought along Uriah's version of Aunt Matt to soften the blow.

"Gordon's Momma, everybody calls her Ms. Bessie, still lives on the family farm with two of Gordon's brothers, Elmer and William. Elmer's the basketball coach here. I'm sure you've seen him around. I guess the others moved away. My daddy says the boys pretty much do all the farmin' now. Ms. Bessie's health ain't so good anymore."

Sandy went on for a few seconds more about the family, Ms. Bessie, and the former governor before finally getting around to the important part. Gordon Riley had no sweetheart to speak of. He was fair game to all of the young ladies at Blacksher.

Knowing that Gordon worked so hard for his momma, the way I did for Daddy, made him even more appealing. He would understand why I felt broken without having to explain a thing to him. Once I learned all of that from Sandy, I couldn't help falling for Gordon. My face flushed and butterflies flew around my stomach every afternoon at 4:45 when I saw him walking down Main Street with his basketball shoes tied together, casually tossed over one broad shoulder. He carried his 5'9" athletic frame with confidence. His dark brown, wavy hair bounced as he walked. As the days grew warmer, he swept his hair back from his face with his strong hands. Standing in the front window, between the mannequins and hat displays, I had to be careful not to stare too long. Sometimes, I steadied myself on the shoulder of the wooden lady next to me as I watched him approach and pass the window.

One afternoon late in April of that year, I left the store at my usual time of 5 p.m. to walk home. Waiting at the corner of Main and Oak, just to the left of the store, was Ray Gordon Riley. My breath caught in my throat when I saw him waiting there, and again when he smiled at me. At the corner, he approached me.

"You're Hattie Andrews, right?"

"Yes," I said.

"I'm Ray Riley, but you can call me Gordon."

"I know," I said and couldn't help smiling back at him.

"Oh, do you? Well then, can I walk you home?" He offered me his arm as he stepped off the corner to cross the street. "You live on 21, right?"

"Um, yes ... how do you know that?"

"Oh, I've noticed you, Hattie," he answered. His chocolate brown eyes twinkled as he smiled at me, "I have definitely noticed you."

"Oh," was the only syllable I could think of before I carefully wrapped my hand through the crook in his arm.

To be honest, I wasn't sure what I was supposed to do with his invitation. What was the proper response? My training in social graces told me I should keep a proper distance from him. If he wanted to spend time with me, he should follow the rules. He should come to my house, introduce himself to my father, and ask permission to spend time with me, but that would mean he would meet Daddy and see inside the house and world I preferred to keep hidden. Momma would have made him work harder before she accepted an invitation. She would spend weeks teasing him as she walked by him without a word, only a coy look to keep him interested. All I knew was how badly I wanted to accept his invitation and to accept him into my life. Actually, I wanted to become part of his. I decided not to play Momma and Daddy's silly game of chicken, and left my Thorsby education and all those well-meaning social graces on that corner. Gordon was kind, playful, and handsome, and I was his from the moment he said my name.

Gordon and I made small talk as we walked down Oak Street to Snowden and eventually, Route 21, the road I began my first life on, the road that would turn into Bowden Street once you hit the Frisco City town limit, the road that I shared with a little white house with cedar trees for columns and Momma. Two years before, my heart had broken in two on that road, standing barefoot on the cold gravel staring at Momma's blood on the back seat of her car. Before that moment, I loved Route 21. Maybe now, Route 21 could lead to something good again.

From that first conversation on the corner of Main and Oak, Gordon and I were together. During that spring and into the summer, I counted the minutes between hours spent with him. After school on Mondays, Wednesdays, and Fridays, I rushed down to the entrance of the gymnasium to see him before he went to basketball practice and I went to the dress shop. At 5 p.m. on the dot, I quickly pinned my hat and pulled on my gloves before meeting him on the corner. We would walk a block down Oak Street, and then, out of sight of the curious shopkeepers and patrons, he would pull me to him and kiss me. The world stopped when Gordon kissed me. And then he would step back, and when I opened my eyes his handsome face was smiling.

Every Sunday afternoon, I hurried through the obligatory after-church meal with Daddy, Meg, Billy, and Albert. By the spring of 1936, I could fry chicken in my sleep and could even keep the flour in the paper sack and on the tabletop, rather than dusting the floor, making clean up much faster. As soon as Meg and I cleared the table and washed the dishes, I ran out front to find Gordon waiting behind the wheel of his daddy's old car. We would drive up to Lovetts Creek, halfway between Uriah and Frisco City. Gordon fished while I laid on a blanket and read, my head resting on his thigh until something inevitably nibbled his line.

On several of our Sunday afternoon outings, Gordon sat, leaned against a tree with my head propped on his leg and his fishing pole in one strong hand. He waited until I was completely engrossed in my book and then reached his free hand down, tickling my waist. I nearly jumped out of my skin with shock. Gordon laughed and then leaned down to kiss my neck. I put up a good fight, purely for show of course, proclaiming that my manners did not allow for such! Gordon then pinned me down and tickled me until I begged for mercy. When he was done torturing me, he sat up to find his fishing pole floating down the creek. He lost quite a few good fishing poles that way.

By the look on Daddy's face every Sunday afternoon when I left the house and later in the evenings when I walked back in, I knew Daddy didn't want me with Gordon. He made comments meant to shame me into staying home, but being with Gordon was more important to me than Daddy's approval. *Where's that boy taking you? That boy's here again. You're too young to be serious about that boy. You're needed here, Hattie, not running around with that boy.*

Daddy always referred to Gordon as *that boy*, never by his name. He certainly never acknowledged his own hypocrisy. Just because Sunday was the only day of the week Daddy chose to be at home with us didn't mean I had to stay home with him. Gordon and Sundays were my escape.

I felt calm around Gordon, as if my life finally made sense again. I wasn't pretending to be someone else or hiding the realities of my life like I did at Thorsby. I told Gordon all about Momma and the trial and Daddy's betrayals. Gordon knew about Mittie and the laundry and the hotel in Grove Hill. He even knew about the illegitimate baby buried in Frisco City. Gordon accepted everything about my family and me. For the first time in over two and a half years, the sadness that pressed on my chest began lifted, albeit just a bit. But, next to Gordon, I could breathe again. Every night, I prayed for him to stay in my life forever. I had found my *Harry*, and now couldn't imagine my life without him.

chapter twenty-seven

Winter 1937
Uriah, Alabama

Late in the summer of 1936, my life with Daddy went from bad to intolerable. Daddy continued his pursuit of trash, both the metal and female kind. He never told us what route he was taking through the county or if he made any sales. At first, in the house on Route 21, he rarely came home for supper, and when he did, he brought home not only a truckload full of junk, but also something dirty next to him in the cab. I never bothered to learn any of their names or even pay much attention to their faces because they were all pretty much the same: short hair, dirty fingernails, reeking of stale liquor. I don't remember much about any of them except my view of Daddy's rotating girlfriends through the kitchen window. I would see Daddy's truck pull around the back of the house with a woman in the cab. Never was she seated politely next to the passenger side door, ankles crossed, hands folded in her pretty lap. No, Daddy's women always slid all the way over to him, like a dog next to its master.

By the end of July, Daddy even stopped coming home for the occasional dinner with his latest piece of trash. He slept at home most nights, stumbling up the front steps long after the rest of us had gone to bed, and check in with us most mornings, but that was it. I told Meg, Billy, and Albert that he was at work. In truth, I didn't know where he was, but I assumed he had a girlfriend tucked away somewhere, and, for whatever reason, didn't want to bring her home.

Right around my birthday that year, Daddy decided to change our lives again. I walked up the stairs to our tiny rented house one afternoon in August to the sound of a woman scolding a child.

"Jerry, you're gonna git the switch if you do that agin!" the woman screeched at the child.

When I opened the door, I nearly dropped the grocery bags. Along with the ingredients needed for dinner, I'd purchased fresh strawberries, sugar, and Crisco on my way home from the dress shop, with the intention of treating myself with strawberry cake for my birthday. I saw a little boy, a toddler, covered in flour with spit running down his face. A woman around Daddy's age was trying to wrangle the child. Daddy was in the kitchen; laughing at the top of his lungs, broom in hand, thick, white flour tracked from door to door. The bag of flour that I purchased and intended to use for my cake wasted on the floor I scrubbed the night before.

"Hattie, Sweetie, come on over here," Daddy said, breathing hard from laughing, "This is Farrish Brisby. And the little ghost is her son, Jerry."

"Good to meet you," I said and offered my gloved hand to Farrish while trying to avoid contact with little Jerry.

Farrish wiped her hands on her skirt, and then, "Your Daddy's told me so much about you."

"Really? I wish I could say the same. Daddy, what happened in here?" I asked, maybe a little more abruptly than I should have, but I was irritated that the floor I had left sparkling before school that morning was now gray with flour, and I would have to work an hour at the dress shop in order to buy another bag of flour.

"Well, Farrish and I were makin' supper, and little Jerry here got into the flour." Daddy wiped beads of sweat off his brow and handed me the broom, "Go on and sweep this up, would you?"

"That's not what we were supposed to have for dinner tonight," I said, looking at the stove, table, and floor. Daddy had given me orders and grocery money for chicken and rice, but I saw the beginnings of country-fried steak, okra and mashed potatoes. "Where did all this come from?"

"I went by Blacksher's. Tonight's a special night," said Daddy.

"Come on, I guess bath time is early tonight," Farrish picked Jerry up and carried him toward our bathroom, avoiding my stare as she left the room.

I stood there with the broom, stunned. I wasn't completely sure what I had just walked in on. Beef was far too expensive the week prior, according to Daddy. Billy and Albert would get Daddy's belt if either of them tracked flour all over the house and, even worse, wasted good money by dumping a whole bag on the floor. I also saw a suitcase in the corner.

"Are you going somewhere?" I asked Daddy.

"No, Sweetie, 'course not."

"Then what's the suitcase for?" I asked and pointed toward the black case in the corner of the room.

"Oh, that, well I need to talk to you about that."

"Uh, huh..."

"Farrish and I have been seeing each other for some time now, and she's in a real bind. So, she's staying with us for a while."

"Oh... and Jerry?" I asked.

"Well, Jerry and Marion, her daughter, and Malcolm, her oldest. Marion will be in Albert's class. That's what all this is," Daddy motioned toward the table and stove, "a nice dinner to welcome Farrish and her kids into our home, into the family."

I was supposed to welcome a bunch of complete strangers into my family? Four more people were to live in this tiny house! Who the hell was this woman?

"And where are all of these people going to sleep?" I asked.

"Hattie, don't take that tone with me. This is my house, and I can have anyone live here that I want. Marion will sleep with you and Meg, and all the boys will stay in the front room. We'll make it work." Then Daddy stood up, brushed off his pants, and headed toward the back porch. "Finish cleaning this up and get supper done. I'm gettin' pretty hungry."

I wanted to run from the house and straight to Gordon, but knew he had promised his mother that he would do the weekly shopping for her that afternoon. For the next hour, I cleaned the flour, sweeping and scrubbing in a futile attempt to get rid of my anger and the pasty mess, and then finished supper. Daddy didn't say another word until he sat down at the table. Before he took his first bite, he introduced the four of us to the Brisby clan. Meg, Billy, Albert, and I crammed in on one side of the table opposite Malcolm, Marion, and Jerry. Daddy sat at the head of the table as usual. Farrish sat on the other end where Momma should have sat. Nine people gathered around the table that night, the handcrafted piece, built to seat six and salvaged from our home in Frisco City long ago. We sat, stared at our new housemates, and waited for Daddy to give us the signal to eat.

Over the next several months, I got to know Farrish and her children well. In his search for every piece of junk in Monroe County, Daddy left very early in the morning and didn't come home until right before supper went on the table, so he only really saw Farrish, Malcolm, Marion, and Jerry on Sundays. Anyone, even the Brisbys, could be on his or her best behavior one day a week.

Living with the Brisbys Monday through Saturday was a nightmare. No matter how many times Farrish threatened to get a switch or pop his behind, Jerry continued to grab anything he could reach off the kitchen table, stove, wardrobes, and dressers. As soon as the object hit the ground, he would try to shove it in his mouth. Once, he nearly burnt himself with scalding water when he reached for the pot I using on the stove. Farrish pretended not to notice as I moved the pot out of his reach just in time.

Malcolm and Marion Brisby ate more than any two children I have ever known. At first, I was surprised by Marion's size. She was more than just pudgy for an eight-year-old. Her chubby cheeks morphed seamlessly into her neck, shoulders, and considerable abdomen. After the third time I caught her rummaging through the pantry only an hour after Sunday lunch, I knew she wasn't going to grow out of her baby fat. Malcolm threw fits every morning claiming that Billy's biscuit was bigger than his, which, according to Malcolm, meant that we hated him and wanted him to starve to death. I thought Malcolm was far too old for fits, but Farrish babied him like he was a toddler. He finally stopped screaming when Farrish gave him her breakfast, too. I doubt that Farrish had eaten a full meal since Malcolm and Marion cut their first teeth. Both of them were behind in school, which was Farrish's reason for refusing to send Malcolm to work with Billy. She insisted that Malcolm needed extra time after school to catch up, which never happened as far as I knew. Sometimes, I was convinced that the little Brisby monsters were going to eat us out of house and home without chipping in a dime along the way.

Farrish was, by far, the worst, though. Along with babying her children to a point that would have made Momma's head spin; she used our house as her beauty salon. As soon as she moved in, so did the smell of burning hair and weird, pungent chemicals. She pushed the kitchen table all the way to the wall, placed a chair in the middle of the kitchen for her clients and occupied what little space the house had to offer from morning until late afternoon, even on Saturdays. Most days, I came home after work to a kitchen floor covered in hair and a table covered in scissors, lotions, salves, shampoos, and curling devices.

One morning, I caught Daddy before he made his daily escape. I complained about cleaning hair out of the sink and off the floor every afternoon in order to cook dinner for nine people. He told me that I was old enough to figure out how to live with the Brisbys and that I was not to interfere with Farrish's business. By March of 1937, I realized that Farrish Brisby and her awful children were in that house to stay.

One night, long after everyone had fallen asleep, I lay awake in my crowded bed, stewing. For God's sake, I was about to graduate high school and was sharing a bed with my sister and some strange, little, fat girl! I couldn't lay there and accept the choices that Daddy had made for me any longer. So, I did something I had never done before. In the dark, I quietly dressed, pinned my hair back with the comb I had bought with a few pennies I was able to save the month before, and climbed out my bedroom window.

My plan was to run the mile to Gordon's house, but when I came around to the front of the house, Gordon was sitting on the front steps. My heart nearly stopped when I saw him, sitting alone on my steps, his shoulders uncharacteristically slumped.

"Gordon," I whispered, "what are you doing here?"

"It's Momma."

Gordon didn't have to say the words. I knew what had happened by the look in his eyes. Bessie Riley had been ill for some time. She had stopped eating a few days before and hadn't been out of bed in weeks. The Rileys didn't have much use for doctors, and without the help of a physician, I knew she wouldn't last long. I was surprised, however, how quickly she died once she decided to. I sat down on the stairs next to Gordon, rested my head on his shoulder, and held him for a long time while he cried—his sobs muffled in my shoulder.

"How did you know I was out here?" Gordon asked after about an hour.

"Um…I didn't. I was going to see you. I needed to talk to you."

What I needed was for him to calm me down. I needed him to tell me everything would be all right and that I wouldn't live like poor Alabama white trash forever, but once I saw him on the steps, knowing that he now knew the pain of losing a mother, my frustrations seemed less important.

"Are you alright? What happened?" Gordon asked.

I couldn't believe it. Gordon's mother had just died, but he was worried about me.

"Don't worry about me," I told him. I wove my fingers through his and ran my thumb along the side of his hand. "I love you, Gordon."

"I love you, too, Hattie."

I squeezed his hand and kissed him lightly on the cheek. Whispering in his ear, I said, "I'm so sorry about your momma. I know what that's like."

"Yes," he said, looking deep into my eyes, "I guess you do."

"The pain is almost unbearable." I kissed him on the lips this time. "Please let me help you. What can I do?"

"Just being here with me, Hattie," Gordon said, "that's all I need."

The next words came out of my mouth before I realized their true weight. "Gordon, I could be your family now... if you'll have me," I told him, and leaned my head against his shoulder again, afraid to look at him in case he refused me. It seemed like hours dragged by as I waited the few moments before he spoke again. My heart pounded in my chest, praying that Gordon wanted me as badly as I wanted him.

"Would you, Hattie?" he asked after a minute or two. "Will you be my family now?" Gordon stared at my face for a moment before he kissed me softly on the lips, stood up, and took my hand.

In silence, we walked over to the playground behind the grammar school building at Blacksher. There, in the darkness, on a pair of old wooden swings, we planned my escape from Daddy's house.

chapter twenty-eight

May 1937
Uriah, Alabama

My last day living under Daddy's roof was also the day of my graduation ceremony from Blacksher High School in May of 1937. I was sixteen years old, had earned my diploma after several breaks in my education, and, unbeknownst to Daddy, I was married.

A week after Gordon's mother died in March of 1937, he and I drove to the Justice of the Peace in Monroeville, Alabama. My friend Sandy and Gordon's friend and teammate Milton Anderson came with us as witnesses. I wore my pale pink suit, cream lace gloves, and a cream wide-brim hat that matched the pearl buttons and collar of the suit. The hat, which actually belonged to Sandy, was my something borrowed, and Momma's brooch with tiny blue stones became my something blue and something old. I had carried that brooch from temporary home to temporary home since Momma died. That afternoon, as I changed from schoolgirl to bride in the ladies' room of the Monroeville courthouse, I ran my fingers across the brooch, feeling the coolness of the tiny stones. I made a wish that Gordon and I would find a permanent home for the brooch and me very soon. When I emerged from the ladies' room, Gordon was waiting in the hallway for me in his Sunday best, looking even more handsome than before. He gave me a white handkerchief embroidered with my new monogram, a small capital H, a large capital R in the middle, and a small capital A to the right—my something new.

After our *I do's* were said and the marriage license signed, Gordon and I swore Sandy and Milton to secrecy. I threatened never to speak to Sandy again if she breathed a word about Gordon and me being husband and wife to anyone. Sandy and Milton agreed to our terms and kept their oath of silence through March, April, and into May.

I was sure that Daddy wouldn't support my elopement with Gordon, and needed to make sure Meg, Billy, and Albert would be all right after I left. I couldn't depend on Farrish to care for them, so I needed time to make my three siblings self-sufficient. Billy made a nice wage in the fields, and Meg was still with the Blacksher Home, so they would have money for food. I knew I could teach Meg everything I knew in the kitchen. She was already a better house keeper than me, and a stickler for the rules, any rules, so I knew she would make sure that Billy and Albert got to school on time and always did their share of the chores. Gordon and I agreed to keep the marriage a secret until graduation. So, by the time graduation day, revelation day, rolled around, they had to be able to take care of themselves. I would never be able to leave if I thought they would fall apart without me, no matter how desperately I needed to get out of that house.

On the morning of my graduation, I readied myself to tell Daddy that I no longer belonged to him. I had kept my promise to Momma and to the stars over Clarke County to care for Daddy and to love him despite his flaws for as long as I could.

I told Meg, Billy, and Albert about my marriage, and that I was leaving with Gordon the night before graduation. I didn't want them to feel blindsided when I left with Gordon after the ceremony instead of coming home with them. They took my news as well as could be expected. Albert cried. He begged me not to leave him with Farrish and the Brisby monsters. He didn't understand why Gordon and I couldn't live in the tiny house in Uriah with all of them. I told him that there was no room for another body in that house, but I would come see him as often as I could. Billy, who was trying desperately to act like a man, shook my hand and told me "best wishes." At least some of Aunt Mittie's good manners had rubbed off on him. All the while, though, he had a very stern expression on his face telling me his true feelings about the situation. He thought I was disrupting his life. He was right. I was.

Meg was the worst. She yelled at me for not taking her with me to Monroeville for the wedding ceremony. I knew she would be hurt by my secret, but I didn't know how much.

"I should have been your maid of honor!"

That was one of many rules that, in Meg's mind, I broke. Tears rolled down my face as I watched my sister's heart break in two. Meg didn't cry though, not a single tear. She crossed her arms, made her blue eyes icy, and stormed out of the room. Billy followed her. Albert stayed by my side and helped me pack my suitcase. When we were done, I hid it under my bed.

"You did what?" Daddy yelled in the kitchen on the morning of my graduation. He stood up from the table so quickly and with such thrust that he knocked his chair backward.

"Daddy, if you'll just calm down..."

"I will not calm down. You had no right to run off like that. He had no right to take you!"

"Gordon didn't take me Daddy. I went on my own."

I tried as hard as I could to keep my voice steady. I had planned out what I would say to Daddy about my marriage and my future plans, but I hadn't planned on him being this angry.

"That boy tricked you!"

"He did not trick me, Daddy."

"What do you know? You're a child!" Daddy said and then yelled for a good ten minutes straight about how I abandoned the family, betrayed him, and how he was going to teach *that boy* a lesson. "I'll teach him to run in and steal a man's child!"

I couldn't tolerate his words anymore. My cheeks burned the same way they did the day Momma died, the same way they did during the trial, but on this day, Momma's voice found my tongue.

"Daddy, I am not a child. I stopped being a child the day we lost Momma," I said in a voice so confident and commanding that I wasn't even sure it was my own. "You will not say these things to me again. You will congratulate Gordon and you will let me go."

"I will not..." Daddy interrupted, but I cut him off.

"No! I have not abandoned you. You drove me away. I did not betray you. You betrayed us by what you did to Momma, by expecting us to accept every piece of white trash you bring in this house. I will not live like this for another second!" I had opened the floodgates and couldn't close them again. "You abandoned us for a year while you were in jail. You wrote me what? One letter? But I'm supposed to stand by you through everything? Well, I can't do that anymore. I won't. You humiliated us in Frisco City. You abandoned us at the hotel. And then you took us away from Mittie!"

"Mittie ain't your mother!"

"Shut up!" I was on my feet and couldn't hold back my rage, "How many women have been in and out of your life, Daddy? Momma, Elsie, Sarah? How many feet away from your bastard child did you bury Momma? How many? And now you bring your latest piece of trash and her children here? Do you plan on marrying Farrish or just play house until you get bored? Not to worry, huh Daddy? Good, ol' Hattie will keep everything in order, right? Ever since Momma died, you expected me to raise your children and keep your house. Well, I am your daughter, not your wife!"

Tears poured down my cheeks. I had not sobbed like this in years, and it felt good. Daddy looked as if I slapped him. For a split second, I was terrified by the prospect of doing what Momma never could, but I knew I had to. I couldn't live as a substitute for her any longer. I had to leave him. I wiped my eyes with a kitchen towel, took a deep breath, and turned back to Daddy sitting in a chair, silenced by my outburst.

"I'm a married woman now. You can't change that," I said, my voice calm and strong, "Gordon has found us a place in Monroeville. We leave next week." I turned to walk out of the kitchen and then remembered, "Oh, and Daddy, don't forget, commencement starts at 2 p.m. in the gymnasium. I would like you to be there."

I went to my bedroom, fixed my face and hair, and slipped the simple gold band that Gordon had given me in March on my left ring finger. I lifted my suitcase, the one with Momma's monogram on the clasp, from beneath the bed, gripped the handle, and walked out the front door. Out front, Gordon stood next to his car, waiting to drive us to the school. He had wanted us to tell Daddy about the elopement together, but after a very long and heated discussion, I convinced Gordon that leaving Daddy was something I had to do on my own.

chapter twenty-nine

March 1963
Mobile, Alabama

A week after my high school graduation, Gordon and I moved into an apartment in Monroeville, Alabama, north of Frisco City on Route 21. Seven dollars a month got us one bedroom, one bathroom, an eat-in kitchen, and a living room. Gordon worked as a clerk for the local grocery store. Mr. Simpson of Main Street Fashions in Uriah put in a call for me to Mr. Donaldson, owner of the largest clothing store in Monroeville, largest, of course, next to the Vanity Fair lingerie factory and offices that had opened a few years before we moved to Monroeville. After hearing Mr. Simpson's recommendation, Mr. Donaldson hired me on the spot as an assistant in the Ladies' Fashion Department. My responsibilities were basically the same as in Uriah, but my hours were much longer. Slowly, over the first year or so of our marriage, we furnished our first home with hand-me-downs from his family and cheap treasures from secondhand stores and classified ads in Monroeville's newspaper. By the fall of 1938, the only new things in that apartment were my new life that I adored, and our newborn son, Ray Gordon Riley, Jr. We called him Ray and loved him to pieces.

Daddy married Farrish Brisby in January of 1938. I have no idea why he married her. Maybe, he thought he needed to provide a better example for Meg, Billy, and Albert. Maybe, he actually loved Farrish. Maybe, she refused to play the role of wife without proper billing. Shortly after their courthouse ceremony, Daddy, Farrish, and their six children moved to a $10.00 a month rental in Frisco City. Daddy continued to peddle junk through the streets and back country roads of Monroe County. Farrish continued doing hair in the cramped, rented kitchen. Momma continued to be buried a short five-minute walk down the road from the newlyweds. I wonder if Farrish knew who else was buried five minutes from her new home.

I thought it was disgusting that Daddy moved Farrish and her three brats so close to Momma. I couldn't believe he thought that Meg, Billy, and Albert wanted to live so close to the little white house that had brought us so much joy and then witnessed much pain. I couldn't believe that in four years' time, this man that I once adored, had gone from being a successful businessman living with his beautiful wife and four children in a home that he built with his own hands, to living in a cheap rental with a tired hairdresser, three brats, and the three children of his own that hadn't left him yet. The man who once owned a hotel and café in Grove Hill now peered out his bedroom window at least four times a night to make sure his truck full of junk was still parked out front.

Within a few short years, Daddy and Farrish's marriage failed, leaving one more woman in Daddy's wake. I never asked him why. He eventually moved south and found the last woman he would marry, Lily. Lily was actually as lovely as her name. She was respectable and, in many ways, too good for Daddy, but I guess she, like so many before her, fell for his charms. Daddy found another café in Foley, Alabama, and seemed content. He ran the café, and Lily kept the dessert counter stocked with the best homemade pies in Baldwin County. Daddy never stopped expecting me to fulfill the role of dutiful daughter.

After a couple of years in Monroeville, Gordon and I moved to Mobile where we loved each other through a couple of moves from apartment to apartment until finally settling in a house in Toulminville, a suburb on the north side. A blonde-haired girl and a little boy with sweet, chubby cheeks came into our lives in quick succession after our move to Mobile. Gordon worked for the Mobile Bus Line for a few years. Then, like so many young men of the time, he enlisted in the Navy. While he was somewhere in the middle of the Pacific, I gave birth to another little girl. I named her after Gordon's mother. Gordon refused to call the baby Bessie. His mother's nickname wasn't pretty enough for the tiny, porcelain-skinned angel. Then, after the war, we had one more girl. Gordon expected nothing but the best from his sons, and doted over his daughters.

Through the years, we had countless fights over too many hours spent fishing and not enough hours in church. Gordon preferred the shoreline to a church pew any day of the week, but especially on Sundays. We argued over money and the kids and why, for the hundredth time, Gordon should get dressed earlier than he did each night so that he wouldn't be late for his job as a night clerk at the Post Office. We took family vacations to the river and made sure the kids knew how to behave in public. We stretched every dime we had as far as it would go. As a thirteen-year-old girl, I had stretched out in my bed and dreamt of a simple life with a man I was wild about, a man who was crazy about me. As a woman, I made sure that dream came true, even if it was just for a few years.

My time with Gordon passed too quickly. On March 4, 1963, my war baby Beth, by then a porcelain-skinned teenager, and I waited outside Sears in downtown Mobile. I was working in the Optical Department, and Beth was enrolled at Murphy High School. Gordon worked the night shift at the post office, so he slept through the mornings and into early afternoon until it was time to pick us up from downtown. When he didn't show up that day, I told Beth he must have overslept. But, in my heart, I knew that wasn't true. In my heart, I knew he was gone.

Beth and I caught the city bus at Stanton Road in Mobile, which brought us north to Osage in Toulminville. The whole time we were on the bus and then while I practically sprinted the two miles down Osage to our house, I kept telling Beth how angry I was that her father overslept. I couldn't bring myself to tell her what was really going on; that I was furious at her father for leaving me. Gordon leaving me so soon was not part of my plan. I wasn't ready. I still loved him too much to lose him. There was so much I didn't know yet, so much that I never had to worry about because I had Gordon. I didn't know how to drive. I had never balanced the checkbook. Gordon managed the finances. Gordon did the grocery shopping. Gordon took care of us. I would never be able to feed and clothe the children on what I made working part time at Sears. Even with Ray off at college and one daughter married, the financial burden would be too great. And I wasn't ready to live without him.

My anger and fear carried me down Osage Street. I ran through the front door of our house, down the hall and straight to the bathroom. Before I saw Gordon, I knew he would be there on the floor, like his father in the cotton field in Uriah. I told Beth to call an ambulance. There was nothing the doctors could do to help, but I didn't want Beth to see her daddy like that. That was the one thing my father got right. I never had to see Momma's lifeless body. And Gordon was lifeless. My sweet Gordon lay on the pale pink tile of our bathroom, dead from a massive heart attack at the age of 42. For a moment, I wanted to lay next to him, to go with him. I told Beth to stay in the hallway, yelling at her to keep her away. I knelt next to him and ran my fingers through his wavy hair. I kissed him and told him that I loved him and that he made my life so much better. Then, I sat on the cold tile until the coroner arrived and took him away.

chapter thirty

February 1993
Spanish Fort, Alabama

A little over three years fell between the day Momma died and the day I married Gordon. In those three years, I learned so much about myself, the world around me, and just life in general. Without knowing, I carried those lessons and everyone who helped and hurt me during those three years through my marriage to Gordon and every day that followed Gordon's death. I didn't really feel the weight of their lessons until after Gordon died, and I had to figure out how to pick myself up from the pink tile floor and carry on without him.

After several horrible months, I slowly started to mend, and I started to listen to the lessons of my past. First, there was Daddy. Daddy taught me the good, the bad, and the ugly of survival. He taught me that I had to take care of myself, that no fall from grace garnered surrender. I sat at our kitchen table and learned to balance a checkbook. I studied the little black ledger that Gordon kept on top of our dresser. The ledger included our monthly budget, meticulously calculated to last penny. I was able to make Gordon's pension, the pension I never knew about until after his death, go further than I first thought possible.

From Daddy's life, I also learned that there is grace in surviving alone. Daddy drifted from woman to woman, terrified to be alone. I didn't want that life. I never loved another man after Gordon. In fact, I never even tried. Why should I drift from man to man when I had everything I wanted from a man in Gordon? In my heart, anyone else would have been nothing more than a stand-in, a pathetic attempt to recreate what I had for twenty-six years. I made a promise to love Gordon always and to be faithful to him until death, and that's what I've done. I kept my promise.

Daddy died in Foley, Alabama in 1973. Our relationship was never what it should have been. He couldn't undo everything I learned during the trial, and I couldn't forget. He may have convinced a jury that he wasn't guilty, but after all I learned during the trial and the years that followed, I couldn't fully declare his innocence. We never could get back to the carefree summer days on the river near Barlow Bend. During the three years following Momma's death, I learned too much about him to love him blindly as a daughter should love her father. I simply knew him too well.

Aunt Mittie lived the rest of her life in the little farmhouse she shared with Uncle Melvin. She lived to the age of eighty, when in January 1980, Mittie Franklin passed away in Luverne, Alabama. Aunt Mittie may have lived her entire life in one county in rural Alabama, scrubbing out the stains from the laundry of generations in Luverne, but she believed I could achieve whatever I set my mind to. She also wanted me to expect more out of my life. I may have only had a high school diploma and bounced from temporary home to temporary home throughout my time in school, but I wasn't the trash some people may have thought me to be. Aunt Mittie taught me that I was something more and deserved more.

A few months after Gordon died, I convinced my boss at Sears to promote me to a management position. I heard Mittie coaching me, "Stand up straight and look him in the eye. Speak firmly, but be respectful. Mind your manners." My boss agreed to promote me to a part-time management position at the new Sears store on the eastern shore of Mobile Bay. I soon became the first woman to manage her own department in that store.

The months and first few years following Gordon's death were the hardest in my life, but I kept the lessons of my past close to me. I conducted myself with dignity, to avoid the trappings of John Howard. Sometimes, my grief was so thick that drowning in the bottom of a bottle was tempting, but I couldn't let myself fall that far. Uncle John ended up in Bryce Mental Hospital to "dry out" for a while. After that, I don't know what happened to him, and I really don't care.

I remember the love shown on Papa Lowman's face when he testified at Daddy's trial. He knew his daughter. He knew her strengths and failures and chose to love her unconditionally. I may not have always made the right decisions in my children's minds, but I always loved my kids the best way I could. They may tell you that my judgments of their choices were sometimes harsh, but hopefully they will also say my love for them was unconditional.

Mostly, I remember everything Momma taught me. A few months after Gordon died, my youngest son taught me how to drive. The heavy machinery under my control terrified me. At first, I was convinced that I would lose control of the car and plummet off a cliff, but after a few terrifying turns, I started to hear Momma's voice. It was probably all in my head, but I think she may have been in the back seat the whole time, window down, fresh air blowing through her hair, smiling from ear to ear. Momma taught me to live without fear. She taught me to choose my own path. She taught me to find my own adventures.

One of my first adventures after Gordon died was to Frisco City. Over two decades had passed since I last visited my childhood home and Momma. With two of my girls, now teenagers, in the backseat, I drove from Mobile to Frisco City. I finally had the money to put a proper headstone on Momma's grave. The stone was simple, but lovely. I chose to engrave only her name and the word "Mother." Any other description of her seemed untrue.

The tiny infant grave next to Momma was weathered, but still remained unmarked. I wondered if inside the grave lay Elsie's baby, Daddy's bastard child and proof of his indiscretions. Surely, he wouldn't have done that? I decided not to ask him. I'd said everything I needed to say about him and Momma on the day I left Uriah to be with Gordon.

After my promotion at Sears, I moved all of us into a pretty, three-bedroom house near Mobile Bay in Spanish Fort and started my new adventure as mother, professional, and soon-to-be Granny. I planted a vegetable garden and eventually screened in the back porch of my modest brick home. I worked at Sears, raised my children, and proudly watched as they began to raise their own families.

I think Momma would be proud of the life I built for myself. And she would be proud of my yard and garden, even though she would say that I need more wildflowers. I prefer the flowerbeds neatly trimmed with monkey grass and perfectly planted with a variety of shrubs, roses, azaleas, and hydrangeas to Momma's wandering wildflowers.

I know she's here with me. When I gather the fallen pecans from under the tree in my yard, I hear her laughing. When I sit on the back porch to snap a bushel of green beans from the garden or pick berries for a new batch of jelly, I can feel her beside me. I wish I could tell her that she taught me well and that because of her, I survived whatever happened at Barlow Bend. I wish I could tell her how much I miss her. But I can't. So, instead, I've told you.

epilogue

Granny told me her story at her dining room table in 1993. I've changed some names and filled in a lot of the details with my imagination, but the basic facts remain true: Addie's death and the suspicions that followed, Hubbard's trial, his second and third marriages, the baby buried in Frisco City, the responsibility placed on Hattie's, my grandmother's, shoulders after Addie's death, and the love she shared with Gordon. Hattie's spirit, her ability to keep moving forward when others may have crumbled under the weight of grief is true. In my heart, that is her legacy.

My grandmother Hattie died Easter Sunday, 1996. At Granny's funeral, Mariah, Mittie's daughter, approached one of my aunts. Mariah told my aunt that her family didn't hold any hard feelings toward Granny's family anymore. According to Mariah, the Lowmans had forgiven Hubbard for whatever happened in the woods at Barlow Bend. Maybe they did, and maybe they didn't. I think some people stay with you your whole life. Some events are never really in the past. Some wounds never completely heal.

Now, I carry Granny with me everywhere I go. Every time my husband and I move to a new town or into a new house, she is with me. When I stand over the stove in my kitchen, she is there. When friends or family push me to my limit, I remember what she taught me. Granny taught me to love without fail. I guess that's what grandmothers are supposed to do: spoil their grandchildren with love. They are supposed to make cookies and take you to the beach and tell you ghost stories. I think mine was really good at all the grandma stuff.

Granny still loves me without fail. Every couple of years since Granny died, I dream about her. The setting of the dream is always the same. Granny sits at her dining room table in her housedress, slippers, and nearly white curls. She does not appear to me as the teenage girl from Frisco City, confused by the tragic circumstances that marked the end of her childhood. She appears as I knew her: a kind, old woman weathered from decades of humid, sunny days in her garden, forever at the ready with homemade treats and stories. In the dream, we sit at her table and catch up over cups of black coffee. We play her old records: Marion Harris, the Supremes, and Bing Crosby. She tells me about heaven and that she is at peace. She tells me not to worry about her. I tell her about my life, the adventures I've chosen and the adventures I didn't choose, but she always seems to know my stories as if she was witness to each one.

Recently in one of my dreams, we were joined by two more cups of coffee, thick and strong, one belonging to Addie and the other to Hubbard. The four of us, my three ghosts and I, sat together sipping coffee and swapping stories. I looked into the faces of my constant companions fully aware that these are the ghosts I will carry with me to each new town, each new temporary home. Sitting at the table, I promised Granny that I would remember their lessons, the good and the bad. Addie asked me if I like my life, if my adventures are fulfilling and carried out on my own terms. Granny smiled at me because she knew the answer would be yes. She's made sure the answer will always be yes.

reading group guide

Discussion Questions

How did Hattie's story make you feel? Did you find her compelling? Was her plight worthy of exploration? Is carving out a simple life still an accomplishment when our modern society seems so enamored with fame and celebrity?

Hattie often chooses to remain silent rather than speaking out when faced with the gossips of Frisco City and Grove Hill. Do you agree with her decision to not engage the rumor mill or challenge these town gossips? Do you think today's society values Hattie's brand of grace?

What did you take away from Hattie and Hubbard's relationship? What effect did that relationship have on Hattie's future actions? What does it say about Hattie that she keeps her father in her life even with all the suspicion and confirmed betrayals?

Do you think Hubbard was guilty? If so, of what? Why? What piece of evidence brought you to your conclusion?

Describe your feelings toward Hubbard's treatment of Millie after the trial. Do you agree with his actions?

Describe the significance of the inscription on Addie's headstone: "Mother." Should the word *wife* be included in the inscription? Is the omission significant?

Do you agree with Hattie's decision to elope with Gordon? What do you think of her decision to never date or marry again after losing him at such a young age? What would you have done in her position?

Hattie faced many tragedies and disappointments in her life. Do you believe she found happiness despite the challenges? Why or why not?

If Hattie were to have one regret, what do you think that regret would be?

What one element of her life do you think Hattie is most proud?

author's note

It was September 2014 in Columbia, South Carolina. With my feet in stirrups, I chatted with my OB. Miracle Baby was on his way, and my book baby's birth was two short months away.

"Oh. You wrote a book." The good doctor did his best to sound interested. "So, what's it about?"

I gave him my elevator speech. *Great grandma killed in odd hunting incident, great grandpa tried for murder...* That got doc's attention. More chatting. More details of my Granny's life revealed until I came to the phrase "Stanton Road in Mobile."

"Where?" he asked?

"Stanton Road. It's in Mobile."

"I know," he said. "As a kid, I spent my summers on Stanton Road. When did your family live there?"

This was the first and by far the oddest—my feet were still in stirrups—encounters that *The Woods of Barlow Bend* led me to over the last several years. What the good doctor and I realized during that checkup is that my mother was the little girl he and his brother played with on Stanton Road during those hot, mid-fifties summers. I also began to realize just how few degrees of separation exist between nearly every person who's ever stepped foot in Alabama. Kevin Bacon has nothing on the people of my home state.

From there, the encounters kept coming. Emails from relatives I've never met—second, third, and fourth cousins. Online comments from Frisco City, Barlow Bend, Grove Hill, and Monroeville residents who remembered the real Addie and Hubbard. Friends of Hattie who outlived her and missed her dearly, happy with the surprise of finding her as the protagonist in her own book. The older man who lived next door to my sister Kellie who came trotting over to her house one afternoon—book in hand—to inform her that he'd worked with Ray Gordon Riley and knew Hattie's beloved Gordon quite well.

All these encounters confirmed that I'd gotten one thing right—research. My educated guesses and pieced-together personalities were accurate. Each chance meeting and comment bolstered my relief that I'd portrayed my grandmother well.

Those educated guesses were based on months of research exploring the shell of a story told to me nearly three decades ago. I interviewed family members, scoured ancestry databases, census records, state records databases, and newspaper archives. A map of rural Alabama from the 1930's held a prominent position on my bulletin board, and my playlist featured singers and crooners from the thirties and forties. I may have developed an obsession with Nellie Lutcher. Look her up. You won't be disappointed.

The research process was not without hiccups. The biggest disappointment was discovering that the trial transcripts were destroyed in a fire in 1957. So, I created the trial based on what I did have. I had the Grand Jury indictment complete with a witness list and census records for those witnesses which told me where the witnesses lived, what they did for a living, and clues as to their economic status. This information gave me an idea as to what they could have testified to pertaining Addie's death. I had the bail hearing record which gave me clues to who was in Hubbard's corner and Clarke County Democrat articles chronicling Addie's death and the trial. I read a handwritten note from Addie to Hattie over and again, finding so much love between the lines.

Then, I found the one piece of evidence no one in my family expected—the death record of a stillborn infant born to the real Hubbard and a woman named Elsie. One family member wanted this piece of evidence to remain a secret. As you know from reading Hattie's story, I chose to include this evidence despite knowing that doing so would upset a member of my family. Why? Because it was part of Granny's story. Finding it proved what I suspected: My Granny exercised unconditional love in a way few in this world do. Some would see Hubbard's transgressions as too hurtful to forgive. Granny didn't. She may have chosen to live her life by a different standard than Hubbard, but she never stopped being his daughter.

Writing Hattie's story was far from a solitary action. So many helped me achieve the goal of published author. Aurelia Sands of Deer Hawk Publications gave me my first shot in this industry. Her humor and patience carried me through the first months and years of this career, this writing life.

My sisters, Kim Frank and Kellie Reid, Aunt Moren, my mother Beth Cain, and husband Jay Smith, graciously read every page as I wrote the original manuscript, stumbling along with me as I figured out how to write a novel. The women listed above share my deep love and grief for Granny. Their trust in me to turn our Granny into the character of Hattie was a gift I'm not certain I deserved.

I would be remiss if I didn't thank Louise Andrews (no relation to the characters in this book). She answered the long-distance call of a total stranger to dig through Clark County Courthouse records for anything useful to my cause. I still consider you my angel in the basement and am so grateful for your generosity and kindness.

One may think that once a book is published, the thank-you's are done. Well, that person would be wrong. As supported as I was in the researching and writing of The Woods at Barlow Bend, I believe I was even more supported after its release. To all the bookstores, libraries, and museums who took a chance on promoting my debut novel, thank you. Being welcomed into your spaces was a treasure.

To my personal publicists (I jest), Uncle Butch and my cousin Leah, how many copies did you purchase? Is there a corner of the Alabama lumber world that has not seen this book? Is there a hunting camp left in Alabama that doesn't have a copy on its bookshelf? I consider it an honor that you two so proudly gave my book to friends, clients, and colleagues. Each time you called or messaged to order books, I felt that faraway hug just as tightly as if we were all together again over a Thanksgiving feast.

To my sounding board, consultant, and confidant, Jay. Thank you for believing in my dream even when I am full of doubt. Our back-porch talks are my favorite minutes of every day.

To Alexa Bigwarfe of Kat Biggie Press and Dr. Kasie Whitener of Clemson Road Creative, thank you for giving this novel new life. I wasn't ready to say goodbye and now I don't have to bid Hattie farewell.

To all of you reading this book now for the first time, thank you for allowing me into your world and for the privilege of sharing my beloved Granny with you. And, to all of you reading this for the second time, thank you for years of encouragement and love. Every comment, customer review, email, and chance encounter gives me joy.

It is for you, my dear readers, that I share this last section. Shortly after Granny died in 1996, my sisters Kim and Kellie, reached out to our extended family for favorite recipes and remembrances. Their goal was to create a family cookbook of Granny's recipes. Our family did not disappoint. Every aunt, uncle, and cousin shared favorite recipes and memories. These were added to Granny's recipe box and compiled into a cookbook, which Kellie Reid recalls on the last page of "Gardens & Gumbo: Remembering Granny."

> *Granny kept all of her recipes in an old, black cookbook she had nearly her whole life. However, by the time the recipes found us, they had settled, cookbook and all, in the bottom half of an old shirt box. If I had never had to look something up in the cookbook myself, looking for something she swore she had written down and stuffed in there, I would not have believed that all the recipes once fit...*
>
> *There were recipes clipped from magazines and handwritten by Granny on everything from hotel stationary to pieces of old envelopes. While shifting through it all, we saw her handwriting getting shakier and realized that some of the recipes were written down quite recently. Why would she write down a recipe she'd made for years and knew by heart? Put simply, she wrote them down for us. She was giving us what we would need, just like she always did. That was Granny's way.*
>
> —Kellie Reid, *Remembering Granny*

recipes from granny

I hope you will try one or two of our favorite recipes from Granny. I cannot guarantee results as Granny was an add-a-pinch-of-this-a-dash-of-that kind of cook. But, maybe a little of the magic found in her kitchen will arrive in yours.

As every family gathering in Granny's house began, let's start with a snack.

HOT PEPPER JELLY

¾ cup chopped or ground bell pepper
¼ cup chopped or ground hot pepper
(Granny preferred jalapenos)
6 ½ cups white sugar
1 ½ cups white cider vinegar
1 bottle Certo
Red or green food coloring (Granny always chose green)

Instructions: Combine peppers, sugar, and vinegar in pan. Bring to a boil. Strain. Add Certo and food coloring. Pour into sterilized jars. Seal with caps or cover with paraffin. Serve with cream cheese and Ritz Crackers.

Granny truly was the queen of snacks. Whenever I stayed overnight, both of us would be up late reading—a passion she passed down to me—and I would listen for Granny's footsteps going down the hall. That was the signal that she was going for a little bite to eat. She never failed to ask if I wanted something too. Now when I read and snack late in the night, I always think of Granny.

We are a family of snackers. It is something that does more that add to our waistlines—it brings us together. And now whenever we meet over bowls of boiled peanuts or chat between the layers of cream cheese and hot pepper jelly on Ritz Crackers, we can thank Granny for giving us this one simple way of keeping our family together.

—Kim Frank, *Remembering Granny*

STUFFED CELERY

(This was my favorite appetizer. No joke. I could live off these.)
Celery, cut into 2-3 inch pieces
1 8oz block of cream cheese, softened
Chopped pecans (I'm guessing 1 cup)

Instructions: Blend together cream cheese and pecans and spread onto celery. (That's it. That's the whole recipe. Sometimes simple is surprisingly wonderful.)

Now that we're all hungry, let's fill those bellies.

GRANNY'S BISCUITS

4 cups Bisquick
1 cup sour cream
1 cup club soda
1 stick Oleo, melted.

Mix Bisquick, soda, and sour cream. Roll dough into walnut-sized balls and lay on baking sheet. With your thumb, press each ball flat in the middle. Pour oleo over biscuit and bake at 375 degrees. (Granny did not say how long to bake the biscuits, so I'd stay close to that oven. Check on them after about 10-12 minutes.)

> *Granny cooked everything so well, it's hard to pick a favorite. But if I had to choose, Granny's chili would have to be the best thing I ever had. I used to get jealous when I saw the care packages Granny sent to the girls (in college) full of frozen chili. I don't know what the recipe was or if it was just Granny's special touch that made her chili so good. As Granny did with almost all foods, she topped it off with a large amount of cheese. That is just the way I liked it.*
>
> —Leo Cain, III, *Remembering Granny*

CHILI

2lb ground beef
1 ½ cup chopped onion
1 cup chopped green pepper
1 28oz can whole tomatoes
1 12oz can kidney beans
2 tsp salt
2 Tbsp chili powder
1 tsp pepper

Instructions: Brown beef. Add all ingredients and cook. (Again, she doesn't say how long to cook this. I simmer mine for about an hour then taste and adjust seasonings if needed.)

> *Granny's garden was a kind of mystical place where, while being instructed not to trip on stems or step on leaves, I was allowed to eat cherry tomatoes right off the vine. We helped pick squash and bell peppers. We pulled radishes and carrots. We took long drives to the Lazerus' farm for corn and peas. And we loved all of it. Some people may think it's odd that many of my childhood memories include fond ones of vegetables. I think it is a blessing. Now, every time I walk into a produce section, I can hear Granny telling me not to pick the largest cucumbers—they have too many seeds.*
>
> —Kellie Reid, *Remembering Granny*

BAKED SQUASH CASSEROLE

8 squash, sliced
1 onion, chopped
4 slices bacon, cooked and crushed
¼ cup melted butter
2 eggs, beaten
1 cup milk
1 Tbsp sugar
1 cup bread crumbs
1 cup grated cheddar cheese
½ tsp salt
¼ tsp pepper
Dash of hot sauce
1 tsp Worcestershire sauce

Instructions: Cook squash and onion in a little water until tender. Drain and mash. Combine with other ingredients and mix well. Put in baking dish and bake uncovered at 350 degrees about 30 minutes.

> *One has not eaten until they have eaten Mother's peas with her vine ripe tomatoes and her fresh cut and fried okra. That has always been one of life's greatest joys for me.*
>
> —Beth Cain

FRIED OKRA

(Seriously the best thing I've ever eaten in my life.)
Okra, fresh from the garden
Flour
Salt and pepper to taste
Oil

Instructions: Wash and chop okra into ½ inch pieces. Roll in flour, salt, and pepper. Put a small amount of oil—cover the bottom of the pan—in a cast iron skillet and when hot, fry okra until very brown. (Watch it close once it starts to brown because it will burn quickly.) Drain on a paper towel and serve.

After all that you'll probably want a nap. Once you've slept off the feast, finish the evening with a sweet treat. And perhaps make it a boozy one.

BOURBON OR RUM BALLS

1 cup chopped walnuts or pecans
¼ cup bourbon or dark or spiced rum
1lb powdered sugar
½ cup melted butter or margarine
8oz unsweetened chocolate
1 Tbsp shortening

Instructions: Soak nuts in bourbon or rum for 3 hours or longer. Combine nuts with sugar and butter and shape into balls. Chill. Melt chocolate and shortening, mix well, then dip balls using a toothpick. Refrigerate until chocolate coating sets. (Please note that these balls pack a punch. The alcohol content is NOT cooked out of them.)

DIVINITY

(My absolute favorite dessert and how I've ruined two sauce pans.)
2 cups sugar
½ cup corn syrup
2 egg whites
1 cup chopped nuts
½ cup water
1/8 tsp salt
½ tsp vanilla

Instructions: Combine sugar, syrup, water, and salt. Boil until thermometer reaches 245-258 degrees. Pour slowly, beating constantly, over stiff, beaten egg whites. Beat until mixture holds its shape. Mix in nuts and vanilla. Drop by teaspoon.

Tips from the woman who has messed up this divinity several times: Don't make divinity on a humid day, don't turn your back on that pot of syrup and sugar for even a second, and keep a keen eye on that candy thermometer.

final thoughts

Occasionally, a reader will ask, *why did you choose to write this story?* At first, I wasn't fully aware of why I desperately needed to write this particular story. Yes, the story my grandmother told me swirled around in my brain and required exploration. Yes, I needed to spend time with her and, in her absence, writing her story brought her to me again. But mostly, I realized I needed to write this for myself. Publishing this novel was Granny's final gift to me.

By 2011, I had switched careers with each of Jay and my Army-mandated moves. After ten years of doing that, I felt lost. In each new location, I found success, but those successes came at the cost of my true self. None of these new paths—puppeteer, seamstress, visual merchandiser, school counselor, instructional program specialist, childcare services outreach director—lasted longer than Jay's military orders. So, with another move on the horizon, this one from Texas to South Carolina, I decided to reinvent myself one last time. During the preparations for that move, I found myself flipping through Granny's cookbook. Near the end of the book, I found my own entry:

> *When I think of Granny, the usual thoughts occur: Family gatherings, great food, relaxing afternoons. However, what I miss most is my childhood friendship with Granny. We used to sit at the table for hours on hot summer afternoons and talk about her childhood... She told me of life in Frisco City, her father's hotel, the family cow, and her fascinating and independent mother. No longer was Granny just a cook and mother. She was a woman who led an amazing, made-for-TV life... There is still so much I could learn from her, but what she told me, her incredible story of endurance, I could never learn from a history book... She told me that she saw her mother's independent spirit in me. That is the greatest compliment I've ever received.*

In that moment, surrounded by moving boxes, I knew what my last new path would be. Becoming a novelist would not be easy, and this path was sure to be riddled with potholes and wrong turns, but it would be mine. Just like Hattie, I needed something of my own. Granny had told me decades before that I had it in me to build the life I wanted. Just as she did. Just as her mother had done. All I had to do was follow her lead and get to work.

about the author

Jodie Cain Smith is the founder of the Mobile Literary Festival in Mobile, Alabama, and the award-winning author of *The Woods at Barlow Bend*. With her husband, she lived in small, Army towns all over the US before finally returning home to Mobile after fifteen years away. And lo and behold, she returned with the sweetest, most adorable boy to ever come out of Heaven in tow.

When she is not living in the fictional worlds she creates via her laptop, Jodie is in her sewing room cursing her machine and geometry, chasing superheroes with her son, or next to the husband on the back porch.

Jodie Cain Smith's short stories, feature articles, and columns have appeared in *The Petigru Review, Chicken Soup for the Military Spouse's Soul, Pieces Anthology, The Savannah Morning News,* and the *Fort Hood Sentinel.*

To learn more about Jodie Cain Smith, visit her website, www.jodiecainsmith.com.

Made in the USA
Columbia, SC
02 December 2021